DECEIT AND DEVOTION

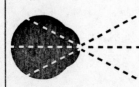

This Large Print Book carries the
Seal of Approval of N.A.V.H.

DECEIT AND DEVOTION

RM JOHNSON

THORNDIKE PRESS
A part of Gale, Cengage Learning

GALE
CENGAGE Learning·

Detroit • New York • San Francisco • New Haven, Conn • Waterville, Maine • London

GALE
CENGAGE Learning®

LIBRARY OF CONGRESS CATALOGING-IN-PUBLICATION DATA

Johnson, R. M. (Rodney Marcus)
    Deceit and devotion / by RM Johnson.
        pages ; cm. — (Thorndike Press large print
African-American)
    ISBN-13: 978-1-4104-4961-0 (hardcover)
    ISBN-10: 1-4104-4961-0 (hardcover)
        1. African American families—Fiction. 2. Urban fiction. 3. Domestic
fiction. 4. Large type books. I. Title.
PS3560.O3834D43 2012b
813'.54—dc23   2012012845

Published in 2012 by arrangement with Simon & Schuster, Inc.

Printed in Mexico
1 2 3 4 5 6 7 16 15 14 13 12

DECEIT AND DEVOTION

1

Monica sat at the bar of a darkened nightclub. The man standing beside her was leaning over, whispering into her ear, as he had been doing for the last hour.

He laughed to himself at something he said. Monica didn't hear it; the techno music in the club was blasting too loud. She threw her head back, laughed with him anyway.

He waved down the bartender and ordered Monica a fourth vodka tonic without asking her if she wanted it.

His left hand was on her bare thigh, just above her knee. Her skirt hiked itself up to just inches below her crotch. Monica was too drunk and too numb to care. No one noticed how the man was touching her anyway. The place was too crowded.

Monica stole a look at herself in the mirror behind the shelves of bottles lining the bar. Her makeup was heavy over her light brown skin. Her eyeliner was dark, her lipstick bright red. Her hair was cropped short, but it had finally grown long enough to cover the surgical scar, where the bullet fragments had been removed from her skull.

Her girlfriends said her hair looked cute. They said they wished they had the courage to cut theirs all off. It wasn't courage that had Monica walking around like this. It was the fact that someone had tried to kill her.

"Here you go, baby," the man said. He was tall, with chiseled facial features and broad shoulders. Good-looking in a very generic way. "Drink up."

Monica did what she was told. Her head spun more. She smiled. As she looked into the man's eyes, he smiled back mischievously.

Yes, he was good-looking, but it wouldn't have mattered what he looked like. Monica had thrown on a tight, low-cut, button-front dress and planted herself on this stool knowing some fool would approach her, start buying her drinks, and give her the attention she needed.

"How you feel?" the man asked. He had told her his name a few times. Monica didn't remember it.

"I'm ready to go."

"Let me walk you to your car."

"Sure," Monica said, standing on wobbly heels.

Outside, the parking lot was quiet but packed bumper-to-bumper tight. Monica leaned against her Jaguar, the man's body pressed against hers.

"You're beautiful," he said.

"Thank you."

He leaned in, attempting to kiss her.

"Don't kiss me," Monica said, turning away, allowing him to suckle her neck.

She felt one of his hands on her breast. She didn't push him away. He quickly undid two of her buttons, and his hand was down inside the cup of her bra, pinching her nipple.

"I'm dizzy," Monica said.

"Let me get you inside the car."

Monica allowed herself to be lowered into the Jaguar. She heard him close the door for her and caught a glimpse of the man hurrying around the front of the car. The passenger side door opened and closed. Before Monica knew it, both her breasts were bared, the man holding them, sucking voraciously.

Monica heard him moving about the small interior, felt his hands move all about her body. She did not look at him. Her head was tilted back, eyes closed.

She felt his warm hands on her bare thighs. She felt his lips kiss her knees. She heard him gasp when he spread her legs.

Monica smiled a bit, knowing it was the shock of discovering she wore no panties.

"I want to taste you," she heard the man say.

"Go 'head," Monica heard herself say back.

She felt his hot, wet tongue between her legs, and now Monica's eyes were open. The dizziness seemed to disappear. She looked down at the top of the man's head. He was working hard, trying to impress her.

Monica moaned, not because what he was doing felt good, but because she wanted it to, needed it to. She wanted to feel something, but she couldn't.

She moaned again. "Oh, baby. It's so good. It's so, damn good!" She pretended. She grabbed the back of his head with both hands, pressed his face deeper into her. "Tell me you love it."

"I love it," the man said, raising his head slightly, just to be heard.

Monica dropped her head back again, staring at the ceiling of her car. She thought about her failed marriage to Nate, about the failed relationship with Lewis that had followed, then the failed attempt at the

10

reconciliation of her marriage. She told herself not to go there, not again, but she could not stop herself. She thought about how no one loved her, how no one wanted her, and she felt herself descending into the place that oftentimes had her crying when she was alone.

"Tell me you love me," Monica said, ashamed, but needing to hear the words from someone, even a total stranger.

She felt the man's head stop for a moment.

"Tell me you love me!"

"I love you," said the man's muffled voice.

"Tell me you need me!"

"I need you," he said, still licking and lapping so much that saliva was dripping down Monica's inner thigh onto her leather seat.

She tried to stop the tears but they kept coming down her face.

The man raised his head, staring at Monica as though she were insane. "Are you crying?"

She wiped at her cheeks with the backs of her hands. "No."

"You are."

"I need for you to go," Monica said, regaining her senses and sliding up in her seat.

"But, baby. We were just —"

"I'm not your fucking baby, and I said I need you to get out!" Monica screamed.

The man blinked. "Fine, crazy bitch. But don't you —"

"Just get the fuck out!"

The man obeyed, climbing out of the car, slamming the door hard behind him.

Monica didn't watch as the man walked back around the front of her car, glaring at her hatefully, flipping her the bird through the windshield.

She lowered her face into her hands and continued to cry.

2

It had been months now since Nate told Monica that he was leaving her for Daphanie.

Nate lamented the decision, but he had no choice. Always wanting his own child, Nate did what had to be done.

On her hospital bed, only days after waking from a coma, Nate told Monica, in essence, that he was leaving her because she could not give him the child that Daphanie could.

Shortly thereafter, Nate found out that Daphanie was lying. The baby she was pregnant with was not his but the child of a married man she used to date, named Trevor.

Now in his mansion, the lights dim around him, Nate lowered himself into a leather chair and took a sip of the brandy he had poured moments ago. It was almost nine at night. Nathaniel, his adopted son, who had just made five years old last week, had been put to bed by Nate's new nanny, Mrs. Langford, leaving Nate free to torture himself with the horrible state of things.

Daphanie had lied to him about the baby he was once sure was his. That hadn't sat well with Nate, so he had gone after her for revenge.

He had accomplished what he had set out to do, causing the woman, he was sure, a pain she would never recover from. But now Nate wondered, what good did that do him? What if he had ignored the rumor that the baby was not his? He would've married Daphanie, and the little baby boy would've been there in the house with the two of them now. Nate wouldn't be alone, trying to raise his five-year-old son by himself.

Or maybe he should've just ignored the knowledge of Daphanie's pregnancy altogether. At the time, he was back with his ex-wife. He loved Monica, she loved him. She had already moved back in. They most likely would've been married again shortly after, but . . . Nate downed the rest of the brandy.

He grabbed his cell phone from the end table, dialed a number.

"Trevor," Nate said. "How are you? Is it too late to come by?"

■ ■ ■ ■

The little boy was beautiful, Nate thought, as he leaned over the crib and softly touched the infant's fat cheek. This was the boy that would've been his, if Nate hadn't called Daphanie back after dumping her for lying to him about the child. When he did call, he did some lying himself, said he would marry her and they would start a family of their own, only if she signed over full custody of her baby to Trevor, the biological father. She did. Nate left her standing at the altar of a huge wedding they had planned, and that's how he ended up here.

Nate leaned into the crib and kissed the baby good night.

When he made his way downstairs, Trevor was there in the living room, pouring a couple of drinks. He was a tall, brown-skinned man. He and Nate resembled each other, both well built, both clean shaven with close-cut black, wavy hair. Trevor was a banker. Recently divorced from his wife after she found out about the baby he fathered with Daphanie, but he was doing well for himself, living in the nice new home he had bought.

Trevor held out a glass to Nate. "You okay?"

Nate took the glass — two fingers' worth of scotch — swallowed it down, gave it back to Trevor for a refill. "Thinking if I played things the wrong way, that's all."

Refilling the glass and handing it back, Trevor said, "You can't do that. Whether it was the wrong way or not, what's done is done." Trevor sat, inviting Nate to do the same. "For the record, I believe it was the right way."

Nate sat. "Your son is beautiful. He's going to be a fine boy."

"He wouldn't be here if it weren't for you. Are you wishing you hadn't done anything? That you could have married Daphanie, been a family?"

"No," Nate said, sincerely now.

"It was wrong of her, lying to both of us like that."

Nate took a sip of his drink. "I know. I've gotten her back for that, but I think I paid a bigger price. I loved Monica. We were together again, and I traded that for a woman I did not love and a child that wasn't mine, even though Monica and I already had Nathaniel. I've lost all of that, and even after everything I've already done, I want Daphanie to pay more. I want to hurt

16

her more."

"So what are you going to do, Nate?"

Nate dug his thumb and forefinger into the inner corners of his eyes and squeezed. "Nothing," he finally said. "I should be done with the plotting, the deception and revenge. Look where it's gotten me. I'm alone and my son and I are missing Monica."

"Well, go tell her that, and win her back."

Nate gave what had been said a moment of thought. In the past he had begged Monica for forgiveness countless times, and somehow she had always found it within herself to give it to him. This time was different. "No. She already told me we were done. I can't blame her."

"So you're just going to give up? Just like that?"

"Yeah," Nate said, standing, taking steps toward the living room's exit. "Only way we get back together is if she comes to me. I know that's never going to happen, so I'm closing that chapter of my life."

Trevor followed him to the front door. They shook hands.

"You can come over and see my son whenever you like, you know."

Nate smiled as best he could, then walked off.

17

3

Austin Harris sat up in bed. He had on boxers and nothing else. The room was dark. He was not in his own home.

A small, shapely woman slept soundly beside him.

He looked at the alarm clock: 10:06 p.m. He slowly lay back down, staring at the ceiling. An hour ago, he had had the woman twisted into a bundle of sweating, trembling flesh. She was screaming his name as Austin grunted, stealing glances at the nightstand photo of the woman and her fiancé.

In the three months that he had been coming here, it had not bothered him. But tonight, this very moment, it had.

Lying in bed, Austin placed his hand on the bare shoulder of the woman lying beside him. "Cindy," he said, nudging her gently.

She turned to him, her eyes opening a little, a sleepy smile on her face. "Hey, babe."

"Hey," he said, pulling her to him so he could kiss her. As he did, he thought about discussing what was on his mind. The no-strings-attached sex was great, but every now and again, he wanted more.

"You leaving me?" Cindy said.

"Why? You want me to stay the night?"

She paused. Austin knew he'd caught her off guard.

"I'm playing with you." Austin smiled, knowing that now would be a bad time to have the conversation. "You know I got work early in the morning."

"Yeah," Cindy smiled, relieved. "Then you better go."

Austin climbed out of bed, grabbed his slacks off the back of the chair, and slid them on, then his shirt. He stood in the mirror. He was a tall, handsome man in good shape with medium brown skin, deep-set brown eyes, and strong chin. As he buttoned up his shirt, he saw Cindy standing behind him.

"Things have been tight again this week. If I don't pay the electric, I think it might be cut off."

Austin stared at her in the mirror's reflection. Cindy lowered her head.

"Sure," he said. "Let me finish getting dressed. I'll give it to you before I go."

■ ■ ■ ■

Austin stepped out of his Mercedes still wearing the gray suit he had worn to work that morning. He grabbed his briefcase and took the stone path up to his house.

The old Hyde Park home was a big gold brick one, with a huge front porch, four bedrooms, three baths, and a full basement. After divorcing his wife ten years ago, Austin had vowed not to be one of those guys that ended up in a studio apartment. He wanted the same lifestyle he had when he was married and wanted a place for his kids to stay when they visited — even though that hadn't happened in quite a while.

Dropping his briefcase at the door and stepping into the dining room, Austin was surprised to see his brother sitting at the table. Caleb was bent over a plate, picking at the corner of a slice of cold pizza. A glass of orange soda sat at his elbow.

"You just coming in from work? It's kinda late," Austin said, taking a look at his wristwatch. "Almost eleven."

Caleb, his younger brother by four years, wore a gray short-sleeved work shirt, his name stenciled on the left breast pocket. He wiped the corner of his mouth with a paper towel before he spoke.

"Naw. Me and Blue went out for a couple of beers. Had some stuff on my mind."

Austin frowned a bit but didn't respond. He walked around the table to a wall cabinet, pulled out a bottle of scotch and two short glasses. He looked at his brother from behind. His hair was long. Either he hadn't had the time or he hadn't had the money for a cut.

Austin set the glasses down and had a seat at the table. "You know, I really don't think you should be hanging around —"

"Austin," Caleb said, raising a hand. "I know you're my older brother, but you're not my father. Pops is dead, remember?"

"Blue was the reason you went to prison."

"I know that. I was the one that went, not you. You gonna pour from that bottle, or what?"

Austin poured a little into each glass. He grabbed a glass and set the other in front of Caleb. "Here's to . . . ?"

"To whatever," Caleb said, kicking the shot back.

Austin drank and set the glass down. "You talk to Sonya lately?"

"Look, Austin, I know we said after a year I'd get out or start paying rent, but —"

"No, no, no. I was just asking how she was

21

doing. You don't have to go."

"I just know that today makes a year I been here," Caleb said.

"It's fine. Really, stay as long as you like." Austin stood from his chair, reaching for the bottle of liquor. "I'm gonna put this away, unless you —"

"Leave it, will you?"

"Things are gonna be all right," Austin said. He dug his hand into his pocket, reaching for his wallet. "Till then, maybe you can use a few dollars."

"Don't. I don't wanna take any more from you. I've already taken enough."

Austin fingered four twenty-dollar bills from his wallet and set them on the table beside his brother's plate. "It's not up for debate."

4

Three hundred dollars' worth of loose marijuana, and three forty-ounce bottles of malt liquor sat on a table. The boys who sat there were all sixteen years old. Bug was chubby but strong, wore an expertly faded Mohawk haircut and a smile on his face. It was his garage the boys were meeting in this late at night, where they always hung out. Toomey was tall, thin, with a few chin hairs, unable to grow a mustache. He had big round eyes that made him appear younger than his sixteen years. Jahlil sat at the head of the table. He was of medium build, baby-faced, and had three shooting stars freshly cut into the side of his buzzed hair.

They all wore baggy jeans, extra large T-shirts, and gleaming white basketball shoes.

Small stacks of plastic wrap cut into three inch squares lay beside them, along with the forties. As the boys talked and drank, they pinched small quantities of marijuana from the pile, placed it in the center of one of the plastic wrap squares, then twisted and tied the ends into a knot.

"You ain't answer the question," Toomey said to Bug. "Your old man ever try to contact you?"

"Naw. He took off when I was five, and fool never looked back. Me and Moms cool without him. I help out with the money I make doing this stuff, so we don't need him."

"At least you knew your father," Toomey said, twisting one of the weed-filled plastic squares into a ball and tossing it toward the growing pile on the table. "My moms said my father left the minute he found out she was pregnant with me. Why they do that, man? Think about how much better off we'd be if we had fathers."

"All fathers ain't good," Jahlil said, looking up from the nickel bag he just twisted.

"Don't always have to be good. All the stuff a grown man knows, all the mistakes he made — sometimes them just being there so we can learn what not to do is better than nothing," Toomey said.

"Why you complaining?" Jahlil said. "You the grade A student, know everything already. What it matter to you?"

"I'd give my grades any day to have a father like you."

"My father is worthless," Jahlil said. "Why you think my moms kicked him out? All the years I known him, he been in and out of prison and looking for a job more than he had one. Now he thinking he's doing something with his janitorial business. He think he ballin' out." Jahlil laughed and reached over to his bottle of brew, twisted the cap, and took two swigs. "You can have him."

"I don't know," Bug said. "I'm agreeing with Toomey. A father is better than no father any day."

Jahlil shook his head and told himself his boys had no idea of what they were talking about. The reason Jahlil was twisting weed into nickel bags right now was that he had seen it done, up close, when he was eight years old.

While his father was in prison for five years, his mother had dated a drug dealer named Craig. The money was good. There were always stacks of it wrapped in thick brown rubber bands. Jahlil, his mother, and Craig lived in the hood. The crib looked like a shack from the street, but it was fancy inside, and they had everything from flat-screen TVs to granite countertops and marble floors. When Jahlil's father got out of prison, he came looking to get his family back.

One night, Jahlil's father busted in on Craig while he was sorting drugs and showing Jahlil how to handle a handgun. Things went bad. Craig ended up holding a 9mm to Jahlil's father's head.

Jahlil picked up the gun Craig had been showing him, pointed it at the back of the man's head, and blew his brains out all over the garage wall.

There was an investigation, but Uncle Austin made sure Jahlil didn't get put into foster care.

Not long after that, Jahlil's father and mother got back together, and the family went back to living in poverty. They had lived that way until separating a year ago.

Jahlil vowed that he would never end up like his old man. He wouldn't be grown and penniless.

That's why he had taken the train up to Evanston, given the white dude with the cloudy eyes the three hundred dollars he, Bug, and Toomey had come up with, for the pile of weed. He had no idea how or where they'd sell it, but the three of them were doing anything they could to make money. One way or the other, it would get sold.

As if reading Jahlil's mind, Bug asked, "You come up with a place to sell this stuff yet?"

"We could do it in the lunchroom at school. Get a table way in the back so no one can see us," Toomey said.

"They catch you selling drugs at school, they'll put you under it," Bug said.

"He's right," Jahlil said. "We don't have a choice. We gotta sell our drugs where drugs be sold."

"Where is that?" Toomey said.

"Over there on Seventy-Seventh Street."

"Oh, hell no!" Toomey stood up from his chair in protest. "That's G-Stone street. They sell there."

"Toomey right," Bug said.

"Then how we gonna get rid of this? We spent a hundred dollars each."

"Find another way," Toomey said. "I wanna make our money back but don't wanna risk my life to do it. Let's just wait for a better opportunity."

"I ain't got time to wait," Jahlil said, anger in his voice.

"You know he got Shaun to think about," Bug said to Toomey.

"Look," Jahlil said. "They don't start selling till afternoon. We go in the morning. No one will see us. Ya'll don't even have to help,

27

just keep an eye out for the police."

"Well . . . okay," Bug said. "That could work as long as we out before someone see us."

"You cool with that, Toomey?" Jahlil asked.

Looking worried, Toomey said, "We get our money, and we get out of there, right?"

"Right," Jahlil said.

5

Austin sipped from his coffee, then set the mug down.

"How is it? Need more sugar?" Marcus asked. He was Austin's younger brother by eighteen months. Other than Marcus being two inches shorter than Austin's six feet, a little broader in the shoulders, and having hazel eyes instead of brown, the two men looked very much alike, with their broad noses and thin lips.

Marcus had been happily married for the past eight years, but things at home had been getting a little uncomfortable since Marcus's graphic design company had gone under.

"Coffee's fine," Austin said. "Thanks for letting me come by for breakfast." Wearing a light brown suit, Austin stood and walked through the dining room, into the large living room of the modest, middle-class family home. He lifted a framed photo of Marcus's daughter, Sophie, and smiled. "You're lucky."

"Really, to have lost my job and have my wife look at me as though she's questioning why she ever married me," Marcus said. "Don't think I'm that lucky."

"I'm talking about this," Austin said, setting the photo down and spreading his arms. "Family. Home. Cooking pancakes in the morning. I miss that."

"Yeah, well . . ." Marcus said, clearing some of the dishes from the table and taking them to the sink. "Things aren't always what they seem. I know you know that, being divorced and all."

"Everything okay with you and Reecie?"

Marcus turned on the faucet for dishwater, then turned to his brother. "We're making the bills. But there's a point where a woman feels she should not be the breadwinner in the family. She says she has a problem being the man. I tell her she's not being the man. I still am. She says, 'Really?' Like she doesn't know. I do everything around here, and she doesn't appreciate any of it. I'm getting tired of this."

"So it sounds like you have a problem being the woman."

Marcus laughed, slipping on a pair of pink

rubber dish gloves, holding up his hands as though he were about to perform surgery. "I am not the woman."

"But you two are fine, right?"

"Yeah, we're dealing," Marcus said, shutting off the water. "How about you? You seem kinda down."

"I'm educated, successful, forty-five, and handsome."

"Really?" Marcus said. "Don't know about the handsome part."

"But I'm lonely. I want what you have — a family again."

"Well, your kids hate you for not spending time with them over the last four years. And Trace has been remarried for that same period of time, but technically, they're still your family. Problem solved."

"Think she'd dump John and take me back if I asked?" Austin said, grinning, grabbing his coffee mug from the kitchen table.

"You're joking, right?"

It took him a moment to answer. "Of course I am."

"You got someone you're seeing, don't you? What's her name? Cindy. How about her?"

"She's just something to do." Austin turned up his mug, finishing the coffee. "My son's birthday gathering is tonight. You and

Reecie coming, right?"

"Yeah. You'll be there?" Marcus said, holding a soapy skillet, sounding surprised. "I'm shocked you got an invite."

"I know. Troy doesn't want to see me," Austin said, sounding disappointed. "But Trace thinks I should show anyway."

"I think you should too," Marcus said, pulling off the wet rubber gloves. "Is Bethany driving up from school?"

"No, final exams she told her mother, but I think she's just trying to avoid seeing me."

"They can't be mad at you forever. You're their father."

"They have a new one of those, remember?"

"Whatever." Marcus walked out into the dining room and gave Austin some dap, and pulled him in for a half hug. He held him there a moment. "But you're good, right? Sometimes I worry about you, man."

Austin felt concern in the embrace and the question. "Yeah. Perfect," he said.

6

Caleb sat in a small wood-paneled office. He felt uncomfortable about his appearance. He wore old jeans, work boots, and his gray work shirt. His hair was longer than he liked. The curls would soon grow into a baby afro. He wanted to get a cut and shave off the patchy beard that had started to grow on his face, but he told himself he would save the few dollars Austin gave him for something more important.

Caleb glanced down at his watch. It read 8:00 a.m.

Last night, Caleb's former longtime girlfriend of almost twenty years and the mother of his child had called him.

"The principal said he wants us to come up there tomorrow morning for a meeting."

"About what?" Caleb said. He had been in the middle of working, cleaning yet another office he didn't feel like cleaning.

"About your son."

"Is he in trouble again?" Caleb asked, praying that he wasn't.

"What do you think, Caleb?" Sonya said, as though he should've known. "Eight o'clock, and don't be late."

This was what had been on his mind last night, why he had had to call Blue to go have some beers.

Caleb looked over at Sonya, who sat in the chair beside him.

She remained thin after all these years, wore her hair the same way — pulled back in a ponytail — and no makeup other than lip gloss and eyeliner. She wore jeans and heels, one of which she nervously tapped against the floor.

Caleb pressed his palm on her knee.

"Relax. It might not be that bad."

Sonya gave Caleb a sarcastic look. "Where is this man? I want to get this over with."

That moment, a boyish-looking man no older than thirty-five walked into the room. He wore glasses, a corduroy blazer, and a smile. His name was Mr. Burke. He extended his hand to Sonya.

"Sorry to keep you waiting, Mr. and Mrs. Harris."

Sonya took the man's hand and shook, neither Caleb nor Sonya bothering to correct him on their marital status.

"Mr. Harris," the principal said, offering Caleb his hand. "I know we're all busy, so I want to get right to the point. Jahlil has been missing school."

"I kept him out a couple of days last week, because he was sick," Sonya said.

"I understand, but he's missed a little more than that." Mr. Burke slid open his desk drawer, pulled out a folder, and examined a page. "Last month, Jahlil missed . . . eight, nine," — the man counted to himself — "eleven days. This month, it's thirteen, and we still have a week to go."

Sonya shook her head. "I'm sure there has to be some sort of mistake. I've never heard anything about this."

"Jahlil was sent home with notices to you. I assume you never got them."

"No." Sonya shook her head.

"Are you sure he's been absent that much?" Caleb asked.

"I checked the attendance records of all Jahlil's instructors and the absences are consistent."

Caleb sat quietly, teeth clamped together, angry.

"Is there any explanation whatsoever for this?" Mr. Burke asked.

Caleb narrowed his eyes and turned to Sonya.

"I don't know," Sonya said, shaken. "A year ago, his father and I —"

"Mr. Burke," Caleb said, interrupting Sonya. "Is this the only problem you needed to speak to us about?"

"Your son's grades have obviously dropped because of the classes he's missed. If he continues, he'll be suspended. And if his grades continue to fall, he may have to repeat his junior year."

"Understood. Thank you." Caleb stood and shook the man's hand. He turned to Sonya. "C'mon."

Outside the school, Caleb walked beside Sonya silently, the muscles in his jaw jumping as he continued to grind his teeth. Sonya stopped beside her aging Nissan Altima.

"Why in the hell didn't you tell me he was missing school?" Caleb asked.

"Because I didn't know."

"But it's your damn job to know."

"He's your son too."

"You put me out. How do I find out about this when I barely see him? This is your fault."

"Come again?"

"You could've let me stay," Caleb said.

"You cheat, and you expect me to let you stay."

"It was one time."

36

"And that makes it right?"

"You pushed me to that."

Sonya chuckled, shaking her head.

"You stopped believing in me, respecting me," Caleb said.

"Caleb, we're past that. That was then. Jahlil missing school is now. You gonna take care of it, or what?"

Caleb turned, sighed heavily, angrily. "I need to be back home, and you know it. We need to be a family again."

"That ain't happening, Caleb," Sonya said, turning toward her car, sliding her key in the lock.

Caleb grabbed her by the arm, spun her back to him. "No! Do you know what I've done for you and Jahlil? When you were about to be thrown out because you were more than half a year late on rent, when there were expenses you had to pay but couldn't afford?"

"What? What did you do for us that was so big?" Sonya asked, as if there was nothing he could say to impress her.

Caleb stared at Sonya, so angry he felt his entire body trembling. He forced himself to calm down. "Nothing," Caleb said. "I didn't do anything."

"Just like I thought. You need to find your

son and talk some sense into him. He needs you."

"Do you still need me?" Caleb said, hopeful.

Sonya stared at him a moment. "No," Sonya said. "I don't."

7

Monica sprang up in bed, her entire body drenched in sweat. She huffed, her heart pounding in her chest as she whipped her head around, looking for the man that had shot her.

Even though this was not the same house she had been shot in, her eyes settled on the bedroom door. It was closed.

In her dream the door was open. She had just stepped out of the shower. Her ex-husband, Nate Kenny — the man she had moved back in with only weeks before, the man she was going to remarry — was in the kitchen, baking cookies with his adopted son, the son Monica was also going to later adopt.

Things were perfect, how Monica had always wanted them.

In the dream, she had heard her husband talking. She thought he was speaking to her, so Monica approached the door.

When she stepped into the doorway, she saw another man. She knew him — Freddy Ford. He was the best friend of Lewis Waters, the man Monica had dated after she had divorced Nate.

Freddy was pointing a gun at Nate. Before Monica could comprehend what was happening, Freddy had shot him.

Monica screamed, then Freddy turned the gun on her. She heard her husband yell and saw a spark of orange burst from the gun. Monica experienced the most extreme agony of her life, as she felt her skull explode.

She always woke up just after that, screaming, sweating, and clawing at the sheets as she had done only moments ago.

Bullet fragments had had to be cut from her brain. She had been in a coma for weeks, but her doctor said she was lucky. It could've been worse. If the bullet had struck a centimeter or two to the right, she would've been dead.

Monica climbed out of her bed and cautiously approached the bedroom door. She grabbed the doorknob and twisted it. It didn't turn. The door was locked, as she had left it last night before going to bed.

She pressed her back against it, relieved, and slid down to sit on the carpet.

Placing a hand to her cheek, she thought about last night, her head pounding from the hangover she was suffering.

She remembered begging some man to tell her he loved her. She remembered sobbing.

How did she get home in that condition? She could've killed herself, she could've killed someone else.

In the shooting, Monica was the victim, the innocent one. She had nothing to do with Freddy or with whatever Nate had schemed against him, yet she was the one that had been near death. She was the one who was without the son she was to adopt with Nate. She was the one who lost the future she was so looking forward to.

It was Nate's fault, yet he hadn't spent even four days in the hospital from his wounds. He still had the adopted boy, his business, the house Monica was supposed to move into with him, and most of all, she was sure he still had his sanity, when it felt like Monica was losing hers.

She was almost certain, if she were to ring his office right now, that he would pick up as if the shooting had never taken place.

Monica stood, her eyes resting on the bedroom phone. A thought skittered across her mind and she found herself standing over the phone, her fist around the receiver.

No. What good would it do? Confirming he was not affected by any of this would only serve to drive her crazier.

Monica lifted the receiver anyway, pushed the two digits to block her call from appearing on the caller ID, and dialed Nate's direct office line.

It rang once. Yes, she was calling him, but no, she didn't really want to hear his voice. At least that's what she was telling herself.

It rang twice, and she thought of hanging up but could not.

The sweat accumulated in her fist as she held the phone tighter. After the third ring, she moved to hang up, when she heard, "This is Nate Kenny."

It felt as though an icicle had been jabbed down her spine.

"Hello? This is Nate Kenny."

Monica breathed heavily, looking over her shoulder as if she were being watched. She opened her mouth to speak but was struck with silent anger. She clenched the phone tighter in her grasp, wishing there was an action she could commit to cause him harm, but there was nothing. She was helpless, and she hated feeling that way. There was nothing more that she could do than slam the phone back into its cradle and forget the man ever existed.

8

Daphanie sat in her SUV, trying not to cry as she stared up at Trevor's house.

She had made the worst mistake of her life, and now she had to fix it.

When Daphanie had gotten pregnant by Trevor, she hadn't known she would have an opportunity to reunite with Nate, the man she truly loved. The problem was that Daphanie knew Nate wouldn't accept her back, carrying another man's child. So she lied, telling Trevor that the baby wasn't really his, and telling Nate that he was the father. The plan worked. Nate told Monica he would leave her to properly be a father to his child, but somehow he found out that Daphanie had lied about the pregnancy.

Nate left her.

But later, she felt she was granted a miracle, because Nate came to her and said he would marry her, give her a family of her own, if she would just sign over her baby to

Trevor, the real father.

A contract was drawn up. Daphanie signed.

In the delivery room, when Daphanie gave birth, she heard her child crying. It broke her heart to tell the nurse she didn't want to hold it, didn't even want to see it.

Daphanie had cried for the loss of her child every day leading up to her wedding. But things would be better once she was married. Daphanie told herself she would start trying to get pregnant again immediately.

On the big day, she waited nervously in her wedding gown for the groom to arrive.

Nate never appeared.

It was a scam. A hoax. A trick to get back at her for lying to him about the baby's being his. Nate had convinced her to sign her baby away, and now Daphanie was left single, with very little money, and alone.

Daphanie saw movement out of the corner of her eye. She turned to look back up at the house she was parked in front of. Trevor stepped out the door. He wore a dark suit and carried a leather briefcase.

Daphanie was out of her SUV, hurrying across the street.

Trevor turned, startled to see her there.

"What do you want?"

"My baby. You have to give him back to me."

Infuriated, Trevor started down the porch stairs toward her. "You lie to me about him not being mine and tell another man that he's his. Then when you're found out, you try to cut a deal, using your own baby." Trevor was in front of Daphanie now, hatefully yelling at her. "Now you think you can have him back! You — you —" His finger trembled before her eyes, as he appeared to hold back from striking her. "Get out of my face!"

Trevor took a step past her. Daphanie grabbed him by his arm. "I want him back! Give me my baby back!"

Trevor spun, pushing Daphanie. She stumbled and fell to the sidewalk.

"You are pathetic. I loved you, and you lied to me," he said, shaking his head. "Today, I'm filing a restraining order against you. Come near me or my child again, I will have you in jail."

9

Jahlil stood in the middle of a block of uninhabited storefronts and run-down apartment buildings. Three cars sat parked on the street; one was charred, had no windows, and looked to have been in an explosion.

Jahlil had not gone to school today. This was far more important. He needed this money.

"Got that fire weed," Jahlil said to an old, bearded man that hobbled by in tattered shoes and a weathered coat.

Jahlil had been selling for about an hour and had gotten about two hundred dollars. Things were going as smoothly as he had hoped. It was still early, around 11 a.m., and he didn't see any other sellers nearby.

Bug was fifty yards down the block, keeping an eye out for the police or any gang members who might roll up. Toomey was on the other end of the street, looking like he was about to wet his pants.

"Gi' me ten dollars' worth." The man who had just passed Jahlil now stood in front of him.

Jahlil fished two five-dollar bags of weed out of his pocket. Casually shaking one of the man's dirty hands, he took the ten-dollar bill, then, grasping the man's other hand, left him with the two small bags of marijuana.

The man shuffled off. Jahlil heard a whistle. It was Toomey. Jahlil looked down the block. Toomey nodded at the two boys who were walking Jahlil's way. They had been sitting on one of the vacant apartment building stoops for the last half hour, watching Jahlil sell.

The two boys wore sagging jeans and hooded zipper jackets, the hoods pulled up over their heads. One stopped twenty feet short of Jahlil, while the other walked right up to him.

Jahlil stared down at the kid, who was barely five feet tall. He looked even younger than Jahlil first thought when he yanked the hood back from his skull. His face was scrunched into a frown. He looked like an infant who had just crapped his diaper.

"This G-Stone corner," the boy said, his voice high-pitched like a girl's.

"Who is you?" Jahlil said.

"Don't matter. This G-Stone corner. You need to be up outta here."

Jahlil wanted to laugh in the boy's face, but he knew the little ones would whip out a gun as big as they were and blow a fool's head off. They were recruited to do dirt, vicious stuff, because if they were caught, they wouldn't do hard time. Jahlil looked the boy up and down. His arms were crossed. He didn't look like he was packing. But his little friend standing in the middle of the street might have been. If the other kid pulled a gun, that would force Jahlil to dig into the waist of his jeans, whip out his 9mm, and although he had never fired it, he wouldn't be taking it out just for show.

Jahlil looked back at the boy in front of him. He wanted to make an even three hundred dollars before he left. "I'll be done in an hour."

"Naw, you need to be done now."

Jahlil took a step toward the boy, towering over him. The other little boy started toward Jahlil. Out of the corners of his eyes, Jahlil saw Toomey and Bug hurrying over from opposite directions, halting a short distance away.

The boy standing before Jahlil looked to his left and right, acknowledging Bug and

Toomey. He looked back up to Jahlil. "You leaving or what?"

"I said an hour, I'll be gone in an hour."

"Yeah, okay," the boy said. He turned, walked over to the other little boy, and they both headed off.

Bug and Toomey rushed over to Jahlil.

"You okay, man?" Bug asked.

"I'm cool," Jahlil said, trying to laugh, although he was shaken. "They get younger every day."

"They wanted you out of here, didn't they?" Toomey said, looking over his shoulder at the boys. "They were gangbangers, weren't they?"

Jahlil laughed. "They were like nine years old. Did they look like bangers? They were trying to cop, I wouldn't sell them none, and little dude was throwing a tantrum, that's all."

"You sure?" Toomey asked.

"Positive."

"So how much longer we staying?" Bug said.

Jahlil looked up and down the street, wondering if the boys truly accepted what he'd told them, or if they were on their way back, with boys much bigger — men. "We made a little over two hundred dollars. I think that's cool for today. What ya'll think?"

"Cool wit' me," Bug said. Toomey agreed. "Then we need to get out of here."

10

AERO was the name of the Magnificent Mile's fine men's clothing store and day spa that Monica owned. Monica had taken money from the millions she'd won in her divorce settlement with Nate and had bought the two-store chain. It was the only positive thing that had come from her union with Nate Kenny, Monica thought as she pulled open one of the double glass doors and walked into her store.

She walked across the granite floor, into what looked like a warehouse-sized loft apartment, with wooden rafters on the ceiling and exposed brick on the walls. The store was busy for a late afternoon. A dozen or so men browsed through the racks of suits. On the west side, where Monica had built the day spa, she peeked in and saw four men in black smocks in the waiting area, reading magazines and watching *SportsCenter* on the flat-screen.

Monica headed back to the front, toward reception, where Roland, her floor supervisor, was now finished with his customer. He wore a pink-and-white-striped Ralph Lauren oxford with a lime green scarf tied around his neck, and a pair of black Gucci eyeglass frames.

Monica walked up the two stairs to the elevated register area, where the tall, thin man gave her a kiss on each cheek.

"Miss Monica, looking radiant as always today." He looked her up and down. "Love the open-toe sling backs. What are they, BCBG?"

"Correct as always. Roland, you should be in New York or Paris somewhere designing your own line."

"Don't tempt me, girl. You know this store would go to hell if I left."

"You know, I think you're right." Monica smiled. "Where's Tabatha?"

"In the back office, acting like there ain't enough work out here for the both of us."

"Thanks, Roland."

Monica walked the long corridor to the back office, feeling exhausted from too little sleep last night. She'd put on the happy face for Roland. She didn't need him worrying about her again. She had gotten enough of that when she first decided to come back to work after the shooting.

Monica opened the door to the back office she shared with Tabatha, her best friend and manager of her flagship store.

"What's up, boss?" Tabatha said, reading glasses sitting low on her nose. Tabatha was slender, wore her hair brushed back, with a long ponytail clip-on. She glanced away from her computer screen at Monica and did a double take. "Geez! You look like hell."

"Thanks, Tab," Monica said, closing the door and setting her purse down on her desk. She walked to the leather sofa and lay across it. "I can always count on you to make a girl feel her best."

"I mean, if you have something, maybe you ought to go back home, 'cause I don't wanna catch it," Tabatha joked.

"I don't have anything," Monica said softly.

"Then what's up?" Tabatha said, walking closer and standing over Monica. "Want me to get you some coffee? Can't be coming in here freeloading on the job. That's what Roland's for." Tabatha chuckled.

Monica said nothing but sniffled a little.

"You okay?"

"Fine." Monica sniffled again and covered her eyes with her hands.

Tabatha sat down on the edge of the sofa,

grabbing Monica's wrists, trying to pull them away from her face.

Monica fought her for only a moment, then let her arms down to expose the tears that fell from her eyes.

"Girl, what's wrong?"

"I went out to a bar last night."

"That's good. I told you you should get out. Get your mind off those loser men you've been dealing with."

"I met a guy, and he started buying me drinks."

"Okay."

"He walked me out, kissed me, and made sure I got into my car."

"A gentleman. That's nice."

"He gets in the car with me."

"Really?"

"Next thing I know, his head is between my legs and he's slurping like I got a Bomb Pop shoved up my coochie."

"Ooh," Tabatha said, biting on a fingernail. "He wasn't forcing himself on you, was he?"

"No. I didn't get that from him at all. But I was pathetic," Monica said, wiping the last tear from her face. "I had been drinking, my head was everywhere."

"Please don't tell me you got all emotional while this man was down on you."

"Yeah, girl. I started off into this nonsense

about 'tell me you love me.' "

"Oh, say you didn't," Tabatha said, slapping a hand to her forehead.

" 'Tell me you need me!' It was a mess. Then I broke down weeping."

"And he looked at you like you were a basket case, and with juice still all over his face, he got the hell out of there, right?"

"Something like that."

Tabatha stared at Monica, shaking her head. "You my girl, but your ass is crazy."

"Woke up this morning, after another nightmare."

The smile disappeared from Tabatha's face.

"Then I called Nate."

"No."

"He was like, 'Hello. Hello!' Then I hung up on his ass."

"Good for you. But why did you call?"

"Because I'm angry as hell. Because everything he did to me, all the ways he mistreated me — I can't get it out of my head. He's over there chillin', living the life, and I'm lost and lonely and suffering. I don't think he should get away with that."

"Get that out of your head, Monica," Tabatha said, rubbing her shoulder. "He's over. That's done with."

"I know, you're right. I've put him out of

my head, and I'll never think about him again."

"Good. And to help you keep your mind off of Nate, I know a guy. A good one. I've already spoken to him about you, and I'm setting up a date."

"No."

"But —"

"Dammit, no, Tabatha!" Monica said, knocking Tabatha's hand from her shoulder. After a moment, she apologized. "Yes, I'm lonely as hell, afraid of being by myself for the rest of my life, and I want to be loved. Who doesn't? But I don't need no fucking men in my life right now. I'm alone because of the men that were *in* my life. I fell in love with two children and had them taken away from me, because of the men *in* my life. I got shot in the head and almost died be-cause of the goddamn men *in* my life!" She looked up at Tabatha and spoke softer. "I don't want them no more. Any of them."

"I see. You don't want another man in your life, but you want to be loved, and you don't wanna be by yourself. How do you accomplish that?"

Monica sat on the sofa and smiled sadly. "I don't know. Just hug me for now, and I'll think about that later."

11

Daphanie stood before the reception desk in the offices of Kenny Corporation, the multimillion-dollar investment company that Nate Kenny started and owned. An attractive, smiling woman wearing glasses and a headset asked, "May I help you?"

"I'm here to see Nate Kenny, please."

"Do you have an appointment today, ma'am?"

"No," Daphanie said, preparing herself for the actions she knew her answer would force her to take.

Still smiling, the receptionist said, "I'm sorry, Miss . . ."

"Coleman. My name is Daphanie Coleman."

"I'm sorry, Miss Coleman, but without an appointment, I'm afraid you won't be able to see him. I can schedule you," the woman said, pecking the keys of the computer in front of her. "His next opening is two weeks from today. Shall I put you down then?"

Daphanie laughed when she really wanted to cry. Her eyes cut across the football field–sized office space. She knew where Nate's office was. She saw herself running through the maze of cubicles, tackled by a security guard who appeared from thin air just before she reached Nate's office door. "Sure, put me down for that one," Daphanie said, then she took off toward Nate's office.

"Ma'am! Miss Coleman, you can't go back there!" Daphanie heard the receptionist call, as she dodged business-suited, paper-carrying employees. She turned a corner, saw the door with raised letters reading NATE KENNY on it. She glanced over her shoulder, saw no security guard in hot pursuit, but heard fast-paced footsteps and the receptionist calling again.

Reaching the door, she grabbed the knob and threw it open, bursting in and almost stumbling to the floor. Nate sat behind his desk, a pencil in his hand. He calmly looked up as though he had been expecting Daphanie. A second later, the receptionist appeared at the door, panting.

"I'm so sorry, Mr. Kenny. I tried to —"

"It's okay, Charlene," Nate said, standing. "I'll take care of this. Thank you."

Charlene gave Daphanie an evil look, then

pulled the door closed.

Nate stepped around his desk, looking fit, dapper in his tailored suit, and — most notably to Daphanie — carefree. "Have a seat, Daphanie. Can I offer you something to drink? Bottled water, juice, something a little stronger?" Nate said, moving toward a fully stocked bar, bottles of liquor in plain view.

"I didn't come here for a fucking drink."

"Fine." Nate walked back to his desk, took his seat. "What can I do for you then?"

"I want my son back."

"That I can't do."

"You can't, or you won't?"

"Daphanie, you act as though I have your boy."

"You took him."

"I couldn't have taken him if you didn't give him away."

Those words cut Daphanie, maybe because Nate had never spoken truer words to her in the time she'd known him.

"Give him back to me."

"You should be speaking to Trevor about this. Go to him."

"I've done that," Daphanie said, willing herself not to cry. "He won't do it."

Nate exhaled loudly and, in an exaggerated motion, shrugged his shoulders. "Then you're done. You've exhausted your avenues. All there is for you to do now is accept the fact that your child is gone."

"No," Daphanie said, feeling those fucking tears crawling down her face again. "No. You have to help me."

Nate stood. "Help you. This is exactly what I wanted. To see you suffer. Now if you'd please, leave my office, before I have security drag you out."

12

Caleb stood in the janitor's closet, watching as scalding hot water rushed into his metal pail. He wore black work boots, Dickies work pants, and his gray shirt from this morning, the one with his name on the pocket. Under it, in smaller letters, PRESIDENT was stenciled.

He had been proud of himself when he pulled that shirt out of the plastic and looked at it the first time, ten months ago. But now it was just a joke to him. President of a janitorial company with just one employee — himself.

Caleb felt his cell phone vibrate in his pocket and quickly dug for it, hoping it was his son calling him back.

On the screen, he saw that it was his old friend Blue and thought about ignoring the call. Blue and Caleb went back almost twenty years. They had hung the streets together, drunk forty ounces of beer, talked about nothing, and ended up robbing a store, which got both of them sent to jail and their friend Ray Ray killed. But that was a long time ago.

"Hello," Caleb said, picking up.

"What up, fool? Wanna get some brews tonight? Go to the strip club? I got a hookup. We can get in free."

"Naw, man. Got some stuff to take care of later. I'll hit you tomorrow."

"You sure, man? Sounds like you need to free your mind a bit. I know a couple of hos there that —"

"Blue, for real, man. I gotta go. I'm at work."

"Oh, okay," Blue said, sounding disappointed. "I'll hit you later."

Caleb ended the call and shut off the water. He had called and left three messages for his son to ring him back. The boy was ignoring him as though Caleb weren't his father but one of his little friends that he could choose not to talk to. Later tonight, Caleb would make sure the boy understood that decision was not his to make.

After cleaning the four bathrooms in the Department of Children and Family Services building, dusting all the surfaces, emptying all the public trash receptacles and the baskets by the desks, Caleb swept all the floors and mopped.

He got this account, nine months ago, after walking through the door and asking to speak to the manager of the building. He gave the same speech he gave when speaking to all the managers of the businesses he visited, trying to win new accounts. He told the manager that he ran his own janitorial company and that he would clean her building for half what the present company was doing it for.

The woman behind the big desk hadn't hesitated when she said, "Do it for a third and we'll hire you."

Caleb accepted. He had only one account at the time, and that was cleaning his brother's law offices every night.

After finding out what he would be getting paid from the DCFS account, he realized he would only be breaking even but told himself he would take what he could get. He would make this business successful one day, even if it was one account at a time.

Finishing for the evening, Caleb stacked all his supplies into the small closet and locked the door. He looked down at his watch. It was 7:30.

He would stop, grab a burger, then make his way over to Austin's offices. Caleb had given his son a job with him working there two nights a week, so his boy could earn a couple of dollars to put in his pocket and get his feet wet. Caleb hoped one day he would take over the company.

Caleb stepped out the back door of the DCFS building and locked it behind him. He walked through the side alley to where he parked his old white Dodge cargo van. He was about to get in when he felt the tip of a gun pressed flush to the back of his head. Caleb froze, his heart accelerating in his chest.

" 'Sup, motherfucker?"

Caleb's pulse slowed some with the recognition of the voice.

"Turn your ass around."

With his hands shoulder high, Caleb slowly did as he was told.

He turned to see whom he had expected, a thin, extremely muscled man, wearing a T-shirt, the sleeves hacked off, tattoos all over his arms and shoulders. His name was Charles. Still holding the gun on Caleb, he bit down on the toothpick in the corner of his mouth, looking as though he wouldn't hesitate to shoot him. There was another man standing a few feet away, a heavier man with a head full of hair, one half sticking up in an afro, the other half tightly cornrowed.

Caleb had never seen him before.

"It ain't time yet," Caleb said.

"We know," Charles said, smiling. "This here just a friendly reminder."

"Then can you please put down the gun?"

Charles smiled wider, looked over at the other man, then back at Caleb. He rolled the toothpick from one side of his mouth to the other, then stuck the gun in the waist of his jeans. "You got the money yet?"

"I'm waiting to hear back about some cleaning accounts I'm trying to get. If I get them, then —"

"I don't wanna hear all that nonsense, and you know Kwan ain't gonna wanna hear it either." Charles paced a short line in front of Caleb. "How many days you got till you settle up with us?"

"Five."

"You can't be late, you know that, right?" Charles said, still pacing.

"I know that."

"Don't know if you seen the news yesterday. Police found some dude in the Dan Ryan Woods with no hands and no head. I ain't saying it was us, but that coulda been this dude who tried to skip on giving Kwan his money." Charles stopped in front of Caleb. "You can't skip on Kwan, and you can't be late. Okay?"

"Yeah," Caleb said, not liking the crazed look in Charles's eyes. "I won't skip, and I won't be late."

13

Jahlil stood in the hallway after knocking on Shaun's door. His phone vibrated in his pocket. He pulled it out, checked the screen to see that it was his father calling. He ignored the call.

He heard a dog barking somewhere on the floor above him. Out of the corner of his eye, he saw movement. He turned his head to see a rat scurrying from one side of the hall to the other. It disappeared into a crack in the wall.

The door opened. His girlfriend, Shaun, stood behind it. She was a cute girl with short, brown hair and dimples. She was seventeen years old but had been held back a year because of poor grades, so she and Jahlil were both juniors. She was normally very fit. She ran track for the school and was a cheerleader — but that was all before she had gotten pregnant.

Her toned, teenaged, size four body was

now stretched into something considerably larger. She was pretty big at eight months pregnant. She stood before Jahlil wearing an extra large T-shirt and slippers.

"Your moms here?" Jahlil whispered.

"No. Come in."

Jahlil stepped into a run-down, sparsely furnished two-bedroom apartment. He kissed Shaun, then smoothed both his hands around her round belly and kissed the top of it twice. "You feelin' okay today?" Jahlil asked.

"My mother trippin' again, talking about me putting our baby up for adoption, or she gonna put me out."

"Don't even worry about her. I'm gonna get you out of here. This ain't no place for you to be raising our little girl anyway."

"You keep saying that, but are you gonna get the money to —"

"Told you, don't worry about that. We gonna be fine," Jahlil said. "Now you got some food in there you can make me?"

"Yeah, but I need some money first."

"Money for what? You on the medical card, and WIC take care of the rest, right?"

"Medical card and WIC card don't pay for bus fare to and from the hospital."

Jahlil frowned, dug into his pocket, and pulled out three crumpled twenty-dollar bills. He gave Shaun two of them.

"Thanks. This money you made from selling today?"

"Ain't make no money. We lost sixty dollars, 'cause we was ran off the corner by some kids."

"Some kids. What kids? How you gonna let —"

"They was representing G-Stone."

"Representing?" Shaun said. "Why didn't you go back, sell some more?"

" 'Cause I said the kids was representing —"

"But they were kids. Jahlil," Shaun said, talking to him like she was his mother, "we eight months pregnant. I'm dropping this baby any week now, and you say you gonna get me out of here, but I'm still up in this nasty apartment. I'm scared Mama gonna put me out, and I'll be on the street with our child, because you letting some little kids scare you away from making the money you need to take care of your family."

Jahlil clenched his jaws. He felt like a child. "They ain't scare me off."

"You gonna make the money we need, or should I have gotten the abortion Mama was telling me to get?"

Jahlil walked up on Shaun, his face just inches from hers. He looked her directly in the eyes and softly, angrily said, "Don't do that to me, you hear me? Don't try and make me feel like no punk. I want our baby, and I'm gonna take care of both of ya'll, just like I promised, okay?"

Shaun stared into Jahlil's eyes. She said, "Then do it."

14

Austin stared up at his ex-wife's house, the house that used to be theirs when they were married.

Four years ago, Trace married another man. His name was John. He was a decent-looking, hardworking guy who owned his own handyman business. Trace refinanced the house given to her in the divorce, with her new husband, and now the house belonged to the both of them.

"You sure you can't make it?" Austin asked. He was talking to Caleb on his cell phone. "The offices will keep till you get to them tomorrow evening. Trust me. We aren't that dirty."

"Sorry, man. Tell my nephew I'll treat him to some burgers, and we'll watch the game on Sunday or something, but I really need to be at work tonight. Okay?"

"Yeah, okay," Austin said, disappointed. He wanted Caleb there so he wouldn't feel like the only unaccompanied one. Marcus was inside with Reecie — Austin saw their Accord parked in the driveway. Trace would be there with John, and Austin was sure Trace would've invited at least one or two of the couples from the neighborhood over.

Austin stepped up to the house and heard laughter through the screen door. From his suit jacket pocket he pulled the birthday card he had bought for his son and stepped inside.

He walked through the hallway into the large living room where Trace and John, Marcus and Reecie, and another adult couple sat drinking wine and laughing.

Troy, who had just turned sixteen, stood in the middle of the room. He was a very handsome boy who had his father's firm jaw-line and chin and his mother's kind eyes, and he was already just an inch shorter than Austin. He was trying on a joke gift — a pair of cheap, plastic shutter sunglasses he had just unwrapped.

"You can wear those when you go out partying with your friends tonight," Marcus said.

"Yeah, just call me Kanye West." Troy laughed.

When the room caught sight of Austin, everyone went quiet.

"Hey," Austin said, trying to sound enthusiastic but failing. "How's everyone?"

"What's up? Late as always," Marcus said.

John pulled himself from the sofa, walked over to Austin, and shook his hand. "How you been, Austin?"

"Good, John. Thanks."

Troy ignored his father, grabbed another gift-wrapped box, and started to tear the paper.

Trace noticed that and looked sadly at Austin. She stood, grabbing empty wineglasses. "I'll get refills, and another soda for you, Troy." She walked over to Austin. "Come help me with these."

Trace had been beautiful when Austin married her, and she remained that way. Her hair was sandy brown and cut shoulder-length. She had gained a few pounds since their divorce but still kept a nice shape, Austin thought as he followed her into the kitchen. He had been a fool to let her go.

Trace set the glasses down on the counter and turned to face Austin. "Why are you so late?"

"I had to get Troy's gift. Anyway, I know he doesn't want me here. I'm not going to stay."

"Austin, it can't just go on like this."

"You think this is what I want? I'm trying

to reach out to the boy, but —"

"Over four years of neglect won't just go away like that."

"I'm sorry. I thought he had John. Every time I wanted to do something with the kids, you said they were doing something with him."

"That happened three times."

"Three times was enough to push me away."

"It wasn't the kids' fault," Trace said.

"I know that now."

"Then it's time to fix it."

Austin sighed. "I'm going back outside. Tell Troy to come out so I can give him his present and we can speak alone."

"Austin, you really should stay."

"Just tell him, please?"

"Yeah."

Austin stepped out of the kitchen and made his way out to the front yard.

Two minutes later, Troy stepped out. He walked down the path and stopped five feet short of his father. Austin admired him. Although Austin constantly called, making attempts to hang out with Troy, the boy always turned him down. It had been over three months since he had seen his son. He was growing into a fine-looking young man.

"Happy birthday, son," Austin said, reaching out to hug him.

Troy stepped back. "Thank you."

Austin nervously combed his fingers through his hair. "You know, about me not being around . . ."

"I don't want to talk about that. Mom said you wanted me to come out here so you could give me a gift."

"Yeah. I did," Austin said, handing Troy the envelope.

Troy pulled out the card and read the store-bought message and his father's signature. There was a folded form in the card, which Troy opened. "What's this?"

"What does it look like?" Austin said, happily. "It's the title to a car."

"What are you talking about?"

Austin pointed to the car he had driven himself over in, the car he had spent most of the day looking for — the car he had bought his son. "It's a 1983 Mercedes C230. It's in mint condition. And it only has sixty-five thousand original miles on it." Austin was smiling wide as he held out the key to Troy.

"I don't want it."

"I looked all over the place for that car. It's perfect. What do you mean —"

"I said I don't want it. I know you're trying, but just because you buy me a car,

doesn't mean I'm going to forgive you."
Troy held out the car title to Austin. Austin
took it from his son's hand. "I know one
day I probably can, Dad. That day just isn't
today." He turned and headed back up to
the house.

Austin slid his hands into his pockets and
looked up to the sky.

A moment later, he felt Trace standing
beside him. She placed her hand on his
shoulder. "It'll take some time. But it'll happen. Long as you don't go anywhere."

"No. I'm not going anywhere," Austin
said, still looking up at the darkening sky. "I
never *should've* gone anywhere. I never
should've left you, Trace."

"Austin, stop."

He turned to her. "I mean it. Do you love
John?"

"Of course I do, and it's too late for us.
So just stop. Just make an effort, you'll find
someone. You're a great guy."

"You mean that?" Austin smiled, placing a
friendly arm around Trace's shoulder.

She wrapped an arm around his waist. "I
do."

"We had some not-so-bad times as husband and wife, right?"

"That's right."

"And we have two beautiful kids to show

for it. We'll always have that together, no matter what?"

"We will," Trace said.

Austin stood in front of his ex-wife and gave her the car title. "Keep this. Tell Troy I bought it not trying to win him back but because he's a great son and he deserves it. Besides, I know my son well enough to know that as soon as he gets his license, he's going to want to drive that thing."

"I think you're right," Trace smiled.

Austin gave Trace a peck on the cheek and said, "Now you need to get back to your party before our son misses you. I'm gonna call a cab home."

"Are you sure? I can drive you back."

"I'm fine. Go," Austin said, pulling out his cell phone. He was about to dial the number for information when he felt Trace touch his arm again.

"I don't know if it matters or not. I just didn't want you finding out from anyone but me."

"Finding out what?"

"I'm pregnant. John and I are going to have a baby."

Austin tried his best to smile. He stared speechless at Trace and thought, At forty-one, you're a little old for that, but said,

"Congratulations. I'm very happy for the both of you."

15

Caleb was emptying the wastebasket beside Austin's desk when he heard someone enter the main office of the law firm. He knew it was Jahlil.

Caleb set down the basket and the plastic bag and walked out of the office.

By the front reception area, Caleb saw his son walking toward him, his head down, his hood pulled up, casting shadows on his face.

"Jahlil," Caleb said.

Jahlil stopped, looked up, pulling the hood down off his head. He looked guilty of something. "Yeah."

"Where you been?"

"Around."

"I called you half a dozen times," Caleb said. "And left you at least three messages. Why didn't you return them?"

Jahlil paused. "I don't know."

"What you mean, you don't know?" Caleb said, taking a few steps toward the boy.

He was trying to remain calm.

"I don't know. I was doin' stuff."

"Your mother and I went up to your school, talked to your principal today. He told us what's going on. So this stuff you're doing, is it the same stuff keepin' you from going to your classes? That's keepin' you out of school?"

"Yeah, that stuff," Jahlil said, under his breath.

"What you say to me?" Caleb said, hurrying over, standing now just a foot in front of his son, doing everything in his power not to snatch the boy up and give him a good shaking. "This is a damn joke to you?"

"No. That's why I'm missing school, 'cause I got more important things to do than to be there wasting my time."

"You're sixteen years old. What the hell in your life right now is more important than school?"

Jahlil looked away and didn't answer.

"Look at me when I'm talking to you, boy! What is more important?"

Jahlil looked his father in the eyes. "Nothin'."

"You damn right nothin'," Caleb said, backing away, calming some. "Son, don't you understand? School is everything. It's what's gonna give you a good future. You see the difference between your uncles Marcus's and Austin's lives and mine. They went to school and I didn't. Uncle Austin owns this office, and I'm cleaning it." Caleb looked at Jahlil, thinking he was actually starting to get through to him. "That's why I'm telling you these things. I'm trying to help you. It's why I started this business, why I have you come up here a couple of nights a week, because I want you to learn the ropes. Then one day, when you finish high school, and maybe go to college, you'll be able to come back and —"

Jahlil laughed.

"What?"

Jahlil chuckled a little more. "You ain't about to say what I think, are you? When I'm done with school, I can come back here and take over your little cleaning business. You a trip, ol' man," Jahlil said, a defiant smirk on his face.

Caleb couldn't believe what he was hearing. He was so frozen with surprise that all he could do was continue to stand there and listen.

"You acting like you imparting some sacred fatherly wisdom on me, when you've been gone almost a third of my life. You been in and out of prison, in and out of work, lying around the house, worthless."

"Son," Caleb said, through clenched teeth. "You better watch what you say to me."

"Can't keep a job someone give you, so you got to make your own. The only reason you in business is because Uncle Austin let you clean up his trash, and you comparing ya'll like there's actually something to compare."

"Jahlil, boy . . ." Caleb said, clenching his fists now, caution in his voice. But he didn't think his son heard him, because he kept on talking.

"And you talk about me coming back, taking this over. I would never, ever do that. Because I'm never, ever gonna be like you. It's the reason why Ma kicked you out, because she no longer saw you as a man."

Before Jahlil could say another word, Caleb had charged him, had him pinned against the wall, one fist wrapped around the boy's throat, the other held back behind Caleb's head, shaking, as though forcing himself not to throw it.

Jahlil's eyes bulged with fear. Caleb's were near tears with fury. He stared at his son, breathing hard, his fist still suspended at the release point of a punch. "I know my life is shit! I don't need you telling me that. I know things ain't right with me and your mother, but I'm gonna fix that, I swear. And I'm sorry that I left you, sorry that I went away to jail," Caleb said, a tear falling from his eye. "But I did it trying to provide for you and your mother. Just like today. Everything I do is for you. I don't want you living this life. I would give my own life for you not to go through what I have. You understand that?"

Jahlil didn't answer, but tears were now in his eyes. He looked hurt, frightened, and he stared at his father as though he were a stranger.

"I'm sorry," Caleb said, finally realizing what his son must've been thinking. He quickly lowered his fist and released his son.

Jahlil glared up at him with a hate Caleb had never seen his son display. Jahlil wiped the tears from his face, turned, and hurried in the direction he had come.

"Jahlil, I'm sorry," Caleb said.

The boy ran and disappeared around a corner.

"I said I'm sorry!" Caleb yelled.

16

After a few drinks, Austin found himself parked down the street from Cindy's house. He sat slumped low in his car seat, waiting for her voice-mail recording to finish so he could leave his third message.

The beep sounded, and Austin said, "I'm outside your house. I want to talk to you when he leaves."

He hung up the phone and tossed it to the passenger seat, eyeing the Dodge Charger that sat in Cindy's driveway. Her fiancé was obviously visiting. Austin didn't care. Hearing that his son didn't forgive him, realizing that his ex-wife truly did not have any desire to get back together, and then hearing the news of her one day soon giving birth to another man's child had Austin needing to talk to someone.

He slid lower in his seat when he saw Cindy's porch light come on. The fiancé backed out the door, and Austin saw a glimpse of Cindy in her bathrobe. The man leaned back in, kissed Cindy on the lips. Austin felt a twinge of jealousy.

The fiancé trotted down the stairs to his car, jumped in, backed out the driveway, and drove off.

Austin was out of his car. Standing, he felt slightly wobbly from the drinks. He steadied himself and walked over to the house.

The front door was left open. Cindy was expecting him. Austin closed the door behind him and looked around. "Cindy," he called.

"Upstairs, in the bedroom."

Entering the room, Austin watched as Cindy made up her bed.

"You got my messages?"

"Yeah," she said, fluffing a pillow.

"I'm sorry. I had to talk to you."

Cindy sat on the edge of the made bed. "So talk."

Austin sat beside her and took her hands. "I want more. You told me you two still haven't set a date. You can break your engagement, and we can —"

"Austin, you've been drinking. I can smell it on your breath."

He released her hands. "This has nothing to do with my drinking. I'm at a point in my life where I want something more, and I've been seeing you long enough to know that I want it with you. You said that you wished you had met me first."

"But I didn't."

"He's out of work. He can't even take care of you."

"I'm taking care of the both of us right now," Cindy said.

"Obviously you're not. I'm giving you money."

Cindy was quiet, taking the remark like a slap across the face. "I'm with him, and I'm going to stay with him."

Austin shook his head, looking around the room. "So you're fine with never seeing me again?"

"I didn't say that. I like what we have. I don't want it to stop. At least not now."

Austin chuckled under his breath. "I see. I'm good enough to get with, but not good enough to be with."

"You're thinking too much into it," Cindy said, starting to unbutton Austin's shirt.

He thought of letting it happen; he could use her comfort right now. But he grabbed Cindy's hands and stopped her. "No. I said I want more, but if you don't want to give it to me, I guess I'm just going to have to get it from somewhere else."

17

In her dark bedroom, Daphanie sat by the window, looking out onto the street. Against her cheek, she rubbed a small white blanket. It was the only thing she had left of her child. The nurses had wrapped her baby in it after he had been delivered.

How could she have been such a fool to have let Nate trick her into giving away her own child?

Daphanie pressed the blanket to her nose, telling herself that she could still smell the child's pure scent, though it had been weeks since the cloth touched his skin.

She had made a fool of herself today. She would never get her baby back like that. She would have to be smarter.

She had looked over the contract several times. There were terms and phrases that she could not fully understand. She wasn't a lawyer, but she just knew there was no way the law would keep her from her child.

Daphanie walked through the dark room to her nightstand and grabbed her cell phone.

The day of the wedding, while she had waited in that back room like a damn fool for Nate, a woman had knocked on the door and entered. It was Nate's ex-wife, Monica, the woman who had been shot and had fallen into a coma.

Daphanie had seen her in the hospital, near death, tubes running in and out of her, half her head shaved. But when Monica walked in that back room on Daphanie's wedding day, she looked much better, beautiful even, and Daphanie could tell why Nate had married her.

Monica told Daphanie that Nate wasn't going to show, that intricate scams were what he was known for, and that the fake wedding was right up his alley.

Daphanie had told Monica everything she had given up for the chance to marry Nate. Monica shook her head, a knowing expression on her face, as if she had been used by him in a similar way. She told Daphanie she didn't know if there was anything that could've been done. Appearing sympathetic to Daphanie's situation, despite the fact that Daphanie had tried to lure Nate away from Monica, she dug through her purse, pulled out a business card, and held it out to Daphanie. "I hear he's a good attorney," Monica said. "You might want to give him a call."

Now, Daphanie called Monica.

"Hello," a voice answered, sounding groggy. Only now did Daphanie notice that the clock on her nightstand read 11:27 p.m.

"I'm sorry. Monica?"

"Yeah."

"This is Daphanie Coleman . . . you know the —"

"Yeah, I know who this is."

"If I'm waking you up, I can —"

"No. I was having a nightmare. What do you want?"

"That day . . . my wedding day, you gave me the business card of that attorney. You said that I should give him a call."

Monica didn't respond.

"Monica?"

"I'm here."

"You remember telling me that?" Daphanie asked.

"Yeah. Did you call him?"

Now Daphanie didn't respond.

"Are *you* there?" Monica said, attitude in her voice now.

"I haven't called. This feels like my last chance and I need him to take my case. You said you know him. Can you go with me, make sure he does?"

"I don't know him. I said I heard he was good, but I don't know him."

"Still, that's more than I have going for me. Can you go with me?"

"Daphanie, look, considering —"

"I know I was wrong for coming after your husband like that while you were in the hospital, but —"

"But what?"

"But I have no one to turn to," Daphanie said, helpless. "Nate stole my baby from me."

"You gave your baby away is the way I understand it."

Daphanie exhaled, trying to remain calm. She told herself she needed this woman's help. "You said scams were Nate's thing. You were married to him. I'm sure he's gotten you once or twice. Monica, please." Daphanie heard Monica sigh heavily on the other end of the phone.

"You don't deserve my help," Monica said.

"I know, but I need it."

There was another long pause from Monica's end. Finally, "Do you know where AERO is on Michigan Avenue?"

"I can find it."

"Meet me there tomorrow morning at nine."

"Thank you, Monica," Daphanie said, only then realizing that Monica had hung up.

18

Jahlil woke up to the smell of cooking bacon. He climbed out of bed, went to his closet, and pulled out a shoebox from the top shelf. He reached in and took out a rolled wad of money, held together by a fat, brown rubber band. Late last night, when he had come home and counted it, the total amounted to a little over $2,700.

For the last nine months, Jahlil, Toomey, and Bug had been doing whatever they could to make money. They broke into people's homes, shoplifted merchandise from stores and sold it on the streets, and robbed people as they approached their cars.

Jahlil wasn't proud of what he was doing, but he needed the money. The few dollars that his father threw at him were a joke.

He pulled the rubber band from the knot of bills, peeled off two twenties and a ten, then wrapped the band back around the cash. He set the money back in the box beside his 9mm handgun.

When Jahlil walked out of his bedroom, he saw his mother at the stove preparing breakfast. He stepped into the kitchen, lifted her coffee mug that was sitting on the counter beside the stove, and placed the fifty dollars of folded bills under it.

Sonya glanced over at the cash as she scooped bacon strips from the frying pan with a fork.

Jahlil sat down at the small kitchen table and watched as his mother came over and spooned scrambled eggs and bacon onto his plate. Sonya set her serving dishes down on a counter and returned with a bottle of hot sauce and her mug of coffee. She sat down across from her son and took a sip from her cup.

"Thanks, Ma," Jahlil said, stabbing a clump of eggs and sticking them into his mouth.

"You saw your father at work last night?"

Jahlil nodded without speaking.

"He tell you we went up to your school and saw your principal?"

"Naw, he didn't, Ma," Jahlil said, not looking up from his plate.

"I find that hard to believe."

"Ma," Jahlil said, giving his mother a stern

look, "I said he ain't say nothing about it. Now can I just eat my food?"

Sonya didn't respond. She stared at her son. "You've been missing a lot of school. I'm worried. This money that you've been giving me, does it have anything to do with that?"

Jahlil set his fork down hard against the plate. "You don't want the money? I'm trying to help you, trying to help us, and you asking me where I'm getting it from. You know what?" Jahlil said, pushing back from the table and standing before his mother. "I can just take it back."

"I'm not saying that. You know we need it."

"Then what you saying?"

"Jahlil," Sonya said, rising from her chair, standing five inches shorter than her son, "you have to be in school. You have to be better than you are."

"I ain't hearing that," Jahlil said, turning his back on Sonya, waving her away with a hand.

"If you're cutting school just to make this money, then you have to stop."

"What if I don't want to?" Jahlil spun, raising his voice. "What if I don't have that choice!"

"Then look around you. You're choosing

to live like this."

The apartment was old, their furniture secondhand, the carpeting on the floor worn and soiled beyond cleaning. A quiet night was when there were screams or sounds of fighting coming from just one of their neighbors' apartments.

"Your father didn't go to school either, and you see all he has to —"

"I don't wanna hear this no more. I'm leaving," Jahlil said, turning.

Sonya caught him by the hand. "Jahlil, just —"

Jahlil spun, raising the back of his hand, as though he was going to strike his mother. She cowered back, raising an arm over her face.

"I said I don't want to hear it, and I meant it!" he yelled.

Sonya slowly lowered her arm, shaking with anger.

Jahlil walked back over to the table and drained his glass of orange juice. "I don't wanna talk about this again, all right?" he said, taking his three strips of bacon and wrapping them in a napkin. "And I don't know when I'm coming in tonight, so don't be calling my cell all worried and stuff." He walked over to his mother, kissed her on the cheek, grabbed his book bag, and left.

19

Austin pushed his way through the doors of the Harris Firm & Associates, a small downtown family law office that employed seven attorneys.

He hadn't slept very well last night, on account of the incident with Cindy. He tossed in bed, wondering if he had been too quick in his decision to end things.

As he approached his office door, he saw Reecie, who was his office manager. A beautiful brown-skinned woman with short-cropped hair and pouty lips, she was hiding behind her desk, her phone pressed firmly to her ear. She was whispering harshly into the receiver. "Look! I told you, I don't want to have this discussion with you now. I'm at work."

Austin stood in front of the desk, his arms crossed, unnoticed.

When the call was over, Reecie looked up, startled to see Austin. She smiled thinly, then set the office phone gently in its cradle.

"Argument?" Austin said.

"Uh, I guess."

"With my brother, I assume."

"The one and only."

Austin shook his head. "Marcus is looking for a job, Reecie. You have to know that."

"I know, but —"

"So please, stop breaking his balls. I see enough of the two of you as it is. I don't want to have to choose which one of you I'll represent in your divorce. Okay?"

"Okay."

"Now, what do I have for today?"

"You have two in the office right now waiting for you, and I'll have your schedule printed up for you in five minutes. It's another busy day."

"Busy days are what I like around here. Thanks, Reecie," Austin said, before stepping into his office. "Oh yeah, and if you really want to trade places with my brother, I could always fire you and hire him."

"Very funny, Austin. But no thanks," Reecie said.

"Good morning," Austin said, stepping into his office, approaching the women, his hand extended. "I'm Austin Harris."

The shorter woman with the short, styled

black hair stood, took Austin's hand, and shook. "Good morning, I'm Monica Rodgers."

Austin looked into Monica Rodgers's eyes, holding her stare and her hand a little longer than he knew he should've, but for some reason, he couldn't pull either away.

"And this is Daphanie Coleman," Monica said, breaking what bond, if any, the two had.

Daphanie reached out a hand to Austin but did not stand. She looked tired and worried.

"Good to meet you, Miss Coleman."

"Please, call me Daphanie."

Austin set his briefcase down beside his desk and had a seat. "Now, tell me what I can do for you."

Daphanie filled Austin in on the events that led her here.

"The contract he had you sign, do you have a copy of it?" Austin asked, very interested in taking a look at the document.

Daphanie dug into her large purse and pulled out the rolled-up contract. She handed it to Austin.

He flipped through the pages quickly, landing on one and giving it a moment of his attention.

"What do you see?" Monica asked.

"It looks in order," Austin said, glancing up at Monica and forcing himself to take his eyes away again.

"That's not good, is it?" Daphanie asked, concerned. "Does that mean you can't do anything?"

"That's not what I'm saying. I'm going to have to make a copy and really give this a good going over. I'm sorry I can't do it now. I have a very busy day scheduled and I'll need more time to look at this."

"That means you'll take the case?" Daphanie asked.

"Yes. Definitely," Austin said, standing from his desk. "Please, leave whatever pertinent information you feel I should have with Reecie outside, along with the address and numbers for Trevor Morgan and Nate . . . ?"

"Kenny," Monica said. "His last name is Kenny."

"Yes, and Nate Kenny," Austin said to Monica. He thought he saw what looked like a smile from her, before she turned to exit the office, but it might have just been wishful thinking.

"Thank you," Daphanie said, as the women walked out the door.

Austin leaned against his desk, telling himself that maybe he should stop Monica, ask her if he could call her. Yes, he would have her personal information in his records, but it would be against his ethics to contact her that way. He would need her permission. But who was he kidding? Just yesterday he had made a not-so-serious play for his ex-wife and then tried to start a serious relationship with an engaged woman, whom he knew nothing about aside from the fact that she was terrific in bed. He was emotionally all over the place. It was probably best he just left Monica Rodgers alone.

"Excuse me."

Austin looked up to see Monica standing just inside his office.

"Uh, yes," Austin said, surprised.

"I just wanted to thank you again for seeing us and taking this case without a second thought. It's a shame what that man did to Daphanie. It should be against the law."

"I agree. And thanks for thinking of my firm for representation."

"Oh, someone had given me a card a while back and . . ." Monica stuck out her hand. "So . . . have a good day."

Austin hurried over and shook Monica's hand again. He looked in her eyes. She didn't look away.

"Forgive me, but are you getting this too?" Austin said.

"Getting what?"

"There's a little connection here, a little . . . electricity, or something. Or am I mistaken?"

Monica laughed. Austin felt her hand almost slip from his grasp but held on firmly. "Yes, you're definitely mistaken. But you're cute."

"Really," Austin said, smiling. "I'll take wrong and cute over right and not cute any day."

"Okay," Monica said, laughing again. "You're funny too."

Feeling there was no better time, Austin said, "I know this is sudden, but what do you think about going out with me?"

"Wow, not one for wasting time, are you?"

"Not when I see something I want."

"I really don't know. I haven't had much luck with the relationship thing, so I've pretty much sworn them off."

"That's why you came back in my office, because you *didn't* want to talk to me again?" Austin said, feeling more confident. "Besides, who said anything about relationships? I just wanna know if you'd like to go out."

"I came back in to thank you for taking the case."

"Then show your gratitude by letting me

take you out."

Monica looked as though she was giving it serious thought. "The best I can do now is a maybe. Your assistant has my info. Give me a call and we'll see. Now, can I have my hand back?" Monica said, smiling.

Austin smiled and released her. "Yes, and thanks for the maybe."

20

Blue and Caleb had been through forms of hell together Caleb hadn't even known existed. Their jail sentences split them, and until eight years ago, they hadn't seen one another for the five previous years, but they always seemed to find their way back together. Caleb was glad about that. He had missed his friend while they were apart.

Blue sat on cement stairs beside Caleb. He was naturally muscular, wore a goatee, and had skin the color of dark, wet dirt. He chewed on a huge wad of bubble gum as he stared up at the building before them.

"I shouldn't even be here," Caleb said.

"You said Kwan's guys were waiting for you yesterday, right?"

"Yeah, but they ain't do nothing."

Blue popped a bubble he had blown. "So what, you think that means they ain't gonna do nothing? That guy with no head and hands — his name was Darryl. I know a guy who knew him. He had a little girl. He was into Kwan for only twenty-five hundred."

"That's five hundred less than I owe him," Caleb said.

"Yeah. That man won't have no problem doing you just like he did the other dude, don't matter if you two went back to grammar school together."

Caleb lowered his head, clamped his hands over his skull. "You did eight years in prison, Blue. Why you even considering this?"

"I ain't got plans of going back, ever. But there's still money to be had. Look at that building," Blue said, grabbing Caleb by the shoulder and pointing to the three-level electronics store across the street. "Filled with all sorts of flat-screens, computers, and video consoles. Me and a couple of guys already got an inside man. All we gotta do is walk in, clean 'em out, and load it on the truck. Don't know how much our share will be for sure, but it's a portion of everything we take. The man who runs the operation said we should get no less than four grand apiece."

"Four thousand," Caleb said, looking up at Blue.

"That's right."

"Who is this guy?"

"Just some dude I met my last year. This is what he does, finds out about moneymaking opportunities, and puts teams together to take advantage, if you know what I'm sayin'."

Caleb looked up at the building again. He thought back to all those years ago when Blue, Caleb, and their friend Ray Ray decided to hold up a convenience store, because Caleb needed the money to help his family.

Ray Ray died in that robbery attempt, and Blue and Caleb were both caught only blocks from the scene.

Blue did eight years in prison, Caleb did five.

Caleb remembered the day the enormity of what he had done finally dawned on him.

He had already been incarcerated. Sonya had visited him and told him she wouldn't be able to do the time with him. She was taking their son and leaving. It was the worst day of Caleb's life. In one bad move, he lost not only his freedom but his family, whose well-being was the reason he had committed the crime in the first place.

Trapped in jail, with five years in front of him, Caleb had felt he had nothing left to live for. But days later, Caleb's father, Julius, who had been diagnosed with terminal prostate cancer, came to visit him.

The man had abandoned Caleb, Marcus, and Austin for twenty-five years and only tried to reconcile with them after learning he was going to die from the deadly disease. But he was there, trying to finally do right by his son. He told Caleb that he would move Sonya and his young son, Jahlil, to California with him and his partner, Cathy.

Caleb hated his father, had every reason to reject whatever he wanted to do for him, but he had no other options.

Julius held the phone to his face, staring at Caleb through the thick prison glass. "I told Sonya that she could get a job there, live with us. We'd help take care of Jahlil. We'd give them everything we can."

Nervously, Caleb said, "What did she say?"

"Nothing at first. But she finally said yes. She said yes, Caleb."

Caleb stood up from the steps now, looking down at Blue.

"So what's the deal? You in?" Blue asked.

"We rolled the dice once and we lost," Caleb said. "I ain't risking that again. I'm forty-one. My family and my freedom mean too much to me now."

"And how about your life?"

"I got a couple of contracts I'm supposed to be finding out about. I get money up front for those if I get them. It'll work out."

"And if it don't?"

Caleb held out his hand to Blue. Blue stood and gave him some dap. "It'll work out," Caleb said.

21

Outside of the Harris offices on the street, Daphanie turned to Monica and extended a hand.

"Thanks for doing that. I appreciate it."

"Don't thank me. I don't know if it'll do any good."

"Still, you didn't have to help me. Especially after how . . . well . . . you know."

"Good-bye, Daphanie," Monica said, about to turn to leave.

"Monica," Daphanie called. "I was just wondering . . . has he asked you back?"

"What?"

"Nate, he ask you to come back to him?"

Monica couldn't believe what this woman had just asked her. "He left me because you lied to him and told him you were having his baby."

"I know, but after he found out it was a lie, I'm sure he asked you back. He would try to hide it, but when he talked about you,

I could hear in his voice that he still loved you."

Monica could hardly comprehend this. After they had divorced, everything Nate had said to her, every time he confessed he still loved her, Monica had felt he was lying. But for someone else to say she could hear the so-called love Nate felt caught her by surprise. Monica told herself to put what she had just heard out of her mind, and she tried her best not to show the struggle she was having with it. "Good-bye, Daphanie."

Half an hour later, Monica walked through a nearby store, looking into the glass display cabinets.

As she browsed, she thought about last night, when Daphanie had called in the middle of yet another nightmare. This time Freddy was in her bedroom with her. Monica had locked her door as she did every night before she went to bed, but somehow Freddy got in the room. When she realized he was there, she sprang up in bed and immediately took a bullet to the head. Monica saw herself, saw the hole the bullet burrowed into her skull, witnessed the thin line of blood as it dripped down the center of her face, between her bulging eyes.

She had stumbled out of bed, fallen to the

floor, crawled across the room, and checked her bedroom door. It was locked. She lay back down, wide awake for another two hours, fearing that someone was standing outside her front door, that someone might come into her house. If someone did, and was standing at the foot of her bed, what could she do?

A bearded man wearing a plaid shirt stepped up behind one of the glass cases Monica was looking down into.

"Welcome back. Your application was approved two days ago. You're all set to buy. See anything you like?"

Once she was out of the hospital, Monica had told herself this was something she wanted to do — needed to do. "Yes," Monica said, pressing a finger against the surface of the glass counter, indicating what she was interested in. "That one."

The man stooped down, unlocked the cabinet, pulled the item out, and placed it in Monica's hands.

It felt good to her. "What kind is this?" she asked.

"It's a forty-four caliber automatic."

"Good," Monica said. "I'll take it."

22

Daphanie stepped back up to the receptionist Charlene's desk. The woman glared at
Daphanie the moment she saw her step off
the elevator.

Nate was clear that he had no desire or
intention of helping Daphanie. If the meeting this morning with the attorney had been
more positive, if Mr. Harris had sounded
more certain that he could get Daphanie's
son back, she wouldn't have come back
here. But she couldn't rely just on him. She
needed to do everything in her power to
reunite with her child, including begging
Nate a million times if she had to.

"Charlene," Daphanie said politely, "I'm
sorry about the last time I was here, but I
really need to see Mr. Kenny again. Do you
think that's possible?"

Charlene strained a smile, then said, "No
apology necessary, Miss Coleman. I'll tell
him you're here." Charlene picked up the

phone. "Daphanie Coleman is here. Yes. Yes. That's correct. Thank you." She hung up the phone, smiling more sincerely. "You can wait right here. It'll just be a minute."

"Thank you, Charlene," Daphanie said. "You don't know how much I appreciate this."

"Sure."

Daphanie kept her eye in the direction of Nate's office, deciding what she would say to him once they were alone. She had no definite words. She would simply beg. She would try to convey how much she loved her child, how wrong it was for him to be torn from her like that, then beseech Nate to do whatever he could to bring them back together.

Daphanie felt a hand on her arm. She quickly spun around to see two security guards standing in front of her.

"Wha—"

"Miss Coleman," the taller guard with the crew cut said, "you're prohibited from entering this office. Will you come with us, please? We need to escort you out."

"But I'm here to speak to Mr. Kenny." Daphanie turned to Charlene. "She just called —"

"Sorry," Charlene said, spitefully smiling.

"It was these guys I just called, per Mr. Kenny's request."

23

Jahlil helped his girlfriend, Shaun, through the door of her apartment, then took her by the elbow and walked her into the small kitchenette. He pulled a chair from the table and gently lowered her into it.

They had just ridden the train back from one of her last prenatal checkups at the county hospital.

"You want something to drink, baby?" Jahlil asked, standing by the fridge.

"Yeah, can you get me a grape pop?"

Jahlil took two sodas out of the fridge, rinsed the tops under water in the sink, wiped them with a paper towel, and popped the top on Shaun's.

"Thank you," she said, after having been quiet all the way from the hospital, despite the positive visit.

"What's wrong with you?"

"I'm fine," she said.

"No, you're not. We about to have a baby

and you acting like it's the end of the world. This is a good thing that's happening to us."

"Is it happening to us, or is it just happening to me?"

"What?"

"How did you act when you found out I was pregnant?"

"That was eight months ago. I was scared," Jahlil explained. "Have I been acting like I don't want this? Have I not been around?"

"All my friends with babies say you acting all excited now, but as soon as the baby come, you gonna tell yourself it's too much and leave us."

"Baby," Jahlil said, taking Shaun's hands and kneeling by the side of the chair. "I know what it feels like to have my father leave, and I would never do that to our baby. I'm gonna be here always to take care of her. To take care of both of you."

Shaun smiled a little and rubbed Jahlil's hands. "And how you gonna do that? How we gonna support our child when I'm seventeen and you only sixteen and we have no skills and ain't even out of school? I live here, and you live there. And you know my mama don't even want me to have this baby. Fact that she hate you don't help either."

Jahlil stood, feeling himself growing angry.

"Why you saying all this negative stuff now?"

"You asked what was bothering me. You really wanna know?"

"Wouldn't have asked if I didn't."

Shaun shook her head. "I love you, Jahlil. I think you're a good boy. But I don't want our baby to be one more child out there suffering, living in poverty like we both doing now."

"She won't. I told you that," Jahlil said, angered at being questioned about this again.

"You need to make sure of that," Shaun said. "Find a way to keep that from happening."

24

It was late afternoon and Austin was in a wonderful mood, still thinking about the beautiful woman, Monica, he had met earlier.

He had seen three more clients after she left. The day was going well, he thought, his feet kicked up on his desk, his arms crossed behind his head when he heard arguing just outside his office door.

He hurried to his door, flung it open to see his brother, Marcus, standing before Reecie's desk, stabbing a finger at her, rage on his face, saying, "If the shoe was on the other foot, I wouldn't make you!"

Reecie was holding her own, her arms crossed tightly over her chest, as she yelled back, "But it ain't. And this isn't about nobody's shoes. This is about you getting a damn job!"

"Hold it, hold it!" Austin said, waving his arms, stepping in between the two. "First of all, this is the Harris Firm office, not the corner of Sixty-Third and King Drive, so I won't have all this yelling up in here. Second, exactly what the hell is going on?"

Both Reecie and Marcus started explaining at the same time, making little sense.

"Okay, okay!" Austin said, waving his arms again. "Marcus, in my office."

"But, I'm just trying —"

Austin raised his voice. "In my office."

Austin closed the door, after Marcus stepped in. "Have a seat."

Marcus flopped into one of the chairs before Austin's desk.

"What the hell is really going on between the two of you?"

"Austin, I'm an artist."

"Yes, Marcus. You're an artist. You've been saying that since you were five years old. What does that have to do with —"

"I have a master's degree in fine art. I can't help that my business failed because of the economy. Does that erase all the years I spent in school?"

"Exactly what are you getting at?"

"Despite how much she insists, I'm not wearing anybody's blue vest or orange smock or green apron."

"In English!"

"I'm not getting a job at Walmart, Home

Depot, or Starbucks."

"Then work somewhere else."

"There is nowhere else that I want to work. Reecie expects me to waste my time surfing job sites all day, going to job fairs, looking for crappy positions that she knows good and well she'd never take. I'm above that."

"But bills need to be paid. You above that too?" Austin said.

"On what you pay Reecie, we're doing fine. All the bills get paid. We even have a little for savings. The woman just has issues with the fact that I'm not out there working some minimum wage job."

"If she has issues, it's your job to resolve them."

"She'll get over them," Marcus said, standing, preparing to leave. "What else can she do? Nothing."

25

Toomey sat in his social studies class, nervous. He kept telling himself that nothing bad had happened to Jahlil, even though he wasn't in the seat next to Toomey's where he was supposed to be. Before class, Toomey had called Jahlil's cell phone three times, but Jahlil hadn't picked up.

Yeah, Toomey knew his friend cut a lot of school, but usually Jahlil would tell him when he was missing class. It wasn't like him to just not show up, especially after what had gone down yesterday when those little boys rolled up on them.

Jahlil said they were just some fools trying to cop, but looking in his eyes, Toomey knew Jahlil was bothered. Toomey didn't know who the little punks were, but they definitely were somebody.

Toomey looked up at the clock, watching the second hand sweep around the clock one final time till the bell rang announcing the end of the period.

He grabbed his books and papers and headed for the door, then to the boys' room. He had to take a leak before physics.

He pushed his way through the swinging door and saw a boy he knew from PE washing his hands at the sink.

"What's up, Toomey?" the chubby boy said.

"What's up, Robby?" Toomey said, heading toward the urinals. "Hey, you seen Jahlil around today?"

"Nope," Robby said, tossing a paper towel into the trash can. "Hurry up. You gonna be late for next period."

Toomey hurried over to one of the urinals and quickly did his business, but when he finished and spun around, he was no longer alone.

Three boys — who by their height, size, and the hair on their faces looked more like men — stood in front of Toomey. They all looked to be at least eighteen or nineteen years old.

The shortest one in the center had a gold front tooth and a green bandanna hanging from his back pocket. "What you ride, fool?"

"What?" Toomey said, trembling. If he hadn't just taken a piss, he would've surely wet his pants.

"What fucking gang you in?"

"I'm not in any gang. I'm just . . . just a student."

The one in the center looked to the other two. The one on the right had a clean-shaved head and wore dark sunglasses.

"He lying," the one on the left said. He had a scar on his face that ran from the inner corner of his right eye to the right outer corner of his mouth.

"I'm not lying. I swear!"

Gold Tooth grabbed Toomey by his throat and forced him back against the urinals. "Shut the fuck up! You speak when you spoken to. Now who the boy that was selling on our street yesterday?"

Toomey was about to lie, say he didn't know, but Scarface lifted his jersey just a little to expose the handle of a small handgun.

"See that?" Gold Tooth said. "It stays where it is long as you don't lie. Now I'm gonna ask you again. Who the boy?"

Trembling, sweat coating his brow, and scared for his life, Toomey said, "Jahlil Harris."

26

Caleb stood in the dirty, dank hallway of the run-down apartment building, knocked on the door, and waited. A moment later, the door opened two inches, a chain stopping it. Sonya peeked out through the space.

"What's up, Sonya?" Caleb said.

"You didn't call. What do you want?"

"What do you mean, what do I want? Let me in."

Sonya stared at Caleb for a moment, then closed the door. He heard the chain being unfastened. The door opened again, all the way this time. Sonya stood beside it, wearing jeans, a T-shirt, and flip-flops.

Caleb leaned in to kiss Sonya. She turned her head to the side, and Caleb pecked her on the cheek. He walked into the living room and looked around. Nothing had changed. The furniture was the same old ratty stuff he had bought from the thrift shop, and although Sonya was always cleaning, the apartment managed to look as though it were covered by a perpetual blanket of grime.

"See you keeping the place up nice," Caleb said.

"Shouldn't you be at work, Caleb?"

"Not for another few hours."

"Then why you here?"

"Did you talk to Jahlil this morning about his absences?"

Sonya walked across the room, rubbing her arms as though it were cold. She sat down on the sofa. "Yeah."

"And?"

"And everything's fine. I told him if he don't start going back, he's gonna be in serious trouble with me and you." Sonya glanced up at Caleb, then looked away. "He said he would do better."

Caleb walked over to the sofa, stood over Sonya, his hands in his pockets. "I know you don't like being hard on him, but it's what he needs. If it don't come from us, where's it gonna come from?"

"I know," Sonya said, looking down.

"Don't worry," Caleb said, resting a hand on her shoulder. "You're doing a good job." Caleb pulled his other hand out of his pocket and held something out to Sonya.

"What's this?"

"It's not a lot, but I just figured you could use it."

Sonya took the money from Caleb to count it. It was twenty-five dollars.

"I don't want it," Sonya said, trying to give it back.

"It's okay. Don't act like you don't need it."

"I don't. Not if it's coming from you," Sonya said.

"You over here working less than part-time, trying to raise our son by yourself, but you don't —"

"I *am* raising him!" Sonya said, coming up off the sofa.

"And you turning down the little money I'm trying to give you?"

"Why you giving it to me, when I know you need it yourself?"

" 'Cause I want you to have it."

"No. You doing it thinking it's gonna get your ass back in this apartment. That ain't happening. I gave you twenty years of my life, and where am I? In this same, torn-up-ass apartment we started in," Sonya said. "You kept telling me what you were gonna do, but you never did it. You ain't done nothing. Not a goddamn thing."

Caleb felt as though his heart had just been ripped from his chest. Sonya always had an uncanny knack of being able to make him feel that way. "You saying when I was here, things weren't better for you and for Jahlil than they are now? That our son wasn't in a lot less trouble when I was here?"

Sonya stared back at Caleb with narrowed eyes. "Since you've been gone, neither of us has missed you one bit."

Caleb grabbed Sonya's hand, pressed the twenty-five dollars back into her palm, smashed her fingers around it. "And you wonder why I went to another woman," Caleb said, then walked off.

27

Jahlil didn't feel like going back to school, but he had to. That worthless principal of his squealed to his parents, and now both his mother and father were on him. Despite how much he hated school, he realized if he didn't at least make an effort to go, his parents would get on him worse, possibly stopping him from making the money he was getting on the side. With Shaun to take care of, and a baby on the way, missing that money wasn't an option.

Jahlil told himself he would attend his last two class periods, then go back and check on Shaun later this evening.

Two blocks from school, Jahlil pulled out his cell phone to make a call. The battery had died.

He walked further down the street, passing a group of four rough-looking boys standing in front of the community center. They were talking low, staring at Jahlil as he approached.

Jahlil caught one of the boy's stares as he passed. He was older, seventeen, eighteen, maybe even nineteen. He had a gold tooth in the front of his mouth. Jahlil nodded at the boy. The boy nodded back.

Jahlil slid his cell phone back into his pocket, hoping that Bug had brought his charger to school today. They had the same phone, and Jahlil didn't like not having access to his cell.

When he looked up, Jahlil saw a boy ten feet in front of him, walking toward him. He had no idea where he came from. The boy wore a hood, had a vicious scar cutting down the side of his face, and he was staring right into Jahlil's eyes as he neared him.

The situation wasn't anything out of the ordinary. He lived in the hood. Every street he walked down, there were menacing-looking dudes hanging out, but something did not feel right to Jahlil that moment. He shoved his hands in his pockets, lowered his head, and thought about taking off, running as fast as he could. But nothing warranted that — nothing had happened. Instead, Jahlil continued on, held his breath, and kept his eyes down as the boy walked past.

A few steps later, he breathed a sigh of relief, thankful that he had made more of that situation than it actually was, when he heard, "Hey, you."

Jahlil halted and slowly turned around. "Yeah. What's up?"

The boy with the scar was now standing in front of him. "Yo' name Jahlil?"

"Yeah. That's my name."

A weird smile appeared on the scarred boy's face. Jahlil noticed his eyes look over Jahlil's shoulder. The boy then nodded his head like he was communicating with someone.

Quickly, Jahlil spun around. When he did, he caught a glimpse of a boy speeding toward him, a demented look on his face, holding a wooden board. Before Jahlil could raise his hands, defend himself, the boy swung the plank like a baseball bat, striking him across his head and the side of his face.

Jahlil's vision blurred, the world spun, and the light around him darkened. The sidewalk shifted below his feet and came up and struck him in the head. He was on the ground. He could hear nothing but the loud ringing in his brain and the muffled sound of the yelling boys as they gathered around him in a circle.

Through the fuzzy vision of his narrowed eyes, Jahlil could see how they jostled each other, trying to get at him. He read their mouths as they kicked and beat him. It looked as though they were yelling "G-Stone! G-Stone!" and throwing up hand signs in the form of *G*s.

Jahlil, seeing the bottom of one boy's boot as he raised it, figured this was payback for selling on G-Stone's street. The boot crashed down onto Jahlil's face, and then all went black.

28

Daphanie paced across the hardwood floors at her best friend Brownie's town house. She and Daphanie had worked together as nurses before Daphanie crossed over into pharmaceutical sales, then lost that job during the recession.

Brownie, who was five-three and curvy and wore her brown hair short, sat on the arm of her sofa, shaking her head. "All they did was throw you out? You were lucky they didn't arrest you. Why would you even go back there?"

"I had to do something," Daphanie said, stopping, staring at Brownie as though the woman was clueless. "I can't just sit while some man steals my child!"

"That happens to be the father of your child. And nobody told you to go trading in your baby like he was a used car."

Daphanie walked up to Brownie and stood right over her. "If you say that one more time to me, I swear I'm gonna hit you."

"Why are you tripping? You're in as good a place as you can be. You said that woman, Monica, helped you find a good attorney and —"

"He's some guy who's earning a paycheck and has no emotional investment in whether I win or lose. And Monica, the woman that was married to the man that was going to marry me — why would she care about me getting my child back? I'm helpless, sitting here waiting for other people to act. With each day that passes, I have less and less of a chance of getting my baby. If you only knew how I felt."

"I'm sorry. I don't."

"Maybe Nate wouldn't be so fucking smug, so callous, if he had the slightest idea of how I was feeling." Daphanie paced across the floor once more, then stopped. She closed her eyes and scratched her chin, then a knowing smile came to her face. "Hell yeah," Daphanie said. "That's what will change his mind." She started quickly toward the door.

Brownie sprang from the sofa, was behind Daphanie, pulling her by the arm. "Hold it, what are you gonna do?"

Daphanie turned to Brownie. "I'm gonna make him feel what I feel."

29

Caleb was walking quickly through the main hospital corridor toward the ER when a woman wearing glasses and a gray pantsuit stepped in front of him. "Mr. Harris?" the woman said. "Can I speak with you?"

"I don't have time," Caleb said, looking over the woman's shoulder at the EMERGENCY ROOM sign. "I have to see my son. Someone called and —"

"I know. That's what I need to speak to you about. My name is Detective Currie." She brought out a billfold, flashed her badge and ID.

Caleb glanced down, then back over the woman's shoulder. "Can't this wait?"

"Just a couple of minutes of your time, sir. It'll help us catch whoever is responsible for this."

"Fine. A couple of minutes," Caleb said, crossing his arms, looking worriedly over the detective's shoulder.

"Is your son in a gang?"

"No. He's not in a gang. Why are you asking me that?"

"Because I spoke to a couple of eyewitnesses, and they believe the people who beat your son were from the G-Stone gang."

"No. I don't believe that," Caleb said, again taking steps toward the ER door.

Detective Currie walked ahead and stepped in front of him, blocking his path. "I'm just trying to find out if he has any affiliation."

"I don't know. Why don't you ask him?"

"I did, and he's not telling me anything."

"Maybe because there's nothing to tell. Now, if you don't mind, your two minutes are up. I need to see my son."

"One more thing," Detective Currie said, grabbing Caleb's arm. She held a business card in the other hand. "If you find out anything, please give me a call. There are too many of our children dying out there on those streets. Let's just be glad, this time, your son wasn't one of them."

"Yeah," Caleb said, taking the card.

Walking through the ER doors, Caleb spoke to a nurse, who directed him to Jahlil's attending physician. The doctor told Caleb that Jahlil had been lucky. He had no serious injuries, but had suffered a concussion. Caleb was also informed that he might be shocked upon seeing his son — they hadn't cleaned him up yet — but not to worry, all of the swelling and bruising was strictly superficial, and Jahlil would recover completely.

Caleb was escorted to triage room 3, where Jahlil was being treated. The doctor told Caleb he would be cleaned up, held for another few hours for observation, then released.

When he pushed open the door of Jahlil's room, his son was lying on a gurney. Both eyes were swollen — one partially, the left completely closed. His skin was marked by bruises of several different shades of red and purple. His bottom lip was split, and a knot the size of a golf ball protruded from the right side of his forehead. A white towel had been placed under his head to catch the blood that spilled from his nose and mouth. Much of it had dried on his face.

Jahlil was alone in the room. Caleb looked at his boy and wanted to break down and cry for not being there to protect him.

He walked over to Jahlil, not knowing if his son even knew he was in the room. Jahlil's eyes were closed.

Caleb grabbed his son's hand. "Jahlil."

The boy stirred. His right eye opened a

little. He turned his head to look at his father.

"What happened to you?"

"I was jumped," Jahlil said. His voice was low, and he spoke as though he had a mouth full of gauze.

"By who?"

Jahlil looked up at the ceiling with his one good eye. "I don't know."

Caleb didn't believe him. Already he felt himself getting frustrated, but he told himself to calm down. "Are you sure?"

"Yeah."

"Were they gang members?"

"I don't know," Jahlil said with a tone that suggested he was tired of questions.

The boy was lying to him. Jahlil was his son, his responsibility and he had gotten hurt, could've even possibly been killed. Caleb felt guilty that he hadn't been around to protect him from that, but he was getting angry that Jahlil was stopping him from doing whatever he needed to do to make sure it never happened again.

"Jahlil, I know you're hurting, but I'm going to ask you one more time. Who did this to you?"

"I said, I — don't — know!" Jahlil said, lifting his head off the towel a little to emphasize his point.

"Fine! You want to play it like that!" Caleb yelled, infuriated, grabbing the boy by the front of his shirt. "Then I'll —"

"What are you doing!" Sonya screamed.

Caleb released Jahlil and turned to see Sonya standing just inside the triage room door.

"He knows who did this, but he won't say," Caleb said, pointing at his son. "I know he didn't get the hell beaten out of him like this for no reason. He's gonna tell me."

"Get out!" Sonya said. "Get the hell out of here! Your son is hurt. He's in pain, and you're questioning him like a criminal. Get out! You never come near him again! Do you hear me?"

The words snapped Caleb out of his rage. Maybe Sonya was right. Maybe Jahlil didn't deserve this. Maybe he was innocent, was in the wrong place at the wrong time. Maybe Caleb had this all wrong. He turned to the boy. "Jahlil, I'm —"

"Just get out," Sonya said, rushing over to Jahlil's side, as if to protect him.

Caleb lowered his head and walked out of the room.

30

A candle sat in the center of the table. The lights were low, and the gentleman that Tabatha had set Monica up with was particularly charming. His name was Kevin. He was fit and had a nice smile. He had thick, freshly cut hair and came well dressed in a collared shirt, cuff links, and a sport jacket. He was a pediatrician. He seemed smart and his conversation was interesting.

Tabatha had called Monica two hours ago.

"So it's set up," Tabatha said.

"What's set up?"

"The date for tonight that I told you about a couple of days ago. It's at the China Doll, on Wells Street. You like Chinese, right?"

"It doesn't make me vomit, but I'm not going on a date. I told you that."

"Because you're so busy doing what?" Tabatha said. "He's a nice guy. He's handsome, and he's a doctor."

"That doesn't matter to me. I have my

own money."

"Really? Not even impressed a little bit?" Tabatha said.

"Okay, it doesn't matter all that much," Monica said. "But I told you, I'm not looking for a boyfriend."

"Fine, then look at it as a free dinner. If he impresses you, screw him, I don't know."

"Really, Tab?" Monica laughed.

"You'll go? You'll meet him there? I vouched for you. Don't have me out there like that."

Monica looked around her house, realizing that if she didn't go, she probably would spend the evening watching TV, eating a pint of ice cream. "Yeah, I'll go."

Kevin was getting comfortable. He had already grabbed Monica's hand from across the table and was rubbing it as though they had been dating for months.

"You're even more beautiful than Tabatha described."

Monica raised her glass of wine, taking a sip. "Flattery will get you everywhere."

"I'm hoping so." Kevin smiled, drinking from his glass. "Would you mind if I'm totally transparent tonight?"

"Honesty is a good thing."

"I just made forty-two years old. I'm not

much into the dating scene anymore, and to tell you the truth, Tabatha had to convince me to come out here tonight. I was actually pretty nervous."

"Oh, did she?" Monica smiled, making a mental note to strangle Tabatha the next time she saw her.

"I'm so glad she did, because I'm having a wonderful time, and if you will forgive me for flattering you too much, in the short time I've known you, I've come to believe that you're a really wonderful person."

"Well . . . I mean, you're definitely entitled to your opinion." Monica laughed.

"I want to see you again," Kevin said, now taking her hand with both of his. "Is that possible?"

There it was, Monica thought. If she said yes, they would date, become closer, screw, say they loved one another, then sometime in the future, if her luck was as it always was, their relationship would crash in flames, like the two she had had before. She didn't know if she was ready for that. But if Monica said no, she would remain lonely, cruising bars at all hours of the night, doing who knows what, with who knows who. Even worse, she might start believing that life was better with her ex-husband and accept him back if he came slumming around for an invitation, as he so often did. She had to admit, that nonsense Daphanie had told her about Nate still loving her had shaken Monica to some degree. But returning to Nate was the last thing in life she wanted, or needed. She had to stay away from him. Maybe Kevin would be just the diversion she needed, till she was fully able to recover from her ex-husband.

"Yes," Monica said, giving it no further thought. "You can see me again."

"Good. Good," Kevin said, releasing Monica's hand. He raised his glass, and Monica raised hers. "A toast," Kevin said. "To the beginning."

"What the hell, the beginning," Monica said.

They took sips from their glasses.

"Not saying that you and I will end up married, but if we do, I just want you to know, I love children and want at least three of them." Kevin smiled.

Monica choked on her wine, spitting some of it back into her glass.

"You okay?" Kevin asked.

Monica set her glass down, wiped her mouth with her napkin, while staring at the man. She figured he thought this was what most single, childless women wanted to hear from a man who was a doctor and interested in marriage. Monica was different. She had experienced that whole childbearing drama with her ex-husband — Nate wanting a child, Monica not being able to produce, and being tossed away because of it. She would not go through that again.

Monica reached for her purse, plucked out a fifty-dollar bill.

"Hey. No, no, no," Kevin said. "Don't you even think about it. I'm covering this."

"No, this is only fair," Monica said, scooting out of the booth.

"Wait, where are you going? I thought you said —"

"Yeah, but I'm saying something else now," Monica said, holding up a finger. "Never tell a woman how many children you're going to have till you find out if she wants any at all. Good-bye, Kevin," Monica said, shouldering her purse and walking away.

31

Austin stepped into his home, still unable to stop thinking about Monica Rodgers. He had gotten her phone number from Reecie as Monica told him he could do. He had to stop himself a few times from ringing her cell phone on the way home. He told himself that could wait. The case he had taken was more important.

Before leaving work, Austin had Reecie reach out to both men involved in the Daphanie Coleman case: Trevor Morgan and Nate Kenny.

Mr. Kenny's office scheduled an appointment for tomorrow morning, but before leaving, Austin had not yet heard back from Trevor Morgan.

Austin set his briefcase down by the front door and was met by Caleb walking into the living room. His brother looked distraught.

"Everything okay?"

"Jahlil was in the emergency room."

"What?" Austin said. "Is he all right? What happened?"

"He'll be fine. He got his ass beat down at school. Spoke to a detective, and she thinks it's gang-related."

"Jahlil's in a gang?"

"No," Caleb said. "Well . . . I don't know. He's not telling me anything."

"Caleb," Austin said, walking over to his brother. "You got to find that stuff out. Look, let me —"

"Austin," Caleb said, "I'm still trying to get my head around this, okay? When I do, I'll open it up for discussion. Besides, there are more important things we need to talk about," Caleb said, nodding his head toward the doorway behind them.

"What are you talking about?"

"Hello, Austin," a voice said from behind him.

Austin turned to see Marcus standing in the dining room entranceway, a suitcase at his feet.

"Marcus, what's up?"

"Remember earlier, when I said there was nothing else Reecie could do?"

"Yeah."

"Well, she kicked me out."

32

It was light outside, early morning, but the sun had not risen yet.

Jahlil wore a bathrobe over his jeans and tank top. He stood beside his apartment building, a patch of gauze taped over one eye, and stitches sewn into the brow over the other. His swelling had gone down only a little and his bruises looked just as fresh and angry as they had moments after his beating, almost eighteen hours ago.

Toomey and Bug stood in front of Jahlil, their hands shoved deep into their pockets, guilty looks on their faces.

Bug had called Jahlil earlier that morning and said they wanted to come by and see how he was doing before school.

"It was the G-Stones who did this to you," Bug said.

"I know," Jahlil said, touching his swollen jaw.

"They cornered me in the bathroom, asking about you," Toomey said, ashamed. "I told them your name. Me and Bug tried looking for you."

"I know. I had to take Shaun to her doctor's appointment yesterday."

"Everything okay with her and the baby?" Toomey asked.

"Everything is cool."

"We're sorry about you getting beat up," Bug said, patting Jahlil's shoulder. "But they said long as we don't show up on they street no more, we square. They ain't gonna mess with us. We ain't gonna show up on their street no more, are we?"

Jahlil looked at Bug with his one good eye. "Did we all of a sudden stop needing money? I know I didn't. I still got things I need to do."

"Jahlil," Toomey said, stepping in front of him, "after what just happened to you, it doesn't make sense to go back on that street, and —"

"I'm not talking about going back out there. We'll just do it how we was doing it before. I don't know, we can get out later tonight. Lay for some folks at the ATM, roll up while they making withdrawals, you know what I'm saying?"

"Tonight?" Bug said, sounding surprised.

"Isn't that a little soon, Jahlil?" Toomey

said. "Don't you need a little more time to get better?"

"How you know what I need? I'm the one that got beat down, not neither one of you. I need some more money, and I'm gonna get it. Ya'll wit' me, or you gonna make me do this one by myself, just like I did the ass whuppin'?"

Bug looked at Toomey as though they had no choice. "Yeah, you know we're with you, Jahlil."

"Good. Tonight, then," Jahlil said.

33

"He was a good one, and you let him get away!" Tabatha said, pacing the office at AERO.

"He wanted a baby factory, just like Nate. I played that game before," Monica said, sitting at her desk. "I'm glad he said that nonsense anyway. He was looking at me like some future wife, and I'm not going there anymore."

"Monica, you're going to let what happened with you and Nate ruin whatever chance at happiness you have left. You said you were going to let that stuff go."

"Nate plotted and paid money to a man to seduce and sleep with me so he could get a divorce and not have to give me my half of what the business was worth. Nate cheated while still married to me. He ruined my marriage, almost got me killed, then, to top it off, just as I wake from a fucking coma, he tells me he's leaving me once again, because he got some trick pregnant."

"I know, babe," Tabatha said. "You had it rough, but —"

"Rough?" Monica laughed sadly. "There are horrible things that should happen to him for what he's done to me, but I'm trying to stay under control and not think about Nate, or any other man for that matter, because right now, all of them are the same. Me not getting emotionally involved with any of them now is the best thing for me."

"Then why were you out at a club?" Tabatha asked.

"I told you, I have needs," Monica said, a sly smile on her face.

"So you're cool with fucking some guy, but nothing more than that?"

"That's how they've been playing us forever. Why not do the same to them? From now on, at least for the meantime, I'll only allow a man to play a physical role in my life, nothing else."

"Then what about the attorney guy you told me about? You don't think he's gonna start talking about relationships?"

"I don't know."

"You might as well not even go out with him, then."

"No. He's cute. I at least want to hear

what he has to say."

"And you don't think he's going to start talking about kids?"

"Hopefully not," Monica said. "Because if someone talks to me about another kid, I swear I'll scream."

"Yeah, right. You don't mean that."

"I'm telling you, girl."

A knock came at the door.

"Come in," Tabatha said.

The door opened, and in walked Lewis Waters. This was the man Nate had paid to seduce Monica so Nate could exploit the clause in their prenuptial agreement. Monica had slept with him, fallen in love with him. They had moved in together and had been very close to getting married before they found out their differences would've made their union a disaster.

Lewis was a muscular, dark-skinned man with thuggish model good looks. He was sharp today in his khaki pants, collared shirt, and fresh haircut. By his right hand, he led his four-year-old daughter, Layla. She was the child Monica had been so looking forward to mothering once she and Lewis were married. Monica now believed that Layla actually could have been the reason she was interested in Lewis in the first place, considering she couldn't have children of her own.

"Hey," Lewis said. "I hope I'm not stopping in at a bad time. Layla had been asking about you for a while, and I was driving by, so —"

Monica said nothing.

"No, no problem at all, Lewis," Tabatha jumped in. She walked over, bent down, and gave Layla a kiss on the cheek. "Hey, Layla." Tabatha turned to Monica, smiling. "I'm gonna leave you guys alone so you can talk." Before she closed the door, Tabatha said to Monica, "Start screaming, sista."

"What did she mean by that?" Lewis said.

"Nothing," Monica said, standing up from her desk. "Bring that little girl over here so I can say hi."

Lewis released Layla. The child ran over to Monica and hugged her. Monica kissed Layla on the cheek.

"Good to see you, Lewis. You look well," Monica said, which was true. He did look good. Fine as he ever did, but she could've lived without seeing him or the little girl. Monica still cared for Layla, but with all the pain the child had indirectly brought her, she thought she might have been able to go the rest of her life without ever seeing her again. It was a chapter in her life she had long been over.

"Thanks. Just trying to keep things in order, stay working. You know," Lewis said.

"Oh, you found a job?"

"Yeah." Lewis smiled proudly. "I work down at the DCFS building in the records room. It don't pay a whole lot, but it's a city job, and it has full benefits, so it's cool."

"I'm glad," Monica said, walking Layla back over to her father. "I wish I had more time, but since I didn't know you were coming . . ."

"No. I understand. Like I said, she was just asking about you."

"Okay," Monica said, walking Lewis and Layla to the door.

Lewis stood before Monica a moment, holding his daughter's hand. He leaned in to give Monica a kiss on the cheek. The look in his eyes said he missed her. "Well, it's been good seeing you."

Monica took the kiss Lewis gave her, then held him by the shoulders a moment longer. Her lips close to Lewis's ear, she said, "I've been through a lot, and I finally believe I'm moving on, so please, don't ever bring that child to see me again."

34

At 10:30 a.m., Austin again looked over the copy of Daphanie's contract as he sat in the reception area outside Mr. Kenny's office. When he was finished, Austin placed the contract in his briefcase. As he feared, it was airtight. Daphanie Coleman signed every single, solitary right she had as a mother over to the father, Trevor Morgan. She didn't even have the right to visit the baby without first notifying Trevor, and it would be his decision whether to allow a visit.

What kind of beast was this Nate Kenny? Austin thought. He had been going to marry Daphanie, which led Austin to believe he had to have once loved her. But if he had feelings for her, why would he knowingly cause her so much pain?

Yes, Daphanie had told Austin she had lied to Nate. Billions of women have lied to men about the same thing. Were they forced to sacrifice their child in repentance?

"Mr. Harris," the secretary said, "Mr. Kenny will see you now."

When Austin stepped into the huge office with the breathtaking view of downtown Chicago, he saw a tall, handsome man, about Austin's height, walking around his desk. He wore an impeccable, tailor-made gray suit. Austin had a similar one in his closet. Nate Kenny was smiling, holding out his hand.

Austin took it and shook.

"Mr. Harris, pleasure to meet you," Nate said. "My name is Nate Kenny. What can I do for you today?"

"Good to meet you too, Mr. Kenny."

"No, please, call me Nate, and have a seat. I only have a few minutes, but you will receive one hundred percent of my attention," Nate said, walking back around his massive oak desk.

"I would rather call you Mr. Kenny."

"Suit yourself."

"Daphanie Coleman retained me as her attorney regarding the situation involving her baby," Austin said, setting his briefcase on his lap and opening it.

"Okay."

Austin took the contract out and passed it over to Nate. "I want to know if you've seen this contract before."

Nate took just a second to look it over, passed it back, and said, "Yes. I had one of my attorneys here draw it up. Do you have a question about it?"

Austin sat in near shock at how cavalier the man seemed. "Are you aware that this contract strips all rights from Ms. Coleman as they relate to her baby?"

Nate laughed, as though he had been asked a trick question. "Yes. I told you. I had it drawn up, and I checked it three times personally to make sure the language was exactly the way I wanted it."

Austin couldn't believe what he was hearing. "You seem proud of what you've done."

"I am," Nate said, sitting up in his chair. "There was an objective and I met it, quite successfully. What is there not to be proud of?"

"I'm sorry, Mr. Kenny, if I seem . . . I don't know, taken aback by how callous and unsympathetic you appear by what you've done to this woman, but please, if you would tell me, why did you do it?"

"That woman lied to me. She knew the most important thing in the world to me was having a baby. She told me Mr. Morgan's baby was mine. She tried to steal that infant away from its biological father in order to marry me. That was unconscionable, and criminal. A woman who is willing to take a child from its father should have that child taken away from her. So that's what I had done."

"But who are you to determine that? You're related to neither of them, and you aren't the law."

"I have power," Nate said, leaning back in his chair. "And powerful men can often impose their own law."

"What you did was wrong."

"What you think doesn't matter, because there's absolutely nothing you can do about it, is there?"

Austin didn't answer right away but took a couple of moments to think. "No," he said, standing. "And to tell you the truth, I don't even know why I came here. The damage you've orchestrated has already been done. It's not as though you even have the authority to affect the outcome either way if you wanted to. You are now outside the equation. Powerless. And something tells me that bothers you."

"Not at all," Nate said. "I've been sleeping soundly from the day Daphanie signed that contract. You're the one tasked with the impossible challenge of getting that calculating bitch's baby back." Nate stood up from his desk, extended his hand out to Austin. "Good day, Mr. Harris."

35

"Hi, Tricia," Daphanie said, trying to keep her voice from quivering. She was nervous that Nate had notified the day care center where he had always taken his son, Nathaniel, that she was no longer involved with Nate — that her name should be taken off the list of people authorized to pick up Nathaniel at the end of the day.

"Hi, Daphanie," Tricia, a redhead with light pink freckles dotting the bridge of her nose, said. "Haven't seen you in a while."

"Yeah, I know. How you been?" Daphanie glanced down at her watch, then over her shoulder. She had more to be concerned with than just her name no longer being on the pickup list. She knew little Nathaniel's nanny, whoever that now was, would be along any minute to pick him up. If that happened while she was standing there, there could be trouble. They might try to hold her, call the police when the nanny told them Daphanie had no business trying to pick up the boy.

"Been good. One day at a time, you know," Tricia said. "Here to pick up little Nathaniel?"

"Yup. Would you go get the little guy, please?" Daphanie asked, thinking either Nate hadn't thought to change her status, or Tricia was being negligent and didn't check the updated list. Either way, Tricia pushed through a swinging, brightly painted door, to the kid's playroom, to retrieve little Nathaniel.

36

"Hello, this is Monica."

"Hello," Austin said, leaning back in his office chair. He had finally dug up the nerve to call her. "This is Austin Harris. You know, the attorney —"

"Yes, I remember. How are you?"

"I've been thinking about you," Austin said, feeling foolish about the huge smile that was on his face.

"Really."

"Yes. And they've been good thoughts."

"As opposed to the bad ones I thought you were having." Monica laughed.

"Have you been thinking about me?"

Monica laughed again. "Well, you're going to have to figure that one out on your own, Mr. Harris."

"Okay, but I'll need some face-to-face time to do that. You're going to have to let me take you out to a cozy spot I know."

"I can do that."

"Tomorrow night. Bijan's on State Street, eight thirty p.m."

"I think I can manage that."

"Excellent. I'll see you then." Austin hung up the phone. He felt energized and boyish as he sat there, but only for a moment, as thoughts of last night — when Marcus appeared at his house after being kicked out of his own — crept back into his head.

Austin had fixed his brother up with a room across the hall from his. He knew Marcus wasn't crazy about being there, but Austin kind of liked it. Having all the brothers under the same roof reminded him of back when they were kids, when their parents were still alive.

Last night, Austin had looked in to check on Marcus before calling it a night.

Marcus was sitting up in bed, staring off into his thoughts.

Austin knocked on the frame of the door. "You okay in there?"

"What if it's not just about me not finding work?" Marcus asked.

"What do you mean?" Austin said, stepping into the room.

Concern on his face, Marcus said, "What if . . . what if Reecie kicked me out because there's someone else?"

That memory forced Austin back to the

present. He stepped out of his office to Reecie's desk. "Order up a nice bouquet of fresh flowers. A big one, a couple of hundred dollars' worth."

Reecie looked up at Austin, a single eyebrow raised. "And send them where?"

"To Monica Rodgers. She came in here a couple of days ago, and —"

"I know who she is," Reecie said, smiling, as she pulled up the online florist on her computer.

Austin continued to stand over the desk, his arms crossed.

Reecie looked up again. "What?"

"You tell me what. What's going on with you and Marcus?"

Reecie sighed loudly. "Why did he go bringing you into this? You're my boss."

"I'm also your brother-in-law and his brother. Now tell me what's going on."

"He refuses to work, Austin. And I just got tired of it," Reecie said. "Don't be mad at me."

"I'm not."

"Really?" Reecie said, surprised.

"I understand. He has a family. He has to do what he has to do. I told him that," Austin said. "But that's all it is, right?"

"What do you mean?"

"Your husband and I are sleeping across

the hall from each other like we did when we were kids, because you're tired of him refusing to work, and that's all, right?"

Reecie looked at Austin as though she didn't appreciate what he was suggesting. "Yeah, that's all."

"Good. You guys will be just fine." Austin smiled. "And take care of those flowers now, okay? I want her to have them as soon as possible."

37

His janitor's supply closet open, Caleb pulled out the supplies he was going to use this evening. He was troubled because he had asked Sonya if they could talk again about them getting back together, and she had said no. He knew if she continued to turn him down, he would have to be more aggressive in letting her know he needed to come back home.

Caleb pulled a broom and a mop from the closet and stood them against the wall when his cell phone rang.

"Hello."

"Mr. Harris, this is Detective Currie. We met yesterday."

"Yeah. What do you want?"

"I'm calling to see if your son told you any more about what happened."

"He hasn't. Jahlil said he doesn't know."

"Can you ask him again? Couldn't he be lying?"

"He wouldn't lie about something like this," Caleb said, telling a lie himself in defense of his son. Caleb would find out in due time, he told himself as he stood in the hallway, looking over his shoulder to make sure no one heard his conversation.

"Detective Currie, if and when my son tells me what happened, I promise I will call and let you know. But right now, I'm at work, so I have to go." Caleb hung up the phone and slipped it back into his pocket. When he turned around, he was startled by the man standing across the hall.

"Sorry," the man said. He was younger than Caleb, well built, and he wore khakis, a long-sleeved shirt, and a tie that hung loose around the opened collar.

"Naw, you all right. I'm just used to being the only one around here at closing time."

"You're a little early today, right?"

"Yeah. Guess you're right," Caleb said.

The man took a couple of steps toward Caleb and held out his hand. "Lewis Waters. I work in the file room."

"Caleb Harris," Caleb said, shaking. "Guess you know what I do." Caleb waved the handle of his mop.

"Yeah," Lewis said. He hesitated a moment. "Everything all right with your son? Sorry. My door was open, and I overheard your conversation."

The man was a practical stranger, but upon first look, he seemed like a fairly decent guy, so Caleb figured he was cool to talk to. "You know boys. You gotta stay on them."

"I got a little girl, myself."

"I wish." Caleb laughed. "Jahlil, my son, is sixteen."

"So he thinks he's grown, don't have to listen to a thing you say, right?"

"Sounds just like him."

"I *was* him. The stuff I got into, not going to school, running with gangs. That was me, all right."

Caleb looked the man over again. "If you don't mind me saying, you seem like you're doing okay now. How did you turn things around?"

"Lucky," Lewis said. "I ran into the right people. I didn't even want it to happen, but I was thrown in a situation with people who had more than me, who were successful. I saw that the way I was doing it wasn't the best way."

Caleb told himself it was his fault his son was surrounded by nothing but down-on-their-luck fools like himself. He wasn't sure how that would ever change.

"But I wouldn't worry, everything's gonna

be cool for your son. You seem like a good guy," Lewis said. "If I can be here, after living in the Ida B. Wells projects just three years ago —"

"You lived over in Ida B.?" Caleb said, reaching out his hand to give Lewis another, more friendly shake. "I live just a few blocks from there, off Cottage Grove."

"Then we were neighbors and didn't even know it," Lewis said, shaking again, more energetically. "Who knows, I probably seen your boy around before and didn't even know it."

"I'm sure you have," Caleb said, smiling at the coincidence.

"Look," Lewis said, sounding uncertain. "You don't know me, but I think I know exactly who your son is and what he's going through. Like I said, when I was his age, I was doing the same things. You never know, I might be able to help some way."

"I don't know what you're getting at," Caleb said.

"I see our boys out there on the streets. They need all the guidance they can get. Maybe one of these days you can bring him to work with you. He and I can hang out, or do something. Not saying you ain't doing a good job yourself, but I'm a little closer to his age, and more important, I'm not his father. I don't know, maybe he'll tell me some things he's been afraid to tell you." Lewis paused, waiting for the answer. After a moment he said, "I mean, but if you think it's a bad idea, I —"

"No, no. I think it's a good idea. He does need to be around positive influences. I just . . . I mean, I can trust you with my kid, though, right?"

"Caleb," Lewis said, "there is no one you can trust more."

38

Daphanie spent the day with little Nathaniel. She had taken him with the intention of causing Nate pain, of making him realize what a hell it was to no longer have his child. But she realized she was causing herself a fair amount of pain, as well. Until now, she had not realized how much she missed his son, and how much she still loved him.

Earlier, when Tricia had brought Nathaniel out to Daphanie, his face had brightened at the sight of her. With open arms he ran to her. She scooped him up, hugged him tight, and thanked Tricia before the boy unknowingly said something that would get Daphanie in trouble.

"I missed you, Daphanie," Nathaniel said slowly, once in the car. He always had trouble pronouncing her name.

Daphanie blinked back a tear as she buckled the boy in the passenger seat. "I missed you too. So much," she said, kissing Nathaniel on the cheek.

She took him to the park, out for lunch, to a movie, for ice cream, and back to the park because Nathaniel asked and Daphanie couldn't deny him. He had her wrapped around his little finger, as he always had when Daphanie and Nate dated.

But it was evening now, and she figured Nate had learned his lesson. She still had little Nathaniel downtown. She wasn't foolish enough to go home. There were probably rescue copters hovering above her condo, SWAT teams scaling the sides of her building, because that was the kind of power and influence Nate had.

She was sure he had already been informed it was Daphanie that had picked up Nathaniel from day care. She was sure he had already called her place a thousand times and probably rung her cell phone even more. She had turned it off for that very reason.

But it was almost eight o'clock, and the boy had already started asking for his father, so Daphanie figured it was time to give him back.

"You ready to go back to Daddy?"

"Yay!" Nathaniel said, raising his chocolate-covered fists. He had been working on a chocolate bar Daphanie had bought him.

"Okay," Daphanie said. She felt sad as she powered on her phone. The twelve missed calls from Nate appeared. She highlighted his number, punched the Dial button, and said, "Yeah," when Nate picked up the phone.

"Is my son okay?" Nate asked. Daphanie was surprised at how calm he sounded.

"Of course. You know I wouldn't hurt him. We had —"

"Hi, Daddy!" Nathaniel yelled.

"We had a good day," Daphanie continued, wiping the boy's hand with a moist towelette she had pulled from her purse. "We went to —"

"I don't care what the hell you did. I just want my son back. You do recognize you made the worst mistake of your life? Where are you? I'm coming to get him."

"No. I'll bring him to you. As long as there are no police waiting for me."

"Fine. There won't be."

"Do you promise?"

"Yes," Nate said.

Twenty minutes later, Daphanie stood at the door of Nate's million-dollar mansion, holding Nathaniel by the hand.

The door opened. Nate stood behind it.

"Daddy!" Nathaniel yelled. He shook Daphanie's hand loose and grabbed his father's leg. Nate lowered his hand to the top of the boy's head. From behind him, an older woman wearing an apron appeared. Daphanie figured she was the new nanny.

"Mrs. Langford, take Nathaniel, bathe him, and prepare him for bed, please. I'll be up to tuck him in shortly."

"Yes, Mr. Kenny," Mrs. Langford said, taking Nathaniel by the hand and leading him into the house.

Nate stepped out onto the porch and closed the door. "He had been kidnapped by that psychopath Freddy Ford. I just got him back. Why would you do this?" Nate said, finally exhibiting the slightest bit of emotion.

"Imagine if you were never getting him back."

Nate stared past Daphanie, as if entertaining the thought. He frowned. "I can't imagine that. I think I would die."

A tear rolled down Daphanie's face. She quickly brushed it away. "That's how I feel. I know I was wrong, Nate. I should've never lied to you. But I loved you once, and I know you loved me too. Do I deserve to lose my child for one lie? You have to help me.

Please," Daphanie said, grabbing his arm. "Please."

Nate took a moment. Daphanie believed she saw something resembling sympathy on Nate's face, before he said, "You did a horrible thing, and you're paying for it. I'm sorry," he said, pulling away from Daphanie's grasp. "What you just did, you're going to have to pay for that too."

Daphanie shook her head. "Do what you will, Nate. You've already done the worst to me. I'm not afraid of you anymore."

39

Nine p.m. and the house was quiet. Austin sat at the dining room table, in the dark, his hands folded on the table's surface, his eyes closed. He listened and heard nothing. Not the sound of his son and daughter playing, not the sound of his wife cooking in the kitchen, calling out to tell him to cut the potatoes.

A small smile spread across Austin's lips as he thought about those memories from so long ago.

"Hey," Marcus said, flipping on the overhead lamp.

Austin opened his eyes, squinting against the light.

"What are you doing here in the dark?"

"Just taking a little time out is all," Austin said. "Where have you been? Kinda late for you to just be getting home."

Marcus pulled a chair out across from Austin and sat down. "Been filling out applications. Went to the coffee shop and was online for a few hours looking, then went to the bookstore and read up on some career books. You know, best interviewing techniques, stuff like that."

"Wow, you're not playing."

"Nope," Marcus said.

"You know if there was anything at all at the firm, I would give it to you," Austin said.

"I know, but I'm not expecting that. And I don't want you to feel obligated," Marcus said. "The crazy thing is, I think it might have taken Reecie putting me out to realize I have to do everything I must to be the man I need to be. I'm actually excited about starting back to work, wherever it is."

"Well, that's what I like to hear. I'm glad for you."

"And how are you? Seem kinda depressed, a little."

"What, a man can't sit alone in his dining room with his eyes closed, the lights off, without being considered depressed?" Austin joked. "Truth is, the more I think about it, the more I want another good relationship. I want to make a woman really happy, be the man she can trust. I want that again."

"So," Marcus said, "are you just telling me that and hoping the information will find its way to some beautiful woman, or are you getting out there and trying to make it happen?"

Austin smiled, thinking about the possibility of him and Monica. "I'm out there trying to make it happen."

40

Monica lay asleep in her bed, tossing in her sheets.

She was back in the courtroom where her shooter, Freddy Ford, was sentenced. Officers stood the thin, muscular man up and walked him out. He would not look up.

Monica needed him to see her. She needed to look in his eyes and see what he was thinking, what he was feeling.

She stood up from her chair, hoping he would lift his face. She wanted to see pain, guilt, remorse — something. She needed that look to replace the one that had been burned in her brain — the expression that was in his eyes when he turned his gun on her.

It was all Nate's fault, she thought.

Nate had blackmailed Freddy.

He had told Freddy if he didn't help Nate in the scheme to get Monica to leave Lewis and come back to him, he would have Freddy's mother thrown out of her house and have the home demolished.

Freddy had helped initially, but toward the end, he had felt guilty and told Lewis everything. It was too late. The plan had worked. Monica went back to Nate. Freddy's mother was tossed out on the street, and the house was demolished, as Nate had said it would be. But that wasn't all. When Freddy's pregnant girlfriend, Kia, found out about all that Freddy had done, she had their child aborted and left him.

Monica knew that was what had brought Freddy to find Nate. But had he been there for her too?

Monica was never able to ask him that, and she worried that one day he might come back and finish the job.

It was the reason why every night before going to bed, she locked her bedroom door. It was the reason why every night she had the same dream of Freddy Ford standing inside her room, his gun pointed at her head.

Tonight, just like all those other nights, at seeing herself killed in her mind, she shot up in bed, sweating, screaming, her eyes wide, her heart racing. She whipped her head about, her eyes landing on the locked bedroom door.

The doorbell rang.

Startled, Monica didn't move, hoping that whoever was ringing would go away.

The bell sounded again. Monica looked at her alarm clock: 10:49 p.m.

She pulled herself out of bed and took her gun from the top shelf of her closet. She walked slowly through the darkened house, the gun held out in front of her.

"Who is it?" Monica said.

"Girl, it's me," Tabatha's muffled voice came through the door. "What are you doing in there? Open up."

Not until Monica opened the door and saw the reaction on Tabatha's face did she realize how she must've looked: her gown soaked through with sweat, sticking to her body. She was still trembling, her eyes wide, the huge gun in her hand.

"What the hell is going on?" Tabatha said.

Half an hour later, Monica was in a robe on her living room sofa, Tabatha beside her.

Tabatha had stopped by to tell Monica about the blind date she had just been on. It had been a disaster, and she thought Monica needed a laugh. She didn't know how right she was.

Monica explained to Tabatha why she had gotten the gun, how she was terrified many nights of being alone in her own home.

"Maybe you ought to see a psychiatrist," Tabatha suggested.

"No." Monica shook her head. "Hell no."

"Something has to be done."

"I don't know why he shot me. I need to know that he still doesn't want to kill me."

"Girl, don't be crazy. He's locked up. Even if —"

"I need to know," Monica said.

"And just how you proposing to find that out?"

"I'm going to go there and talk to him."

41

At almost midnight, Jahlil stood in the shadows around the corner from an ATM. The machine was attached to a Jewel food store, in a shopping plaza off Ninety-Fifth and Stony Island Avenue. The grocery store had closed a couple of hours ago, but there was a gas station nearby, leaving just enough traffic to have an occasional person coming by wanting cash, but not so many that Jahlil and his small crew couldn't quickly rob someone without being noticed by onlookers.

Jahlil had been standing in that dark corner for almost half an hour. He wore a black hooded zip-up and a black ski mask pulled over his face. The bruises and swelling had healed some, but they still hurt. He kept a bottle of aspirin in his pocket to stave off the ever-threatening headache.

His 9mm rested in the small of his back, under his shirt. He punched the tiny keys on his phone, sending a text to Bug.

Bug sat behind the wheel of his car, a silver revolver in his lap. He and Toomey were parked thirty feet away, off to the side of the ATM, out of sight of the camera that recorded the area just in front of the machine.

"What did he say?" Toomey asked, sitting in the passenger seat of Bug's 1986 Chevy Impala. The license plates had been pulled off and stuck in the trunk just after they had parked.

"It says, *Ya'll better not go to sleep.*" Bug laughed, and spoke aloud what he texted back to Jahlil. "*Sorry . . . we . . . ain't . . . get . . . this . . . text . . . cause . . . we . . . already . . . sleep.*" Bug giggled and pressed Send.

Toomey was stone-faced.

"What?" Bug asked.

"He damn near got killed yesterday. He's fresh out the hospital and already got us back out here robbing. Why does he need money that bad?"

"You know he got a kid on the way. You act like we ain't getting money. Like we don't need it too. You need it too, right?"

"Yeah, so?"

"And my mother so broke, if I wasn't making this money, I probably wouldn't eat,

I wouldn't have no clothes, no shoes — nothing. So why you trippin'?"

Toomey slumped in his seat, watching a car roll past the ATM. "What if that was you who got beat up, or me? And what if instead of just getting beat up, one of us died out there. We didn't even make all of our money back that day. You trying to tell me that's worth our lives? Yeah, I kinda need the money now, but I'm going to college. I got a future to think about, so —"

Bug spun in his seat. "You smart, and we all know it. We glad you going to college, but right now, you need to decide what you gonna do here. We about to stick a gun in some fool's face. Anything can jump off, so we need your head here, not wondering why we doing this in the first place. You know what I'm sayin'?"

It took a minute for Toomey to answer. "Yeah," he finally said. "I don't like it, but I know what you saying."

"Good," Bug said. He looked down at the glowing screen on his phone. *We got us one. Ready?* it read. Bug looked over his shoulder to see a big man step out of his car and walk up to the ATM. Bug texted Jahlil back. *Let's do it!*

Around the corner of the building, Jahlil slipped the phone in his pocket and grabbed his gun. He carefully peered out from behind the wall and saw the man punching numbers into the machine's keypad. Over in the parking lot, he saw Bug jumping out of his car. Toomey slid over to the driver's seat to act as a lookout and getaway driver.

Bug walked alongside the wall of the building, his gun tucked under his sweatshirt in the front of his pants. He wore dark sunglasses but no hood or mask. If he had, he would've probably triggered the suspicions of the man they were about to rob. At ten feet away, the big man had already stopped punching the keys and was watching Bug as though he knew he was up to no good.

Bug stopped three feet short. "You got the time?"

"Get the fuck away from me," the man said, stomping a foot at Bug like he was shooing a dog away.

Bug giggled.

The man heard a click and spun to his right to see the masked Jahlil, pointing a gun at him. When the big man turned back to face Bug, Bug's gun was drawn too.

Jahlil stood still, not wanting to be picked up by the camera.

"We do this right and fast, and you won't end up dead. You hear me?"

"Yeah," the man said, starting to turn toward Jahlil.

"Don't look at me! Your business is on that machine. Withdraw the max, five hundred dollars. Walk over and hand it to my boy on your left."

"What if I don't have five hundred?"

"You better have five hundred, broke-ass motherfucka," Bug said.

The man went about withdrawing the money. He walked the few steps, out of camera shot, over to Bug.

"Easy," Jahlil warned him from behind his mask.

With one hand holding the gun, Bug took the bills with the other.

The Impala pulled up to the curb.

"Go," Jahlil said, prompting Bug to run around the car and jump in the passenger seat. Next, Jahlil demanded the man's car keys.

"What?" The man said, his eyes wide.

"I ain't jackin' you, man. Just give me the keys, so you don't try following us. I'm gonna drop them out the window on the corner of Ninetieth and Stony. Now give 'em up."

The man fished the ring of keys from his pocket and tossed them to Jahlil. Jahlil walked backward, keeping the gun on the man till he lowered himself into the Impala.

Toomey sped off.

Inside the car, Bug howled with excitement. "Clockwork, baby! Just like the pros do it. Five hundred smackeroos!"

"Yes, sir!" Jahlil said, peeling the mask from over his head. "We ain't no joke. We want money — get money. Five hundred, three ways. How much that come to, Toomey?"

"One hundred and sixty-six dollars and sixty-six cents," Toomey said, driving but not sharing in the celebration.

42

So this was the other man keeping Daphanie from seeing her child, Austin thought, first thing in the morning, as he sat in Trevor Morgan's office.

Austin was there to reason with this man, ask him to search his conscience, maybe find it in his heart to allow Daphanie to share the responsibilities of raising their child.

"Please have a seat," Trevor said, only briefly looking up from his paperwork. "I'll be with you in just a moment."

Austin looked around the large office and at the clean-shaven, neatly dressed man. Austin could see how Daphanie could get away with telling Mr. Kenny the child was his, for he and Mr. Morgan bore an uncanny resemblance to each other.

Trevor slid the paperwork into a drawer and gave his attention to Austin. "I received your message. I was going to have my secretary call you back and find a good time for us to meet."

"I'm sorry about coming here unannounced," Austin said, not sorry at all. He believed the man had no intention of calling him back, which is why this morning he told himself he would go to the bank where Trevor worked and not leave until he had spoken to the man.

"It's okay," Trevor said. "This is important, right?"

"Yes, very important. As I'm sure your secretary told you, my name is Austin Harris. I'm representing Daphanie Coleman in regard to regaining custody of her child."

Trevor sighed heavily. "You know the story then."

"Yes."

"I really wish things hadn't happened this way," Trevor said, sounding sincere. "But when she found out she was pregnant, she told me it was mine. Then she changed her story. I knew she was lying. I could feel it in my soul, that baby was mine. I loved that child from the moment she told me she had conceived."

"And don't you think Daphanie loves the child too?"

Trevor appeared troubled. He stood up from his desk and walked over toward his office windows. "I don't think about that, and I don't have to. She signed the contract, and if you've read it, you'll see there's nothing she can do. Nothing anyone can do."

"I know that, Mr. Morgan," Austin appealed. "But is this really what you want, for Daphanie not to know her own son? For your son not to know his mother?"

Trevor stared silently out the window. "You know I loved her once," Trevor said, facing Austin again. "My wife didn't want any children. When Daphanie said she was pregnant, I gave it a lot of thought, and decided I could leave my wife for her if it came to that. But then she pulled that stunt."

"Do you still love Daphanie?"

Appearing tortured by the conversation, Trevor said, "How could I after what she's done? She didn't want me. She wanted Nate. And how fitting that Nate was the one that got her to sign over our child to me."

"You didn't answer the question," Austin said, standing. "Do you still love Daphanie Coleman?"

Trevor's jaw tightened. "I don't want to, but yes, I do."

43

Daphanie rose from her bed, stretched, and felt hopeful for some reason. Last night, she'd gone to bed thinking how much fun she had with little Nathaniel. While asleep, she dreamt that she had gotten her son back. In her dream, she had taken her baby everywhere she had taken Nathaniel yesterday. She cradled him in her arms, kissed his cheeks as he laughed and kicked and used his little hands to grasp at her face.

Daphanie lowered her legs over the edge of her bed, wondering why she'd had such a dream. She knew it was because of those brief moments of thought Nate had last night after she'd asked him what he'd do if he thought he'd never see Nathaniel again. She'd reached him. She had penetrated the man's cold, hard armor and reached the man she used to know and love.

Of course there was no guarantee that Nate would help Daphanie, but something deep inside her told her he would. She smiled at the thought and stood up from her bed feeling better than she had since the day all of this had started.

She grabbed her robe from the foot of her bed and pulled it on, when she heard a knock at her front door. It was odd, considering she lived in a condo building and anyone visiting her would have to buzz from downstairs in order to be let up.

Daphanie stepped out of her bedroom and headed toward the front door, telling herself that it had to be her neighbor from down the hall, considering her alarm clock had only read 8:01 a.m.

At the door, she looked through the peephole and was surprised to see two uniformed policemen.

Her heart skipped and she tumbled away from the door, obviously making enough noise to prompt one of the officers to knock again.

"Miss Coleman, this is the police. We hear you in there. You need to open the door."

She held her breath. She felt trapped. The thought of running out the back occurred to her, but that was ridiculous. She wasn't a fugitive. "What . . . what do you want?"

"Open the door, ma'am."

Daphanie walked back to the door and,

with a trembling hand, opened it. "Yes," she said to the two officers, "how can I help you?"

"Daphanie Coleman," the mustached, dark-haired officer said, "we're here to arrest you for the kidnapping of Nathaniel Kenny."

44

Caleb had been consumed with worry over what he needed to do to help his son, but he could not lose sight of the fact that in three days, he would owe Kwan the money he had borrowed from him.

Kwan's men had made their threats, but Caleb was not as worried as he felt they wanted him to be. He had known Kwan since grammar school, and he had borrowed money and returned it late before. Yes, that was ten years ago, when the man didn't have such a ruthless reputation to uphold, but if Caleb didn't get him the money the second he needed it, he was sure Kwan might cut him a little slack.

Caleb felt uncomfortable in the tie he was wearing. He hated ties, never wore them, but today he was waiting to hear if he had gotten the cleaning contract for the small paper company whose offices he was in now.

Mr. Butler was the name of the bookish-looking man that walked into the office and greeted Caleb.

"Have a seat, Mr. Harris," Mr. Butler said. He sat on the front edge of his desk and pushed his glasses back up on his nose.

"So did you have a chance to review my offer?" Caleb said, hopeful. "I know it's the cheapest one around." If Caleb were hired, he would work a deal with Butler, give him like ten percent, maybe even twenty percent off if he agreed to pay Caleb for the first six months up front. This way he would have no problem paying Kwan on time.

"I did look at your offer," Mr. Butler said, "and you're right. You do undercut everyone else, but I've decided to go with a more established company."

"What?" Caleb said, surprised. If he didn't get this contract, he would only have one chance left with a small building that housed a nursery school and day care center. The woman he spoke to there initially was named Mrs. Jackson. She had stared at Caleb as though she didn't trust him, so Caleb didn't have a good feeling about winning that contract. "It's cleaning," Caleb finally said to Mr. Butler. "Can someone be more established at cleaning a toilet or sweeping a floor?"

Mr. Butler smiled, extended his open

hand. "I'm sorry, Mr. Harris, but I've made my decision."

Caleb stood outside on the street corner, squinting against the sun, and yanked the tie from around his neck. He would have to start knocking on company doors again.

He looked up the block, trying to remember where he had parked his van. He saw it across the street. He stepped off the curb but was almost run over by a black Dodge Magnum that sped up, then came to a screeching halt beside him.

The driver's window, tinted as black as the car's paint, powered down a crack, and Caleb saw Charles, Kwan's flunky, staring out at him.

"Get in the car, fool," the man said around the toothpick sticking from his mouth.

"But I got three days. I said I'm gonna have —"

"I said get in the car. Or I'm gonna have my man get you in the car," Charles said, lowering the window so Caleb could get a look at the same heavyset man that was with Charles last time they'd found Caleb. The man held an Uzi in his lap, pointed up at Caleb.

Caleb pulled open the back door and climbed into the dark cabin. "Where you taking me?"

"Where ever the hell we want," Charles said, shifting the car in gear.

Kwan was a short man. He stood five-five if he stood an inch. He compensated for his lack of height by lifting weights, which gave him the stance of a VW Beetle.

Kwan walked around the large back room of the small building where he operated a corner candy store. From the front of the building, he sold treats to the neighborhood kids, and from the back, he did his loan-sharking, drug dealing, and whatever other dirt he conducted.

Wearing a skintight T-shirt to show off his cannonball biceps, he leaned on a baseball bat like a cane.

Caleb stared at Kwan from the wooden chair he was told to sit in. His hands had been tied behind his back, and Caleb could feel sweat accumulate at his brow as he glanced at the frightened-looking man who sat tied to the chair ten feet in front of him.

"Why am I here?" Caleb said. "I got three days."

Kwan looked up at Charles. "Does he know that, Charles?" Kwan questioned. "Does Caleb really know he got three days?"

"I don't know," Charles said. "He sho'

ain't acting like he do."

"How is that?" Caleb said, trying to pull his hands free. They were tied tight. "I don't gotta act no way. All I gotta do is give you your money back on the day it's due."

"Naw. That's where you wrong," Kwan said, walking over, placing his face just in front of Caleb's. "I been doing this for a long time. And there's a way a man act when he got the money to give back, and the way he act when he ain't. That's why I have my boys watch my indebted clients. When the clock winds down, the men who ain't got my money often take off, get lost."

"I wouldn't do that," Caleb said.

"I know, because I got you here, and I'm gonna let you know what happens to men who consider skipping without paying me my money."

Kwan stood up, swung the bat over his shoulder, and walked over to the other bound man.

The man's eyes ballooned and he started to struggle, trying to free himself from the ropes that tied his wrists and his ankles to the chair. "I swear, I was just going to my cousin's to get yo' money," the man said, tears coming to his eyes.

"Your cousin in Philly, right?" Kwan said, smiling at Charles and Lamar. Both men chuckled.

"What are you going to do to him!" Caleb yelled.

"Same thing I'm gonna do to you if you try getting over on me," Kwan said, grabbing the bat with both hands and swinging it with all his might. The motion was sweeping and powerful, and the bat didn't come to a halt till it struck the bound man's right shin. There was a loud crack, and the man screamed out like a tortured child.

"What are you doing!" Caleb yelled, kicking his feet, rocking on the legs of the chair.

"Work, motherfucker," Kwan said, walking to the other side of the man, pulling the bat back up over his shoulder. "I'm doing work." He swung the bat again, snapping the man's other leg. Again the man cried out, but the scream was clipped. The man's eyes rolled in his head, and he looked to have passed out from shock. His head fell limp, his chin resting on his chest.

Caleb sat quiet, dumbstruck by all that was happening. His pulse raced, and sweat poured from his brow into his eyes as Kwan stepped over to him.

"I'm gonna have your money," Caleb said. "I swear. I'm gonna have it."

"I know you will, or we gonna have to go green on your ass," Kwan said.

"What? I . . . I don't know what that means," Caleb said.

"Before scooping you, Charles and Lamar went to the store and bought me some Hostess cupcakes," Kwan said. "Got my cakes, Charles?"

Charles grabbed the plastic bag off the counter behind him, reached into the bag, and tossed Kwan the package. Kwan took out one of the cakes and ate it.

"White folks always talk about recycling plastic, use it over for different things. That's what we do around here. Give him an example, Charles."

Charles took the handles of the plastic bag in each of his fists, walked around behind the unconscious man, threw the bag over his head, and pulled back on the handles.

"No," Caleb said, horrified. "No!"

The man sat unconscious at first, but then, under the plastic mask, he sprung, howling to life. Caleb could see the bag draw into the man's open mouth, muting him. It shrunk to the contour of his face, his nose, his eye sockets. The doomed man whipped his head frantically back and forth, lurched forward and back in his chair. Grimacing against the man's efforts, Charles continued to pull on the bag, suffocating him till there was no more fight.

After another moment of struggle, the man's body went limp. Charles stood, a smirk on his face, leaving the bag over the man's head.

"Well done, Charles," Kwan said. He looked over at Lamar, nodded the man an order.

Lamar walked over to the back of Caleb's chair. Caleb's heart skipped until he realized Lamar was knifing the ropes away from his wrists.

"Get me my money," Kwan said. "Or you gonna experience this firsthand."

45

Monica heard Tabatha's words echo in her
head as she was led down the long hallway
by the white-jacketed counselor.

"Are you out of your mind?" Tabatha had
said, last night. "He tried to kill you, and
you're fool enough to go there and visit
him?"

The counselor, a young woman with red
hair pinned up in a bun, stopped and
opened a door with the word VISITATION
painted in small black letters on it.

Monica stepped into a room that looked
more like a 1950s grade school classroom,
with its old vinyl tile floors and ancient light
fixtures, than the visitation room at Oak
Park Psychiatric Institution.

There were four identically upholstered
sofas that sat against each of the four walls,
and at least a dozen wooden chairs were
scattered about.

"Have a seat anywhere," the counselor

said, smiling at Monica. "We'll bring Mr. Ford right in."

The door closed, and Monica felt trapped. She wondered if she had made the right decision. She told herself to relax and lowered herself onto one of the sofas.

A moment later, she was startled by the door opening again. A large, square-shouldered man walked in, wearing a white uniform. Behind him walked Freddy Ford.

Monica shot up from the sofa, wishing she had never come.

The uniformed man held Freddy high by his arm, leading him over to the chair nearest Monica, and helped him into it.

Monica looked not at Freddy but at his handler.

"Ma'am, are you okay?"

Monica managed to speak. "Yes."

"I'm not leaving the room. I'll be right there by the door. If you need me, just say."

"Okay," Monica said, feeling herself trembling. She sat back down as the man took his place by the door.

Monica stared at Freddy's feet. He wore beige house slippers and what looked like white pajama pants. Her eyes moved up to a red T-shirt. A peeling, iron-on decal of a white rabbit was on the front. TRIX ARE FOR KIDS was written under the picture. Freddy was thinner than she remembered. His hair was shorter, and he had a full, curly beard that looked as though it had taken months to grow.

When Monica finally found the courage to look into Freddy's eyes, they gave no insight into what he was thinking.

"Why you here?" he said. "What do you want?"

Monica felt her lips trembling. "You . . . you shot me. You tried to kill me."

"I was there for your husband."

"But you shot me. You —"

"You came outta nowhere. I ain't know what was happening. I turned, and the gun just went off," Freddy said. He looked away, scratched his beard.

"Do you want to kill me?" Monica said, looking over at the uniformed man near the door.

Freddy laughed a little. "You having dreams. Post–traumatic stress disorder, or some shit."

"Something like that," Monica said. "I just need to know."

Freddy leaned back in his chair. "Just said shootin' you was a mistake. Never wanted you dead, don't want you that way now."

Incredibly, Monica felt as though the weight of a lifetime of fear had been lifted from her shoulders. "I'm glad to hear that."

"But your ex-husband needed to die. I'm sorry I couldn't make that happen."

"You don't mean that."

"Who you talkin' to? My mom's living in a room, sleeping on a twin bed. Her house, my house, been torn down. My girl left me, killed our baby. And Joni, the girl I still loved, never stopped loving — Joni is dead. And it's all because of Nate Kenny. So who you talkin' to?"

"I understand how you feel."

"You don't understand shit, Monica, so don't say that to me."

"I do," Monica said. "There are times when I wish I could kill him myself for what he's done to me, but I would never try it. Look where it's gotten you."

"I won't be here forever," Freddy said under his breath.

"What? What was that?"

"I said I won't be in here forever, and when I get out, all the motherfuckers who went against me gonna pay. They need to be looking over they shoulders now. Even from here, I got pull on them streets."

"I don't understand," Monica said, starting to feel uneasy.

"It's not for you to understand. Just know I'm making my list," Freddy said, lowering his voice again. "Nate, he's number one. I saw his brother in Atlanta where my girl got shot. Don't know his name, but he gotta go down too. And Lewis, it might be over for him, and maybe his little girl. Just depend on how I'm feelin'."

"What! No!" Monica said, shocked. "You wouldn't!"

"I have nothing, because of —"

"I'll tell the police," Monica said, standing.

"Sit yo' ass down!" Freddy said, his voice hushed.

Monica glanced at the man at the door. The man raised his brow, as if asking if she needed him. Monica shook her head, then slowly sat back down.

"Tell the police what?" Freddy said. "That I want Nate Kenny dead? They already know that. I tried to kill his ass, remember? And even if they believe you, which they won't, 'cause I'm supposed to be crazy, what they gonna do? Put me in jail for something I say I'm gonna do? I'm already in jail."

Monica sat there speechless, feeling helpless, the room starting to spin around her. "Then I'll tell Nate, I'll tell Lewis so they'll know to —"

"Then I'll have to rethink what I said a

minute ago."

"Rethink what?"

"The part where I said I didn't want you dead," Freddy said, standing up from his chair. He looked over at the uniformed man at the door, then leaned over to Monica. "You safe as it is. Say one word and that shit might change." Freddy straightened up and turned to the guard. "Yo, I'm done. Get me the fuck outta here."

46

Bug and Toomey sat parked outside a small apartment complex just outside the Beverly area.

The buildings looked clean, the grounds kept neat, and no one hung around outside the front doors looking like they were ready to mug the first person that walked in or out. There were a couple of little white kids in the park across from the building that Jahlil had just walked out of. This spot was nothing like anything Bug or Toomey had ever seen.

"What are we doing over here?" Toomey said.

"I don't know," Bug said. "Maybe he got some little shorty who live there."

"Why doesn't he just tell us?"

"Don't know that either," Bug said.

Before they came here to the apartment complex, the three boys had stood across the street from a house they had been watching for the last few days. It was across the street from Bug's apartment. Bug told Jahlil that he had seen the man who lived there move in a brand-new sixty-inch LCDTV the other night. Bug knew the guy had other nice things in there too. He didn't know what the man did for a living, but he knew he lived alone and was often gone for hours during the night. Jahlil made it known he wanted to rob that house tonight.

Now Bug watched as Jahlil approached the car with some pamphlets in his hand. Bug turned to Toomey. "You gonna tell him you want out of the crew?"

"Don't know."

"You gotta tell him."

"I know," Toomey said.

Jahlil pulled on the door handle and jumped into the back seat. He was smiling, damn near jubilant.

"You got a shorty in there, don't you?" Bug said, grinning up at Jahlil through the rearview. "You just got you some?"

"Nope."

"Then what?" Toomey snapped.

"Damn," Jahlil said. "Somebody funky today." He passed up the pamphlets he was holding. They were informational brochures from the complex. Inside were floor plans, prices, and a list of amenities the community offered.

"What's this?" Bug said.

"You see that two-bedroom floor plan? I'm gonna be living in that in like a month."

"What are you talking about?" Toomey said.

"You see that park? You see? There are little kids out there playing, not like where we live. My kid gonna be playing out there."

"It says it's like nine hundred dollars a month," Bug said, reading the pamphlet. "You can't afford that."

"Why you think I got us doing all this work?" Jahlil said. "I'm gonna give them a crazy down payment and have my old man sign the lease, and then —"

"Thought you said your old man has bad credit," Toomey said.

"He does. That's why I'm saving up the big down payment."

"And what if you don't have enough?" Toomey asked.

Jahlil looked at Toomey with attitude. "Like I said, that's why we putting in all this work."

"I can't do it no more," Toomey said.

Jahlil looked at Toomey like he had no idea what his friend was talking about.

"It's not worth it, Jahlil, and you know it. For a few hundred bucks here, and a few

211

hundred there, it's not worth the risk."

"What risk?" Jahlil said. "You see how easy we took that five hundred off that dude last night? We do this in our sleep."

"He right, Toomey," Bug said.

Toomey shot Bug an evil look. "That's the attitude I'm worried about. What if we think we're so good that one night we slip, and something happens? It just isn't worth it."

Jahlil fell silent. "Toomey, don't do this to me, man. I need this money. I really need this money to get that place."

"Is it so important that you're willing to risk your life?"

"Ain't nobody dying, Toomey. Damn!"

"What if we get caught?" Toomey said. "You want to be locked up? Is it worth that?"

"Yes!" Jahlil said, without even having to think about it. "My girl is having our baby. She depending on me. Yes, it's worth it!"

Toomey shook his head. "I would do anything for you, Jahlil. You and Bug my best friends. I've known you for more than half my life, but —"

"Then this last one," Jahlil said. "This one, tonight. Bug said the dude got some expensive stuff in there, and he never home. It'll be easy. We get in, get out, sell the stuff, make the money, and you can be done."

Toomey shook his head silently.

"You said you'd do anything for us, Toomey," Bug said.

"Shut up, Bug," Toomey said.

"You did say that," Jahlil said. "This last time, and I promise. No more."

Toomey looked up seriously at Jahlil. "You will never ask me to do any of this stuff with you again?"

"Never. I promise."

"Okay," Toomey said. "Then tonight will be the last time."

47

Daphanie had been handcuffed and driven to the nearest police station. There, all her property was taken from her, and she was fingerprinted and stood before a bond hearing officer, where her bond was set at $5,000. She then received a court date a month out.

Finally given the opportunity to make a phone call, Daphanie called Mr. Harris. He came to the station, paid her bond, and she was released.

In his car, after starting the ignition, Austin turned to Daphanie and said, "Now tell me exactly what happened? Kidnapping charges?"

"I picked up Nate's son from day care and took him out for the day."

"You did what? Why? I told you I would handle this, and you go and kidnap —"

"It wasn't kidnapping. That's what I was trying to explain to the cops. My name was on the pickup list. Tricia, at day care, gave him to me. How could it be kidnapping when Nathaniel was given to me?"

Pulling up to a stop sign, Austin said, "Fine. We'll argue that on your court date, but it still makes absolutely no sense for you to have done that. What were you thinking? That man has no control over this situation."

"He's the one that stole my baby from me," Daphanie said softly, slumping in the passenger seat.

"Well, he can't get him back."

That was an hour ago. After a good cry and a hot shower, Daphanie decided she needed to get out, drive down to Water Tower Mall, buy a pair of shoes or a dress — do something to try to make herself feel better.

Finding a pair of cute, peach-colored, open-toed heels, Daphanie walked the box up to the counter to pay for them.

She had been wrong about Nate. She thought she had reached him, but she had not. She should've known she hadn't when he said she might have to pay for taking little Nathaniel. But to have her arrested?

As she set the shoe box on the counter, she gave a quick smile to the associate in front of her. While reaching in her purse for her credit card, Daphanie asked herself what she could do to get back at Nate for the embarrassment, inconvenience, and money he had just cost her.

"Debit or credit?" the woman asked, taking Daphanie's card and punching numbers on the register.

"Credit," Daphanie said, realizing she'd best take Mr. Harris's advice and leave Nate alone. She had tried playing his game to get even with him and lost. Daphanie just wasn't evil enough, calculating enough, at least not by herself.

"Ma'am," the associate said, "I'm sorry but your card has been declined."

"Run it again, please, will you?" Daphanie said, having had the same problem with this card being declined on the first swipe, then accepted on the second, in the past.

The associate did as she was asked.

Daphanie heard a short buzz from the register.

"I'm sorry. Would you like to try debit?"

"Sure," Daphanie said, entering her PIN on the punch pad in front of her. Again, she heard the buzz, and again the associate said the card had been declined.

Daphanie tried the two other credit cards she had. They were also no good.

"No," Daphanie said, worry starting to

consume her. She took the third card from the associate with a quivering hand and hurried toward the store's exit, which led her into the mall. Walking fast, almost trotting, Daphanie rushed toward the first ATM she saw, praying, begging under her breath. "Please, don't have done this. Don't have done this to me, Nate."

She pushed her bank card into the ATM slot, stabbed her pass code into the machine, then pressed the Balance Inquiry option.

Daphanie was living off her 401(k). After losing her job, she had taken the money, stuck it in her account, and she had been living off that. She had a little over $22,000. It was all she had to her name.

"Don't have done this to me, you bastard," Daphanie said one last time, brushing a tear from her cheek.

The balance screen popped up. She stared, mouth open, at the figure displayed in red. That figure was $0.01.

48

Lewis slid into the opposite side of the booth in the downtown café. He was wearing khaki pants and a button-down shirt. He must've just been getting off work, Monica thought.

"Hey," Lewis said, smiling. He picked up the plastic menu, glanced at it. "Surprised to hear from you after the last time."

"I apologize for that. You know I love Layla, it's just . . ."

"No problem. I know you didn't mean it," Lewis said, the smile still on his face. "What're you eating?"

"That's not why I called you here," Monica said. "I thought you should know, I just spoke to Freddy Ford."

Lewis dropped the menu to the table, the smile disappearing from his face. "What do you mean? You called —"

"I went there, to the institution, to see him."

"Why? What for? He shot you," Lewis said, flustered. "What in the world would you have to talk —"

"I was having nightmares. I needed to confront him, but that's not important. Lewis, I'm not supposed to be telling you this, but he blames you for everything that happened."

"Me?" Lewis said, surprised. "Nate was the one —"

"He blames Nate the most. Says he's going to get him, Nate's brother, and you."

Lewis sat still, quiet for a moment, his eyes steadily focused on Monica. "What do you mean he's going to 'get' me?"

"That he's going to come after you when he gets out."

Lewis remained silent for another moment, his eyes focused on his thoughts, then he chuckled some, as though suddenly not worried at all.

"What? What's so funny?" Monica said.

"He can't get me. He's never gonna get out of there, and even if he does, I would like to see him try coming after me. He will get his black ass whupped."

"Lewis, I think you need to take this seriously," Monica said. She wanted to tell Lewis that Freddy had mentioned his little girl, but she didn't want to worry Lewis more than necessary. "You see what he did to me, to Nate."

"He won't do that to me," Lewis said, standing up from the booth seat. "I appreciate you telling me this, but it ain't nothing I have to worry about. Okay."

"Look, just sit down so we can talk about this more. Have something to eat, my treat," Monica said.

"You said that ain't why you called me here. Besides, I ain't hungry no more. You told me what you had to tell me," Lewis said, sounding almost angry. "I appreciate it. Now I'm gonna go."

"Okay, Lewis," Monica said, not wanting to let him go. "Just be careful, okay?"

Lewis forced a confident smile, then said, "Yeah, see you around."

49

Eight forty-one p.m., and Jahlil wished he had listened to Toomey's warnings.

Jahlil crouched behind a long sofa inside the dark house they were robbing, his hands shaking around his gun. He felt he couldn't breathe. He pulled the mask up over his face, stared at Bug, who was crouching beside him. His face covered with sweat, the boy looked more frightened than Jahlil had ever seen him.

"Where's Toomey?" Jahlil whispered harshly. "Where is he?"

"I don't know!" Bug whispered back.

It wasn't supposed to have gone like this.

Jahlil, Toomey, and Bug had pulled up forty minutes ago, at the exact time the owner of the house was backing out of his driveway.

They waited half an hour, made sure there was no movement inside, then the boys approached the house from the back entrance.

All the windows had bars on them, but after breaking one of the small glass squares on the back door, making more noise than Jahlil would have liked, Toomey was able to fit his hand through and unlock the door.

Jahlil, Toomey, and Bug, black ski masks pulled over their faces, walked slowly through the dark house.

"Where does he keep the TV?" Jahlil whispered to Bug.

"I don't know. We gotta find it. Maybe upstairs."

"I'm not liking this," Toomey said from behind them.

"Shut up," Jahlil said, looking over his shoulder. "Just come on."

They walked through a narrow hallway that opened into the dining room. There was nothing of value, just the table and chairs.

The boys came together at the doorway of the living room.

"I can check upstairs," Bug whispered.

"Maybe we should just get out of here," Toomey said.

"No!" Jahlil said. "We ain't —"

Just then, they heard the sound of a chair skid across the hardwood floor and topple over. There was a flash of orange fire and a cannon-like explosion. The window to their left shattered. Toomey threw himself behind a chair on one side of the room. Bug dived behind a sofa. Jahlil fired two shots in the direction of the shotgun blast, then dived behind the sofa with Bug.

"What happened?" Jahlil said, frantic. "What's happening?"

"I don't know, man. I don't know!" Bug yelled.

Jahlil looked around but couldn't locate Toomey. He peeled up his mask. "Where's Toomey? Where is he?"

"I don't know!" Bug yelled back.

There was another shot. It tore through the middle of the couch, sending splintered wood and cushion stuffing into the air. Bug threw his hands over his ears. "What the fuck! What the fuck!"

A second later, Jahlil heard the sound of shifting, as though whoever just fired at them was trying to find a better position to take a better shot. Jahlil knew if they stayed too much longer, they would all wind up dead or in jail. He didn't want to experience either.

He scooted over closer to Bug. The boy looked as though he was about to cry. "Listen," Jahlil whispered. "We gotta get out of here now! We gotta go. You got your cell."

"Yeah."

"Pull it out. Text Toomey. Make sure he ain't hit."

Bug did what Jahlil told him. Seconds later, Bug's screen lit with the return text.

"He's okay."

"Tell him on two, we breaking for the back door. Okay. One, two — we going."

"Okay."

Jahlil looked at Bug's trembling fingers as he quickly pushed the buttons. They were shaking so badly he could barely type. But they would get out of this. Toomey would know what to do, and they'd all get out fine.

Toomey's text came in. Bug looked up at Jahlil. "Okay. He's ready."

"Are you?" Jahlil said, a hand on Bug's shoulder.

Bug swallowed hard. "Yeah."

Jahlil pulled the mask down over his face, gripped the gun tighter, and pointed it in the direction of whoever fired at them. "One . . . two!" he yelled, loud enough for Toomey to hear.

Bug was up faster than Jahlil had expected and was around the sofa. Jahlil sprang to his feet and was right behind him. He heard furniture toppling over and saw Toomey appear from behind a chair.

They were halfway into the dining room

when Jahlil heard the cock of the shotgun.

"Hurry up!" Jahlil cried, pushing as he looked over his shoulder. He saw the eruption of fire behind Toomey. He heard the blast of the big gun, and almost at the same time he saw Toomey's mouth fall open, his face go blank, as the fire from the shotgun opened up his best friend's chest.

Droplets of blood sprayed Jahlil's face, as Toomey's body flew forward, dropped at Jahlil's feet, then slid, lifeless, across the floor.

The world went silent that moment. For that second, Jahlil was deaf, and all he could do was stare as the shadowy figure in the dining room cocked the shotgun again, and took aim.

50

After knocking on Nate's door, Daphanie told herself not to throw herself at him and claw out his eyes for what he had done. She didn't have proof, but she didn't need it.

After seeing that she had a balance of one cent in her account, she called the bank. Whomever she spoke to said Daphanie herself had electronically transferred the money out.

"I'm telling you, I didn't take out that money!" Daphanie yelled into the phone. "Why would I be calling, telling you the money was missing if I had taken it out myself?"

The representative took a moment to answer, then finally said, "I don't know, ma'am."

She had also found out that her bank-issued credit card had been maxed out, along with her two other credit cards.

No, she didn't have proof, Daphanie

thought, her fists clenched at her sides, hearing the locks on the other side of Nate's door being undone. But this was his work, him "making her pay" for taking Nathaniel.

When the door opened, Daphanie was surprised to see not Nate standing in front of her, but Nate's private investigator, Abbey Kurt. She was a short, stout woman, with hair pulled back into a bun and a stern look of business on her face. She wore a pantsuit and square-toed, black, low-heeled shoes.

"May I help you?"

"I'm here to see Nate."

"Mr. Kenny is unavailable."

"Tell him I need to speak to him. I know what he did. He can't just act like he didn't do it."

"I don't know what you're referring to, Miss Coleman, and I'm sure Mr. Kenny doesn't either."

Daphanie stared at Ms. Kurt. Her teeth clenched, her eyes narrowed, she searched her mind for a way to appeal to this woman. "I don't know how he did it, but he maxed out all my credit cards. He stole all the money I have and left one fucking cent in my bank account. I have nothing. Please, let me see him."

"I'm sorry," Abbey Kurt said, not seeming to care about a thing she'd just heard. "He's unavailable."

The woman was fit, angular, and muscled, looking as though she worked out daily. But she was short, shorter than Daphanie. If she wouldn't let Daphanie see Nate, Daphanie would force her way in.

Daphanie made a move toward the woman.

In two quick movements, Abbey brushed her jacket back to expose the Glock handgun on her hip, then wrapped her fist around it, ready to draw.

Daphanie froze.

"Miss Coleman, you're threatening to trespass. I'm hired to protect this property. I would be within my rights to shoot you. Please leave."

Daphanie didn't respond. She looked over Abbey's shoulder, hoping she would get a glimpse of Nate. She stepped back, looked up at the windows.

"Fine," Daphanie said, feeling she could do nothing more.

She headed back down the path toward her car but felt the strange need to turn, to take another look at the house. When she did, the woman was no longer in the doorway. Nate stood in her place. He glared at her, shaking his head slowly. "I told you you would have to pay," she heard him say.

51

It was late, and Caleb was still cleaning Austin's offices. He dragged the mop across the floor, but his mind wasn't on his work. Caleb still couldn't shake the image of that dead man's head hanging limp on his chest.

After he had been released, Caleb had jumped in his van and called Austin.

"You all right?" Austin asked.

"Yeah . . . I just . . . I —"

"You're not okay. What's going on? Is it Jahlil?" Austin had said.

"No, he's fine."

Caleb thought of asking for the money right then. That was the reason he had called. But he had been living in Austin's house for the past year, and at last count, Caleb was into his brother for at least twenty grand. It was a debt that had been accruing over a number of years. How would he look, begging for more money? He'd look like a loser.

"Nothing. Nothing's wrong," Caleb lied, telling himself he'd try his best to come up with the money first, and if he couldn't, Austin would be his last resort. "I just called to say I'll be a little late coming into work tomorrow evening."

"That's fine," Austin said. "The mess will still be here."

Caleb spun around when he heard a noise behind him. His son had just walked in the front door of the office.

It was Jahlil's night to come in, but Caleb hadn't expected the boy, given the beating he had taken and their last conversation.

"Jahlil, I would've understood if you didn't come in tonight," Caleb called.

Jahlil stood silent at the other end of the offices in the shadows. His face was hidden by his hood.

Caleb set his mop against one of the office desks and took a couple of steps toward his son. "Hey, is everything all right? No one been messing with you at school again, have they?"

Still, no response came from Jahlil.

There was something definitely wrong. Caleb moved quickly over to the boy, taking Jahlil by his shoulders, and was shocked to see that his face was covered with tears.

"Jahlil —"

"He's dead. He's dead, Dad!" Jahlil said, throwing himself onto Caleb. Caleb hugged his son. He could feel the boy's body trembling against his.

It was approaching 11:30 p.m. when Blue opened the door and let Caleb into his apartment.

Blue glanced down at his watch. "Did I forget we was supposed to be hanging out tonight? Gimme a second to finish this beer and we can roll."

"Naw, we weren't supposed to hang out," Caleb said, lowering himself into the tattered sofa. A forty-two-inch flat-screen stood on a cheap wooden stand, muted. A boxing match played silently. "You got another beer?"

"Yeah," Blue said, going to the fridge and grabbing Caleb a beer, then handing it over. Caleb drank more than half of it without stopping.

"Dude, you gonna be drinking like that, we gonna have to go to the store."

"Kwan had me grabbed earlier today, man."

"What?"

"Took me to his store, tied me up."

"They ain't do nothing, did —"

"Naw, not to me," Caleb said, as if in a trance. "But they had some other dude tied up. Some dude who didn't pay and tried to leave town." Caleb looked up at Blue. "They killed him. They put a plastic bag over his head and suffocated him right in front of me. Said they'd do the same thing to me if I don't pay."

"Fuck, man! You gonna be able to pay 'em, right?"

"Contracts ain't come through," Caleb said, staring helplessly at nothing, his eyes glassed over.

"Forget all this. Just ask Austin for the money."

"No," Caleb said. "I already owe him too much, and I'm gonna need more than just what I owe Kwan."

"What do you mean?"

"Jahlil came to work all messed up, crying, saying someone was dead."

"Who's dead? What's the boy into?"

"I don't know," Caleb said. "He wouldn't tell me anything. Just kept saying he's tired and things are messed up. All I know is I need to be back in that boy's life. I need to be back at home. And I can't go over there broke, telling Sonya to let me back. I need money. My family needs money. So I need to do a job. You said it's an easy one, we won't get caught, 'cause I can't go back to jail, Blue."

"Naw, man. No risk. We all good."

"So can you call this man, or what?" Caleb said, impatient.

"Yeah," Blue said. "I'll call him."

52

Monica sat alone at Bijan's, her head buzzing.

Carrying around that disturbing news from Freddy Ford made her want to do nothing more than go home and roll up in a ball. But she honored her word by meeting Austin Harris for their date.

On the drive over, Monica had told herself again not to worry about Freddy and the possibility of him going after the people he felt were responsible for his imprisonment. She forced herself to see things exactly how Lewis saw them. Freddy could make all the threats he wanted, but he couldn't carry them out from behind the walls of a mental institution.

After stepping in the restaurant, Monica was greeted by a very handsome Austin, who had been waiting at the bar wearing a brown suit with a crisp white-collared shirt. He stood, gave Monica a hug and a soft kiss on the cheek. He smelled good, and his strong chest felt even better as it pressed ever so slightly against her breasts.

"I want to thank you for the flowers you sent," Monica said. "They were beautiful."

"Not as beautiful as you are tonight."

"Smooth talker, smooth talker." Monica laughed, waving a finger at him.

They had a martini at the bar while they waited for their table.

Monica asked how Daphanie's case was progressing.

"Not great. I don't know if she'll have many options," Austin said. "And this jerk, Nate Kenny. You know, let's not talk about this. I feel myself getting angry already."

"I completely understand," Monica said.

After they were seated, they shared a bottle of white wine with their seafood dinners.

Monica found herself smiling for much of the date. She told herself to calm down, because she didn't want to start feeling Austin Harris, then later find out he was a repeat of her last date.

"So," Monica ventured, still smiling, "what do you think about kids?"

Austin's face brightened. "They're wonderful. I always wanted kids."

"Oh."

"And now that I have them," Austin said, "I wish I could take them back. No, I'm joking. They're great."

"Oh! So you already have children?"

"Yeah. Two. Troy just turned sixteen and Bethany is away at college," Austin said. "With their mother getting remarried a few years back, I've been more distant with my kids than I should've. I've been a better father in the past, but I'm working on that."

"I'm sure you're a great dad." Monica smiled. "You planning on having any more?" Monica held her breath.

"I'm fine with the kids I have," Austin said. "Not to get ahead of myself, but if some way lightning strikes and we do end up together, I hope you're okay with that."

Monica smiled. "I think so."

Outside, in front of the restaurant, Austin's Mercedes had already been fetched by the valet. Austin waited with Monica for her car to be brought around.

It was a beautiful night, and the two stood very close to one another.

"Why are you smiling?" Austin asked.

Monica found Austin to be a perfect gentleman. He pulled out her chair every time she sat, and stood each time she stood. His dinner conversation was interesting, funny, and just flirtatious enough to have Monica clamping her legs together under the table, wondering what the man would be like in bed. "For the same reason you're smiling," Monica said, smiling more, trying not to give away her thoughts.

The valet stepped out of Monica's Jaguar, and held the door open.

"Well, I guess this is the end of a good night," Austin said. "I know you gotta get up early for work tomorrow."

"I don't. I own my own business. I go in when I want."

"So what does that mean?"

"That means this isn't the end of a good night," Monica said, not imagining herself just yet butt naked, bent over Austin's dresser, but loving the option of choosing that path if she wanted. "Not if we don't want it to be."

"I don't want it to be."

"Neither do I," Monica said, the alcohol still giving her brain warm fuzzies.

"Okay," Austin said. "I was just on my way home, and —"

"Let's do that, then."

"Really?"

"Yeah, really."

Half an hour later, Monica sat on the edge

of Austin's bed wearing nothing but panties. Austin stood naked in front of her, his head thrown back, moaning as Monica stroked him.

"Are you ready for me?" she asked, knowing he was by the stiffness of what she held in her hands.

"Yes," Austin breathed.

"You have protection?"

"Yes."

Monica took Austin's hand and pulled him to bed. He climbed in and reached over toward the nightstand to grab a condom.

Monica pushed her panties down off her hips, let them fall to the floor. She slid under the bed linen and tried to calm her desire.

She had not had sex, not real sex, in over two months. Her body was telling her it was time.

Austin lay next to her and kissed Monica's lips. She pressed her body to his, pulled his tongue into her mouth, and relaxed as she felt him slide a gentle finger into her. Monica closed her thighs around his arm, kissing him harder. "I want you," Monica panted.

He continued to pleasure her with his hand, till the sensation became too much. She didn't want to go this way. She reached down, pressed a hand on his arm, looked into his eyes, and said, "I want *you*."

"Okay," Austin said, and Monica thought she detected the slightest bit of uncertainty.

She opened her legs, closed her eyes, let her head fall to the side on the pillow, and breathed heavily as she felt Austin's weight upon her.

Then nothing.

Monica opened her eyes just a little, looked up to see that he was still there. She reached down between her legs, felt for him, and he was as firm as he was a moment ago. "You okay?"

Austin gave her a look filled with angst, rose off her, and lay down on his back. He pulled the sheet up to his chest, folded his hands on top of it, then said, "I don't want to. Not like this."

"Huh?" Monica said, sitting up in bed.

"What would we get out of this?"

"I don't know about you, but I was hoping for an orgasm."

Austin gave Monica a look that said he wasn't joking.

"Sorry, but what more are you looking for?" Monica said.

"More than sex. I just came out of a relationship like that, and . . . and . . . I deserve better. I'm a good man. I think a better man than I've ever been, and I want to share that with a woman. I guess I'm looking for a relationship."

"Ohhh, Austin," Monica said, plopping backward onto her pillow. She slapped her hands over her face. "You were perfect, and now you wanna screw it up with the *R* word. Say it ain't so."

Austin rolled up on his elbow, pulled one of Monica's hands away from her face. "I thought all women wanted a good relation-ship."

"Then I'm the one woman on earth that doesn't. I just came out of a relationship, and there was absolutely nothing good about it."

"It was the wrong man."

"And the 'good relationship' before that one failed too."

"Again, another wrong man," Austin said. "It could happen."

Monica leaned forward, laid a palm on Austin's cheek. "I like you, so can we please not mess this up?"

"Mess what up?"

"The chance at a great . . . whatever we want this to be, with no talk of commitment and the future, and where we're gonna vaca-tion next year. I told you, I've done that, and it's really nothing I'm interested in."

"Not even the chance of one?" Austin said. "You're telling me there's absolutely nothing I could do to make you interested in starting something with me."

"Well," Monica said, her eyes dropping to the bulging imprint in the sheet below Austin's waist.

"You're joking."

"Does it look like I'm joking?" Monica said with only a hint of a smile.

"This is performance-based is what you're saying?"

"Yes, sir. Show me you can do the work and I'll give you a shot at the job," Monica said, turned on by the playfulness of all this.

"Well, okay. This one time. But remember you asked for this," Austin said. He leaned over and lowered himself down to kiss Monica. It was a long, passionate, sloppy kiss that had Monica's eyes closing, nipples hardening, her body squirming, and her insides aching. He placed his palm low on her pelvis, the tip of his middle finger ever so slightly grazing her most sensitive spot, and continued to kiss her till she nearly exploded.

Monica's eyes slowly opened. She saw that he was kneeling between her legs, rolling on the condom.

"Close your eyes," Austin said.

"What?"

"I said close your eyes. You don't have to see. All you have to do is feel."

Monica did what she was told. She felt Austin's warm palms on her inner thighs, spreading them. She felt him kiss her belly, take one of her breasts in his mouth, then slowly, lovingly insert himself into her.

She moaned deeply, thinking she would succumb and lose it that moment. But she held on, telling herself that if he was always as good as he was feeling that moment, she would be seeing a lot more of Austin Harris.

53

Lewis thought he had heard his name being called, but he was too far into his thoughts to pull himself out.

"Lewis." It was his girlfriend, Eva, shaking his arm.

Lewis finally turned to her, blinking a couple of times as if he had just come out of a trance. Lewis's daughter, Layla, and Eva's daughter, Tammi, had both been put to bed, and Eva and Lewis were watching a Netflix movie that had come in the mail that morning.

"What were you doing?" Eva asked.

"Watching the movie," Lewis lied.

"Okay, what was the last thing Jeffrey Wright said?"

Lewis had no clue. His mind was back at the restaurant where he had met Monica. For every minute, it seemed, after that meeting, Lewis had questioned just how concerned he should've been about Freddy's threats. He wasn't terribly bothered, but the more he questioned those threats, the more concerned he became. "Jeffrey Wright just said . . . uh . . . that he was gonna whup up on dude if he didn't give him the bag of money," Lewis guessed.

"Really, Lewis? That's what he said? Wrong. Now you wanna tell me where your head was at? Where it's been since you came home from work today?"

His head was on wondering whether he should tell Eva about Freddy. Lewis had been pretty much honest with Eva so far. When they first met a few months before, he had told her he'd done a little time in jail, but he'd also said all of that was in his past. At the time, Eva appeared relieved, and she later told him she was happy he was no longer into any shady business, because she had a little girl to care for and wasn't into making time for men whose stuff wasn't together.

Lewis kept telling himself he had nothing to fear from Freddy. But if the man did ever get out and happened to see Lewis and Eva walking down the street and approached them, shooting off his mouth about some craziness, Lewis figured Eva would appreciate having had a heads-up. But then again, telling her about Freddy might have her second guessing if being with Lewis was a good idea.

"I'm thinking about tomorrow," Lewis lied again. "Remember I told you about that man, Caleb Harris, I met at work?"

"Yeah, the janitor."

"He asked if he could bring his son by after work tomorrow. I told him I would hang out with the kid. He's into a little trouble, and I thought I might be able to reach him. I don't know, make a difference somehow."

"Aw," Eva said, leaning over the sofa, taking Lewis's face in her hands, and giving him a kiss on the lips. "How was I so blessed to find a man as good as you?"

"Lucky, I guess," Lewis said.

54

Monica awakened to the sound of someone knocking on her front door.

"All right," she said, stretching. She sat up in bed and rubbed her eyes. She looked at the clock. It was 7:48 a.m.

Shocked, she was happy and relieved that she had not been tormented by yet another Freddy Ford nightmare. Maybe speaking to the man had actually worked.

The knocking came again.

"All right! I'm coming!" Monica yelled. "Damn."

Tying her robe and opening the front door, Monica was surprised to see Daphanie standing in front of her. She looked like she had been up all night.

"What are you doing here?"

"It's early, I know. I'm sorry," Daphanie said, "but I need to talk to you."

"I said, what are you doing here? I did what I said I would, now I'm done."

"Your ex-husband . . . he . . ." Daphanie said, looking lost and victimized. "Can I come in?"

Monica looked pitifully at Daphanie, then reluctantly stepped aside.

Daphanie walked in and fell down onto the living room sofa.

"What happened?"

"I picked Nathaniel up from day care without Nate knowing about it. I wanted to teach him a lesson, scare him. I only kept Nathaniel for part of the day, then I called Nate and took Nathaniel back to him. The next morning, Nate had me arrested, then he had all my credit cards maxed out and stole all of my money from my account."

Monica gasped. She thought of asking Daphanie if she was sure he was behind it, but she knew Nate's vengeful spirit, and Daphanie did play games with Nate's son.

"I have nothing," Daphanie said. "I won't be able to live, and I won't get my baby back."

"How do you know that?"

"I called the lawyer this morning on his cell, asked him what my chances are. I told him to be blunt with me."

"And?" Monica asked, even though she remembered that Austin told her last night Daphanie's options would be few if any.

"He said the contract is binding. I can't get my baby back. I can't even see him."

"There's nothing that can be done?"

"The lawyer said no. Now I have to focus on living. I'm going to try to get my money back from Nate, but I'm sure it's gone for good. The man's a millionaire, yet he takes my twenty grand." Daphanie sighed, stood up, took three steps, then shook her head. "Mr. Harris suggested I go back with Trevor. He said he still loves me, that he'll take me back."

"With the father?"

"Yeah."

"Do you still love him? Have you ever?"

"No. We were fucking, and that's it. And now, in order to see my own child, to be with my baby, I have to submit to a man I don't even have feelings for? Because of Nate?" Daphanie said, her eyes starting to tear. "I think . . . I sometimes think . . . I want to kill him," Daphanie sobbed.

Monica walked over to Daphanie, put an arm around her, and comforted her as much as the circumstances would allow. That moment, she couldn't help but think of Tori Thomas, the other woman who wanted Nate dead. But she hadn't just *wanted,* she'd acted. Nate's old secretary and mistress, Tori, had been done as terribly wrong by Nate as Daphanie and Monica had been, but Tori showed up at his office with a gun, pointed it at him, then, at the last minute, turned it on herself and pulled the trigger. Thankfully she had not died. Last Monica heard, she was in California somewhere.

"You don't want to kill Nate," Monica said, pulling her arm from around Daphanie.

"But I do. He took away my child and everything else from me. He needs to pay. You of all people should agree. The things he's done to you, how he treated you. He almost got you killed. You were in a coma, for Christ's sake, and you don't want him to feel any pain for that?"

Monica thought about the horrible ways he had treated her. Yes, if there was anyone who wanted revenge against Nate, it was herself. "No," Monica lied. "What's done is done."

"Bullshit," Daphanie said, staring Monica in the face. "I can see it in your eyes."

"You don't see anything," Monica said, trying her best to disguise her pain. "I have millions of dollars because of him."

"Yeah, yeah. You're a millionaire, but that doesn't mean you aren't hurting. We could do something," Daphanie said, desperately.

"Think of a plan to get him back. He's not the only one that can scheme."

"No. I told you, it wouldn't work."

"But —"

"It wouldn't work. You've tried it once and look where it's gotten you! You've lost your child, for God's sake!"

Daphanie was silent. "So I should just go back to Trevor, submit to a man I don't love in order to be with my baby?"

"Is there any other way for you to be with your child?"

Daphanie sighed heavily and lowered her head. "No."

"Then I think you've answered your own question," Monica said.

55

Standing in front of his school wall locker, Jahlil kept thinking that he really hadn't wanted to break down in front of his father, but he couldn't help himself. Everything had just become too much. After work, his father had driven him back home, grilled him all the way there. At one point, he even started yelling.

Jahlil didn't say another word, just climbed out of the car, once they reached home.

"We aren't done with this," Caleb had said.

Still in front of his open locker, Jahlil jumped at the hand that was pressed on his shoulder. He turned to see Shaun standing behind him, her round belly jutting out in front of her. "Hey, baby," she said, giving Jahlil a quick kiss on the lips. "You okay?"

Jahlil took her hand. "Can you cut this

period? I really need to talk to you."

Two blocks away from school, in a quiet public park, Jahlil sat on a bench with Shaun.

"Jahlil, what's going on? You starting to scare me."

"I did something bad, something really bad, but you have to promise not to tell nobody."

"What? I won't tell, I promise."

Jahlil tilted his head toward the sky, blinking tears away. "Toomey's dead."

"What!"

"He's dead."

"How?"

"Me, him, and Bug broke into this dude's place."

"You didn't tell me about this one."

"I know," Jahlil said, lowering his head. "I didn't want you all stressed with the baby coming."

"Did you make sure the guy was gone?"

"He was gone. We saw him leave, but there was somebody else there. When we tried to leave, Toomey . . ." Jahlil tried to choke back his emotion. A tear fell from his eye, which he quickly brushed away. "Toomey got hit. He was killed right then."

Shaun reached out for Jahlil. He threw

himself into her, held her tight, and cried. Shaun rubbed his back, kissed the side of his face.

"I . . . I just . . . Toomey's gone, and I just can't . . . I can't do it anymore."

Shaun continued to hold him but stopped smoothing her hand across his back. "What do you mean?"

Jahlil looked up. "I mean, I can't do it anymore. It's not worth it."

"I understand that you scared, but how else you gonna make money? I thought you was doing this so we can someday live together like a family. What about the place you gave me the pamphlet to? I thought you was doing this for the baby. You saying our baby ain't worth it?"

"That's not what I'm saying, Shaun," Jahlil said, pulling away from her.

"Then what are you saying?"

"That could've been me in there. If on the next job I get killed, there won't be no new place to live, and there sure as hell won't be no family, because I'll be dead." He stood up angrily from the bench. "You all right with that?" He turned, took a couple of steps away.

Shaun walked up behind Jahlil, hugged him from behind. "You know I ain't saying that, and you know I love you. But you been robbing for almost a year now, and this is the first time something bad happened. Somebody slipped last night, and you just gotta make sure it don't happen again. But we gotta keep making money. You don't, and where am I gonna stay? Mama gonna either put me on the street with our baby or force me to put it up for adoption. You want either of those things to happen?"

Jahlil was silent.

Shaun released Jahlil, walked around so she could look into his eyes. "Baby, you want either of those things to happen?"

"No," Jahlil said, feeling anger that he must continue what he knew might one day get him killed.

"Then you gotta do what you gotta do for your family."

56

Austin sat in his office, the phone pressed to his ear.

"She thinks she's going to go back to Trevor."

Austin listened, hearing anger in Monica's voice. "I know. I recommended that," Austin said.

"That makes no sense to me."

"She has no other recourse. It was either that or never see her baby again."

"You don't know how angry that makes me. I mean, really angry."

"I'm sorry. But there was really nothing else that could've happened."

Monica was silent. "It's not right."

"I know."

"I'm mad at you for even suggesting it."

"I'll make it up to you," Austin said.

"I don't know. What are you suggesting?"

"Take off work tomorrow, spend the day with me downtown. We can do breakfast, a carriage ride, a museum or two, and top it off with a couple of waffle cones. What do you say?"

"I didn't hear anything about sex. The way you handled yourself last time, I thought I'd give you another go at it."

"You enjoyed yourself?"

"I guess you can say that," Monica said.

"Which means, the idea of a relationship is something that you'll consider now."

"Just pick me up at the store tomorrow morning."

"Okay, see you then," Austin said, even though he realized Monica had avoided answering his question. He hung up the phone, smiled, and leaned back in his chair. He had been thinking about this woman much more than he knew he should've, especially considering she told him from the beginning that she wanted nothing more than a sexual deal with him. He told himself not to worry. Besides, he figured, once he threw enough of the old Austin charm on her, she would start to develop feelings for him, just as he knew he would for her. Everything would be fine.

A knock came at the door.

"Come in," Austin said, sitting up at his desk.

Marcus stepped in, looking perturbed. He

closed the door, then sat in the chair in front of Austin's desk.

"How's the job search? Find anything yet?"

"Are you kidding me? Do you know what it's like out there? A guy just served me coffee at a bookstore. He has a freaking PhD in economics."

"I'm sorry, man."

"It'll pass. The important thing is now I have the right mind-set, and at least I'm trying."

"True."

"But unfortunately that's more than I can say for your office manager out there," Marcus said.

"What's up with you and Reecie now?"

Marcus scooted his chair closer to Austin's desk, leaned in, lowering his voice. "The other day, I told her I was really out there, searching for jobs. I told her I missed her and Sophie and I wanted to come home. She said no, that I laid around the house for two years, and she didn't think I learned my lesson after just a few days."

"Ouch."

"I know. I think there's something going on. Like, maybe another guy."

"What?" Austin said. "Don't be ridiculous. Reecie loves —"

"I've been doing some investigating."

"Investigating, Marcus. Really?"

"Yeah. I got a source."

"A source. A source? C'mon. Who is it?"

"Our babysitter, Kendra."

Austin stood up from his chair. "Okay, you know what, Marcus? I really have better things to do than to —"

"No, no! Sit down," Marcus urged.

Austin did.

"Reecie has been asking Kendra to babysit for the last three nights in a row. She's going out every night. I followed her last —"

"You followed her! Marcus, enough!"

"I lost her at a red light. But I'm going again tonight, and I want you to come with me."

"I'm sorry, I have a late business-related social function tonight, but even if I didn't, I would've lied and said that I did. You're crazy."

"I'm not crazy," Marcus said, standing, leaning over Austin's desk, pointing a finger down at his brother. "She's out there doing something. Something that's stopping her from letting me back into our family, and I'm gonna find out what it is. Tomorrow night. Come with me then?"

"I got a date tomorrow afternoon, Marcus."

"Good. Kendra said she's not babysitting till nine p.m. I'll pick you up at your place at eight thirty. Okay?"

Tired of trying to talk sense into his brother, Austin said, "Fine, Marcus. Eight thirty it is."

57

Jahlil sat down at a table in the back of the crowded high school cafeteria. Bug looked sheepishly left and right, as though afraid they were being watched, then set his tray of food down. They were alone at their table, even though all the other tables were filled with loud, talking and laughing students.

Bug was about to speak when Jahlil interrupted and said, "We need to set up another job. Maybe at another ATM, maybe outside the mall."

Bug looked both shocked and angry. "You crazy!" He whispered harshly, looking around to make sure no one was listening. "Toomey just got killed."

"It happens."

"It happens? What the hell is with you? He was our best friend. That don't mean nothing to you?"

Of course it did. Inside, Jahlil's heart was

still torn to shreds because of the death of his friend, but he had responsibilities. Shaun made sure he knew that, and he wasn't about to shirk those, like his father so easily had done. "It means something. But he's dead, and we gotta keep on living. It takes money to live, Bug. I thought you would've learned that by now."

"And what if we get caught on the next one? We ain't even clear of the last one yet."

"Nobody knows."

Bug shook his head and pulled his phone from his pocket. He punched a number of keys on the device to get online. He pulled up video from this morning's news. "You haven't seen this," Bug said, handing the phone over to Jahlil.

The volume turned way down, Jahlil listened to the faint newscaster's voice as he watched the video of the house they robbed last night.

". . . a robbery at a South Side home. One of the intruders, Toomey Peters, was killed by the homeowner's vacationing friend. There is an ongoing investigation and search for the other assailants. Linda Perez reporting for —"

Jahlil handed the phone back to Bug, slapped an angry palm to his skull. "Fuck!" he hissed. "What do we do?"

"Don't panic," Bug said. "I already called my boy, Mike. He said we can say we was chilling at his house last night if the police come asking questions," Bug said. "You know they might come, right?"

Jahlil looked over his shoulder as if expecting police officers to walk in and start blocking the exits to the lunchroom. "I gotta do another job and that's all there is to it."

"No. We can't do this no more," Bug said. "You know that. I know you gotta do for your girl and your baby, but this ain't the way. It's gonna catch up to us, and I don't wanna be in prison or dead. I ain't really realize that till last night."

"So what you saying?"

"I gotta be out, Jahlil. But I need for you to say that you done too."

"I can't just —"

Bug came around the table, sat down next to Jahlil, and grabbed him by the arm. "Do you wanna be dead? Do you wanna get locked up?"

"No. Hell no! But you gonna feed my kid when it comes? You gonna take care of my girl, find us a place to stay?" Jahlil said, raising his voice. He drew momentary looks from students at other tables.

Bug waited for them to turn away before he said, "Jahlil, we can find help, okay?" Bug pleaded, "You don't even have to say you'll never do it again, just think about it, till after we find you some help."

Jahlil stood up from the table, shook his head as he stared down at his friend, and said, "Yeah, I'll think about it."

58

Monica walked slowly up and stood in front of Nate's office, raised her hand to knock, but did not do it.

She had told herself to forget this man, put him out of her thoughts for good. Even considering the abuse and mistreatment she had suffered from him, she made out okay — the millions of dollars she now had, her stores.

But there was the evil thing he'd just done, taking Daphanie's baby. For Monica, it wasn't really even about Daphanie. She could give less than a damn about that woman after she tried stealing Nate from her. It was about Nate's doing something so god-awful as swindling the woman out of her child, then simply thinking nothing more of how he had just ruined her life, as he had done so many times with Monica. The trend had to stop.

Monica prepared herself again to knock

when the door opened up in front of her. Nate stood behind it.

"My receptionist called and said you were coming back. I was going to find out what was taking you so long," Nate said, like they were good friends, like he had never cheated her, cheated on her, and left her for not being able to give him a child.

Monica walked past Nate and stood in the center of his office, shaking her head. "It just doesn't stop with you."

"What are you talking about, Monica?" Nate said, closing the door.

"You were fucking her, were going to marry her, left me for her — didn't that mean you cared the slightest bit?"

"Not you too," Nate said, walking across his office to his liquor bar. He poured himself a quick drink. "Want one?" he said, looking back at Monica.

"No."

Nate took a sip from his glass. "She came by here like there was something I could do, even had some pompous, arrogant attorney asking questions. And now you? Like I told both of them, I can't get the child back. What's done is done."

"Then undo it, Nate," Monica said, angry. "I know she lied to you, she deceived you, but it's nothing more than you've done a thousand times to a thousand other people."

"It's different," Nate said, turning his back on Monica, walking toward the sofa at the other end of his office.

Monica hurried behind him, grabbed him by the arm, spun him. "How?"

"If she hadn't told me she was having my baby, I would have never left you, okay?" Nate said.

Monica was stopped by the sincerity and regret she heard in Nate's admission — so much that it took her a moment to say, "She didn't make you leave me. The decision was yours. It's over now. Now you have to make right what you did wrong. You took her child, and you have to find a way to give him back."

"I can't."

"You can, Nate. I know you. You found a way to take him, you can find a way to get him back."

"Fine," Nate said, downing the last of the drink. He set the glass down on his desk. "Come back to me, and I'll see what I can do."

Again Monica was forced into silence, but only for a second. "You disgust me. You could possibly reunite this baby with his mother, but only if you get what you want out of the deal."

"I know it hasn't always seemed like it, but I still love you, Monica," Nate said, taking her hand.

Monica snatched her hand away from Nate's grasp, as if he had assaulted her. "Don't ever say that to me again, and don't you ever touch me."

"Nathaniel misses you. You can come back," Nate said. "I promised myself I would not ask you, but if you wanted to come back, I'd let you."

It was becoming all too much for her, the nerve of him, his resistance to undoing possibly the worst thing he'd ever done, and then his trying to make a deal to win her back in the same breath. "Will you talk to Trevor about the baby, see what you can do?" Monica said, ignoring Nate's request.

"I already told you, if you come back, I'll do everything I can to get Daphanie's son back to her."

Monica narrowed her eyes on Nate, wanting nothing more than to spit in his face. She suppressed that urge and said, "Then Daphanie will never get her child back."

59

Daphanie sat in her car, only the single penny Nate left her to her name. She was older than she should've been to have had a baby, and by the grace of God, the child turned out healthy. Daphanie knew she would not be having another.

She looked out her window, up at Trevor's house. What other choice did she have?

She had called him up an hour ago to ask if it was all right if she came over so they could talk. He said it would be fine. Daphanie knew her visit there would be not to have a conversation but to accept the terms that would allow her back into her baby's life. She figured Trevor knew that too.

It was the right thing to do. It hurt now, but in fifteen, twenty years, when Daphanie would no longer need Trevor's permission to be with her child, she would know, definitely, that she had done the right thing.

Daphanie crossed the street, walked up to the house, and rang the doorbell once. The door opened almost immediately, as if Trevor had been waiting there behind it.

He looked good, and Daphanie could almost remember what had initially attracted her to this man. In his arms, he held their beautiful baby boy. The child smiled and reached out a hand to her. The gesture almost made her cry.

"It's good to see you, Daphanie. Please, come in," Trevor said, stepping aside so that Daphanie could enter.

60

Mrs. Ford opened the door and tried to smile as Lewis walked past her into Freddy's uncle's house. She closed the door, turned, and accepted the kiss Lewis gave her on the cheek. Lewis had called Mrs. Ford this morning, after not being able to keep Freddy's threats out of his head.

Standing in the records office at work, the phone pressed to the side of his face, Lewis had said, "Yeah, Mrs. Ford, I know it seems like a while since we've spoken. I want to know if I can come by there and speak to you."

Mrs. Ford had said yes, that the company would be nice, and she was looking forward to seeing him.

Stepping back from Mrs. Ford now, all Lewis saw in the older woman's face was pain.

"We can talk in the kitchen," Mrs. Ford said. "I can make you some lunch."

"You don't have to do that," Lewis said. "I can get something on the way back to work."

"No, you won't. You gonna sit and have some decent food to eat," Mrs. Ford said, leading the way down a narrow hallway toward the kitchen.

Fifteen minutes later, Lewis finished the last corner of a delicious turkey sandwich. He wiped his mouth with a napkin, crumpled it, and set it on the plate. Mrs. Ford sat at the table across from Lewis.

"Was it good?" she asked.

"The best," Lewis said, patting his belly.

"You said you wanted to talk about something. It's about my son, ain't it?"

"Yes. Has he contacted you? You spoken to him lately?"

"I went to visit him a week ago. He wouldn't come out. I waited and waited, told the man there I needed to see him. The man went, told Fred what I said, then came back and told me Fred said never to come back. That he didn't want to see me no more," Mrs. Ford said. She reached for one of the napkins on the table, folded it, then dabbed the corners of her eyes.

"I'm sorry, Mrs. Ford," Lewis said, squeezing one of her hands. He thought about telling Mrs. Ford about the threats

Freddy had made, asking her if she thought he had any reason to worry, but it seemed this woman knew no more about what Freddy was thinking than he did. "Do you . . . do you know when they're supposed to be letting him out?"

"My baby is gonna be locked up for three years. Are you going to visit him?"

Lewis relaxed some, his thoughts being validated. The only thing Freddy could do from behind the walls of that institution was make threats. Lewis stood, thanked Mrs. Ford for her time and the food, then said, "I don't think I'll be making it over there, considering how we ended. I . . . I hope you understand."

Mrs. Ford looked saddened by what Lewis said but nodded. "Yeah, I understand."

61

The day had been wonderful, just as Austin had expected. The sun was shining, and the temperature was a perfect seventy-five degrees. As they rode the tour boat that glided along the Chicago River, Austin found himself staring at Monica, wondering what kind of future they would create.

Monica turned, noticing Austin's gaze. "What are you looking at?"

"Nothing," Austin said, smiling and looking off.

They had lunch at an outdoor café on Rush Street, cabbed it over to the Art Institute on Michigan Avenue, and walked the quiet halls together, staring up at the beautiful, ancient paintings of da Vinci, Michelangelo, and Rembrandt.

From there, they walked to a small ice cream shop. Austin bought two waffle ice cream cones — cookies and cream for him, butter pecan for Monica.

They continued their stroll along the lake-front to Buckingham Fountain.

Licking her cone, Monica turned to him. "You're checking me out again?"

"No, I'm not," Austin lied. "There was . . . this dog over there and . . . it was looking at me . . . so . . ."

"You didn't want to be rude, so you looked back at the dog, gave it a little eye contact. Is that right?"

"Yeah." Austin smiled. "That's right."

"You're cute."

"Is that why you walked back into my office, after you had left?"

"I don't know what you're talking about." Monica grinned.

"Yeah, you do. You left, and you came back in, and that's when I asked for your number."

"Well, before I left, I don't know, I had gotten the feeling that you wanted to ask but you didn't. Something told me you might have been in there kicking yourself, so I wanted to give you one last shot at it."

"That was generous of you."

"I have my moments."

Austin reached over and took Monica's hand.

Immediately Monica stopped walking, looked down at their clasped hands, and said, "Uh . . . do we really need to take it there?"

"What?"

"The hand holding. Really?"

"Monica," Austin said, letting go of her hand and stepping in front of her, "we've already had sex."

"Sex is just physical, holding hands involves emotions. I thought we were clear on this, Austin."

"Yeah, we were," Austin said, feeling as though he had just been scolded. "We are."

"But it doesn't mean I like you any less," Monica said, taking Austin's face in her palms. "I still think you're cute. Does that work?"

"Sure," Austin said. Then under his breath, he added, "But I don't know for how long."

62

After Jahlil's last class, he walked down the hall, then halted, shocked to see his father waiting at his locker. "What . . . what are you doing here?"

"Grab what you need. You coming with me," he said.

Moments later, Jahlil sat in the passenger seat of his father's van. "Where we going?"

"To the DCFS," Caleb said, steering the van, his eyes on the road.

"Why you taking me there?"

"There's someone there I want you to meet."

"I ain't meeting nobody," Jahlil said, reaching for the handle of his door. "Let me out."

Caleb brought the van to a screeching halt along the curb. He turned to Jahlil. "Tell me what's going on. Who beat you up, and who did you say was dead?"

This was his father's attempt to get close

to him, be the buddy he had never been to Jahlil. It was too late for all that. "Ain't nothing going on, and ain't nobody dead, okay?" Jahlil said, turning and facing his window.

Caleb stared at him a moment longer, then threw the van back in gear and pulled off. "Fine, if that's the way you want it."

When they arrived at the DCFS building, Caleb introduced Jahlil to Lewis Waters.

Lewis stuck his hand out to shake. Jahlil rolled his eyes, till he felt his father's hand heavy on his shoulder, squeezing him till it came close to hurting. Jahlil shook the man's hand.

"Good to meet you, Jahlil," Lewis said. "If you'd excuse me, I'm gonna talk to your father a sec and then we'll be ready to go."

Jahlil didn't answer, just watched as Lewis and his father walked to the other side of the lobby.

Jahlil wandered a few steps toward a reception window and looked in through the teller glass. He saw desks and papers and envelopes. He knew this place, the Department of Children and Family Services building was where families with all sorts of problems came to hash out their business. This would be where, if Jahlil was a deadbeat like his father, Shaun would come to file for child support. But he wasn't no deadbeat. He thought about what Bug said, about his ultimately getting locked up or ending up dead if he kept on robbing. Jahlil saw an image of Shaun holding their blanketed newborn, stepping up to this very window, asking for assistance, because Jahlil had gotten shot like Toomey.

He would never let that happen.

"Ready?"

Jahlil turned to see Lewis standing behind him.

"Where we going?"

"We just hanging out."

Jahlil looked past Lewis to his father, who stood ten feet behind them.

"Go with Mr. Waters," Caleb said. "You'll have fun."

Walking out to the parking lot, Jahlil did not feel unsafe with this man. He trusted his father enough not to allow some dude that was dangerous to take him. He just thought the guy was kinda goofy with his back-to-school outfit, khaki pants and oxford shirt. But Jahlil's opinion changed when Lewis clicked the alarm on the big, black Cadillac Escalade. The alarm chirped twice and the parking lights blinked.

"Get in," Lewis said.

"That's you?"

"Why? You like the ride?"

"It's a'ight," Jahlil said, swinging the door open and jumping in.

They drove twenty minutes, listening to Lil Wayne, and Jahlil thought this Lewis guy couldn't be all that bad.

Lewis parked the SUV outside some South Side project buildings.

"Why we stopping here?" Jahlil said, looking out the window. It was a spot not too far from his building, but the area was much worse.

"C'mon, get out," Lewis said, climbing out of the Escalade.

Jahlil jumped out, walked around, and joined Lewis on the sidewalk.

"See that building right there?"

The buildings before him were all boarded up. The street curbs were lined with trash, and what grass had once grown was all brown and dead. There weren't many people on the street — an unshaven man wearing a soiled white T-shirt shuffled by, and two kids riding bikes too small for them played a short distance away. Jahlil had driven by here before, and he knew it was the hood. "Yeah. I see it."

"That's where I used to live."

"You used to live in the projects?" Jahlil

said, surprised, given the Cadillac and the church clothes.

"Yup." Lewis stared sadly at the building, lost in his thoughts. "Seems like another whole life ago."

Lewis bought Jahlil a cheeseburger, fries, and a large pop, and bought himself a gyro and fries. They sat in the small fast-food joint off Thirty-Fifth and Indiana, not far from the projects they had just visited.

While they ate, Lewis filled Jahlil in on his life story — how his father had abandoned him when he was young, how he hadn't finished high school, and how he had been to jail a few times for stealing. "The last time was just stupid. But I had to do it for my little girl."

"You got a kid?"

"Yeah. Her name is Layla," Lewis said proudly, digging into his wallet and pulling out a snapshot of her and sliding it across the table.

"She's a little cutie," Jahlil said, handing it back. For a brief second, he had the urge to tell Lewis that he was expecting a child, but he didn't even know this man, so he stopped himself.

"How is it?" Jahlil asked. "You know, having a kid."

"Best thing ever happened to me. It makes a man out of you, lets you know what's important. It makes you wanna do the best you can do. It's one of the reasons I ain't got no problem walking around in these clothes every day — why I'm almost proud."

"I feel you," Jahlil said, sincerely, thinking that this man's life hadn't been much different from his own.

Back in the Cadillac, Lewis stuck the key in the ignition. "So, we've been where I wanted to go. I got an hour till I have to be back home. Anywhere you wanna go?"

"What you mean?"

"I mean, you got a chauffeur-driven Cadillac you sitting in, and the driver's saying he'll take you anywhere in the city you wanna go — for free. You don't want to take him up on that?"

Half an hour later, Jahlil and Lewis sat on a park bench across from the apartment complex Jahlil had hoped to live in. The sky was darkening outside, but there was no threat, no cars racing by, no music blasting, no gunshots, no police sirens. In the distance, only a lawnmower could be heard, and the faint sound of children playing.

Jahlil sat peacefully.

"Why did we come here?" Lewis asked.

" 'Cause it's the opposite of how I grew up, and it's where I wanna live one day."

63

Lewis sat parked in his SUV two doors down from Freddy's old girlfriend's father's house.

After Lewis dropped off Jahlil, he'd thought of going home, but Freddy was still on his mind. Going to see Kia, thinking that Freddy might have contacted her, was a long shot, considering Kia had broken up with Freddy and, worse, aborted their child. That had devastated Freddy and was probably the last straw that sent him off to try to kill Nate Kenny. But still Lewis knocked on the door of the mini-mansion, only to be told by Kia's father that she wouldn't be home until later this evening, after her classes.

Lewis thanked her father but decided to wait for her in his SUV.

After an hour, Lewis spotted Kia's BMW pulling into the driveway of her house.

He stepped out of the Escalade and

started down the block. Lewis and Kia had never been great friends. He hadn't liked the way Freddy had dumped Joni for Kia, and that always came across whenever Lewis spoke to her — he always thought she could sense his dislike — but he would try to hide his opinion of her today.

Lewis continued toward the passenger side of her car, when he saw her climbing out of the coupe. She hadn't seen him. She walked away from the car, toward the walkway of the house. When Lewis caught a full body glimpse of Kia, he froze in his tracks, gasping loudly, unable to believe what he saw.

Kia must've heard him. She turned, then immediately moved her huge purse in front of her stomach, in a failed attempt to hide her round, growing belly. Lewis wasn't an obstetrician, but he knew what a six-to-seven-month-pregnant woman looked like.

"What are you doing here?" Kia said, shocked.

"You ain't . . . you ain't get rid of it?" Lewis said, marching quickly toward Kia. He stopped in front of her, staring down at her belly, still unable to believe what he was seeing.

"What are you doing here?" Kia said, her arm guarding her belly.

"Freddy told Monica he's going to get the people who got him locked up."

"I don't blame him. That man, Nate Kenny," Kia said, hate on her face, "something needs to happen to him."

"It ain't just him Freddy says he's gonna get. It's me."

"You?"

"He say any of this to you?"

"Me? He hasn't tried to talk to me. He hates me."

"I wonder why that is," Lewis said, staring down at Freddy's baby. "That is his, right? You never aborted it."

"I tried. But I couldn't."

"But you told him you did," Lewis said. "You fucking lied to him and told him you did. You ever think that was what drove him over the edge, had him acting all crazy, landing him in the fucking asylum?"

"Don't put that on me. He started that nonsense way before I told him that. What you think had me wanting the abortion?"

"Tell yourself whatever you need to to be right with Freddy sitting in some cell, making threats about going to get people. Lucky he can't back up none of that shit he's talking," Lewis said, anger on his face. He turned away from Kia, started walking.

"Lewis," Kia called.

Lewis stopped, looked back.

"Don't be so sure he can't back it up."

"What?" Lewis said, taking a couple of steps back to Kia, a scowl on his face. "What did you say?"

"Crazy or not, Freddy doesn't say stuff he don't mean. If it's just to get under your skin, or he really means to come after you, Freddy don't say stuff just to say it."

"So what are you saying?" Lewis said, and for the first time, he gave those threats serious concern.

"Maybe you need to talk to him and find out exactly what he's talking about."

64

"Okay, that's them," Blue said, from behind the wheel of his Buick Regal. He wore a black leather jacket, dark sunglasses, and a red bandanna tied around his neck, hanging under his chin.

"Where?" Caleb said, sitting up to get a look out the windshield. His sunglasses lay on the dashboard, and he too wore a bandanna.

"The black Monte Carlo pulling to the curb. Those two guys gonna go in, then one is gonna come back out." Blue waited till both men exited the car, then pointed to the taller, blond man. "He's the lookout. The other one stays inside and trades the money for the drugs. When that's done, he comes out too, they get back in the car, and go. I mean, that ain't gonna happen tonight, 'cause we gonna jack they ass." Blue smiled. "But that's normally how it goes every two weeks."

"How many people inside?" Caleb asked, no longer feeling certain this was something he wanted to do.

"Two guys, three tops. They never gonna know what hit 'em." Blue reached into the glove box, pulled out a gun, and handed it to Caleb. "Here."

"What? I don't want that," Caleb said, moving away from it.

"When the buyers go in, we roll up on opposite sides of that door. When the first one comes out, you put the gun on him, I go in and steal they shit," Blue said. "You gotta have the gun. Now take it."

Caleb didn't reach for the weapon.

"Take the fucking gun, Caleb!"

Caleb stared down at it but still did not move.

"What you gonna do? We don't go now, you don't get your money, and you deal with Kwan tomorrow. It's your call." Blue pressed. "They about to go in the building. Make up your mind."

Caleb prayed that everything would be fine and took the gun from Blue. "Soon as they go in, you take the right side of the building, I'll take the left."

Blue pulled his bandanna over his mouth and nose and snatched his two guns from the waist of his jeans. Caleb pulled up his scarf, slid the dark shades on, and tried to calm himself as best he could.

"Okay," Blue said. "They inside. Now!"

Blue and Caleb opened their car doors and ran, heads lowered, hunched over, to the building. From behind the corner, Blue stuck his head out and whispered loudly, "As soon as dude comes out, you roll up on him, and I'm going in."

Caleb felt dizzy with anxiety. His hand was trembling around the gun, and he wished he could just shut his eyes and disappear, but he heard the door opening, saw the first man step out.

His back was to Caleb, so Caleb darted out from around the corner as quickly and quietly as he could. Before the man could turn, the barrel of Caleb's gun was pressed to the back of his skull.

"Don't move. I don't wanna have to kill you," Caleb said, his voice less than convincing. The man slowly raised his hands over his head. Caleb reached around, patted his torso for a weapon, and grabbed the gun from the holster he wore under his left arm.

Blue appeared from around the other corner and ran to the door. Caleb saw Blue's eyes smiling, as he gave him a thumbs-up, before Blue pulled the door open and disappeared inside. Caleb could hear Blue's muffled voice as he yelled, "A'ight, bitches. This is a stickup! Hand over the shit!"

An hour later, Blue and Caleb had taken the drugs and the money to Blue's contact and had been paid what they were owed.

"Easiest four grand you ever made, huh?" Blue said.

Caleb didn't respond. He was still too wound up from what had just happened. "It wasn't easy."

"But it worked. Now you got the money to give Kwan and still got a thousand to blow. Kinda like the old days, right?"

"Those days I never want to go back to, Blue."

"So you sayin', if dude wanna use you for another job, you don't want no part of it?"

"Yeah. That's what I'm saying," Caleb said.

65

Marcus brought his Honda Accord to a stop across the street and a number of car lengths behind his wife's car. They were parked across the street from a fine Italian restaurant.

"She's just going to dinner," Austin said, still not knowing why he had foolishly agreed to accompany his brother on his insane chase. "I'm sure she's just meeting girlfriends."

"Dressed like that?" Marcus said, jealously gripping the steering wheel with both fists.

Austin had to admit, Reecie was dressed provocatively. She wore sexy high heels and a tight-fitting dress that hung just above her knees and exposed too much cleavage. "Girls like to look nice. What do they say, 'Women don't dress for men but for each other.' "

"Whoever said that was a liar," Marcus said, shifting the car into park. "Well?"

"Well, what?" Austin asked.

"Well, I'm gonna wait here while you go in there and find out whether I'm right or not."

"What? Why me? This is your crazy —"

"You know I can't go. If she sees me, she'll know I followed her. That'll screw up any chance I have of her letting me come back home."

Austin looked out his window at the restaurant.

"You have to go," Marcus said. "It's no big deal. She's probably in there with her girlfriends just like you said, and if she spots you, just say you were meeting somebody for a drink."

Austin pulled on the car door handle and set a foot on the pavement. "And when I confirm she's not in there with some man, you have to promise never to ask me to do something this foolish again."

"Promise. Now could you go?"

Austin walked across the street and into the restaurant. It was fairly dark and cozy inside. He had never heard of this place, but he grabbed one of their matchbooks on the way to the bar, thinking he would have to take Monica here one night.

The hostess smiled at Austin from behind

a podium and asked if he wanted a table for one.

"No." He smiled back. "I'm . . . uh . . . meeting a party," he said, looking into the dining room.

When Austin entered the small bar area, he saw three single men sitting on bar stools, and two couples, but no Reecie. He looked over his shoulder, wondering if there was more to the restaurant, when his cell started to vibrate in his pocket. He pulled it out. It was a text from Marcus. *See her yet?*

No, Austin texted back. He told himself he would take a look in the dining room, then leave, letting his brother deal with this insanity on his own, but first he needed to use the men's room.

Austin walked down the corridor, pushed his way through the door marked MEN. Inside he did his business, washed and dried his hands, then stepped out into the dimly lit hallway to notice a woman walking ahead of him with a nice shape. For only a split second, Austin admired the curves of her hips and the way she walked, until he realized he was staring at Reecie.

He suppressed the urge to call to her, tell her about his mistake, so they could have a laugh; he let Reecie continue until she turned the corner.

She turned toward the bar. Austin followed cautiously, stopping at the doorway.

He saw one of the single men at the bar, a decent-looking guy, chubby, a little shorter than Marcus, stand, take Reecie's hand, kiss her on the cheek, and help her back onto her bar stool before sitting himself. Austin quickly stepped back around the corner and pressed himself against the wall, hating the position he was now in.

Outside, he climbed in the car without looking at Marcus.

"Well?" Marcus said, anxious.

"Well, what?" Austin stalled.

"Was she in there or not!"

"Of course she was in there. We saw her go in. It's not like she just disappeared."

"Dammit! Was she in there with a man?"

Austin slid down in his seat some, wanting to lie, wishing he could. But he dropped his head, and softly said, "Marcus, don't do anything you're going to regret."

"She's the one who's going to regret this," Marcus said angrily, grabbing hold of the door and flinging it open.

66

The next morning, Austin stood in his office, staring at Reecie. She stood before him, her eyes downcast, dark half circles hung under them. Austin assumed she hadn't slept much. She was deserving of a far worse punishment than lack of sleep.

"Just give me one reason why I shouldn't fire your ass this very minute," Austin said.

"Because my marriage to Marcus has nothing to do with this job."

"It has everything to do with this job," Austin corrected. "If you weren't working here, I would've never introduced you to Marcus. If you weren't working here, I would've never known you, thought you were good enough for him. Obviously, I was wrong."

"I'm sorry you were there to see that, but Austin, this is between Marcus and me, and you know it."

"He's my brother. You think I'm going to

stand by and let you do this to him? How serious are things between you and that clown from last night?"

"Like I said, that's between my husband and me."

Austin spun angrily away from her, trying to suppress the urge to tell her exactly how he felt. Turning back, he said, "The only reason I don't get rid of you is then both of you would be out of work, and I won't have my niece suffering for your stupidity."

"I was wrong," Reecie said. "I'll fix things."

Austin stepped over to his desk. He picked up a couple of envelopes, glanced at them, then tossed them down. "If you don't, I will."

67

Toomey's services were held in a small South Side funeral home. Only a handful of people showed. Toomey's mother was there, his sister, and his aunt. There were four or five students as well — classmates of Toomey's that Jahlil didn't know. And in the back of the room, there were two old men leaning on canes. Jahlil didn't know who they were either.

Bug sat in one of the folding chairs next to Jahlil. Neither of them wore dress clothes because they didn't have them. They sat there in their jeans and long-sleeved shirts, the collars buttoned at the top. He felt that their clothes might have been disrespecting their friend, but the important thing, Jahlil figured, was that they showed.

The funeral director spoke, then Toomey's mother. She cried at the podium, constantly looking down into the casket at her dead son. Afterward, she had to be helped back to her chair. More family spoke, and there was a lot more crying. Even Bug shed some tears. The whole event was just too much for Jahlil. He still couldn't believe his best friend was gone, and he couldn't believe that it was his fault that he was.

After the funeral director said final words, he asked if anyone wanted to view the body before the casket was closed.

Jahlil turned to Bug.

"I ain't goin', man," Bug said, still smearing tears from his chubby cheeks. "I just can't. You?"

Jahlil looked up at the short line of loved ones, viewing Toomey's body for the last time. "I have to."

"I'll wait for you outside," Bug said.

Jahlil joined the end of the line, taking slow steps toward his slain best friend. When he made it to the casket, Jahlil did not look at his friend at first but inhaled deeply, tried to ready himself for what he might see, then finally turned to gaze into the casket.

Toomey was dressed in a dark blue suit, his hands stacked on his chest. His face was waxen, covered with makeup. He looked good but fake, like a mannequin.

Jahlil wanted to reach into that casket, shake Toomey by the lapels, tell him to stop playin', but this was no joke. Toomey was dead. Jahlil wiped at the tear that rushed down his face and was about to tell his friend how sorry he was, when he was interrupted by a tug at the elbow of his shirt. He turned to see Toomey's mother. She was a heavy woman, wearing a black dress, gloves, and a large hat. She pressed a hand onto the little girl next to her, Toomey's little sister, as though she needed the child to keep her upright.

"It was you," Toomey's mother said. "Always in trouble, always dragging my son in it with you."

"I'm sorry, Mrs. —" Jahlil tried apologizing.

"If it wasn't for you, my child would not be lying dead in this coffin," Toomey's mother said, raising her voice, drawing the attention of everyone in the funeral home. The little girl looked away, embarrassed. "You . . . you should be the one lying in that coffin. You should be the one that's dead."

"I'm sorry," Jahlil said again. "I don't want Toomey to be dead."

"Don't matter what you want. My son is gone," Toomey's mother sobbed. "And I hope and pray, hope and pray, you gonna be next."

68

After the funeral, Lewis had shown up at the apartment just as he had told Jahlil he would when he dropped him off after their last visit. Jahlil answered the door, saw that it was Lewis. Ashamed of his home, Jahlil tried to hurry out before letting Lewis see the place.

"Hold it, is that the man your father told me about?" Jahlil's mother said. "Invite him in. I want to meet him."

Reluctantly, Jahlil did as he was told.

Lewis walked into the ragged apartment but didn't seem like he thought he was above the place. He smiled at Jahlil's mother, shook her hand, and introduced himself.

"So you work over there with Jahlil's father?" Sonya said.

"Yeah, we only met a little while ago, but he's a nice guy. I like him. Turns out we lived around the same neighborhood."

"Oh, okay," Sonya said, not seeming impressed with the bit of information Lewis offered. "You're gonna take good care of my boy, right?"

"Yes, ma'am," Lewis said. "Just taking him to my place to have dinner with my family and bringing him right back."

Once there, Jahlil met Lewis's daughter Layla, his girlfriend Eva, and her daughter Tammi. They sat down in the living room of Lewis's four-bedroom, three-bathroom home. The space was as big, it seemed, as Jahlil's apartment and filled with stylish furniture that looked as though it had just come from a furniture store. The house was in a quiet neighborhood, with cut grass and no graffiti on the sides of buildings, and the family had dinner just like people did on TV. Until that moment, Jahlil didn't really believe there were black folks who actually lived that way.

Afterward, Lewis and Jahlil went downstairs to watch a little TV on the big flatscreen, before Lewis took Jahlil home. They talked about Jahlil's grades for a while, then the conversation landed on Jahlil's girlfriend.

"My father never married my mother. I think that's wrong," Jahlil said. "I don't wanna do that to Shaun."

"You must really love her," Lewis said.

"I do. But it costs money to be married, to live in a house like this, and I ain't got it."

Lewis chuckled. "You're only sixteen. You don't need much money."

"I do."

"Why?"

Jahlil stood. "I think it's probably time for you to take me home."

Lewis grabbed Jahlil's arm. "Hold it. Is everything okay?"

Jahlil looked Lewis in the eyes. He knew he shouldn't tell him, but the man seemed to know what Jahlil was going through, seemed as though he had gone through the same things when he was Jahlil's age. Now he had everything that Jahlil wanted. Maybe by hearing his story, Lewis could help him find a way to get those things too.

"Shaun's gonna have our baby."

Lewis didn't say a word, didn't look like he was disappointed in Jahlil. "When?"

"Two weeks, something like that."

"Your father told me about you getting beat up at school. Did it have anything to do with Shaun and your baby?"

"Trying to make money," Jahlil said, not looking at Lewis but staring off into the distance. "Sold a little weed on the wrong corner. Thought I could get away with it but didn't."

"That's not the right way to make money, Jahlil. I think you know that."

"Tell me another way. Tell me how I can take care of my girl and my baby, move us away from my mom's crappy-ass apartment, and live a halfway decent life. Tell me!" Jahlil said. " 'Cause if you can't, I'm gonna have to go out there and do it again."

"Okay," Lewis said, trying to calm Jahlil down. "You know where I work. I see and hear about all sorts of programs that pay to help folks who want to get married and get places so they can raise their kids the right way. There's all sorts of assistance, so you won't have to go back out there."

"I don't know about any assistance."

"I do. Tell you what. Me and Eva, we're gonna look into it for you, okay? We're going to find a program that's going to take care of you, your girl, and your baby. We're gonna work this out."

"You serious?" Jahlil said, wanting to feel hope but feeling more skepticism than anything else.

"I promise."

"You won't be mad if I don't believe you till it happens," Jahlil said. "It's just . . . I can't be looking forward to stuff like that, and it not happen."

Lewis smiled. "Trust me. I understand. But we gonna make this happen."

"If you say so. And don't tell my father about this. Since he don't care about his own kid, I don't want him knowing about mine."

69

At the end of the day, all the customers were gone, and Monica had let Roland and Tabatha leave early. She was in her office, shutting down her computer, preparing to close a little early and get out of there herself.

An hour ago, she had gotten a call from Austin. "Can I see you tonight?" he'd said.

"Two days in a row?" Monica had joked. "You really are a go-getter, aren't you?"

"Yeah . . . there's something I want to talk to you about. I'll come by you. Around ten. I have your address."

Now as Monica grabbed the store's mail from her desk, she heard someone outside her office, in the store, saying, "Hello. Anyone here?"

"Oh great," Monica said, shouldering her purse, clicking off the office light, and closing and locking the door, wishing Roland had locked the front door when he stepped out. As she walked down the hallway that led to the store, again she heard, "Hello?"

"Sorry, we're closed," Monica said, not yet emerging from the corridor. "You'll have to come back tomorrow."

"And what if I don't want to come back tomorrow?" her ex-husband, Nate, said, standing in the center of the store, his hand in his pocket.

"What are you doing here? We said all we needed to say the other day," Monica said, surprised to see Nate, of all people, in her store.

"I need to say more."

"Fine, say it, then get out of my store," Monica said.

"I was wrong to do to you what I did. To leave you for Daphanie just because I thought she was having my child."

"Uh-uh, Nate," Monica said, waving a hand in front of him. "Don't think you can come over here, admit how foolish you were, and then expect me to take you back, just because I didn't go for your little deal."

"I'm not thinking that."

"Really?"

"I just came to apologize for how thoughtless, selfish, and foolish I was. I saw how you responded to me and to what I asked you, so I'm rescinding that offer," Nate said,

307

pulling his hand out of his pocket and holding his fist out to her.

"What?" Monica said, staring down at his hand.

"Take it."

Monica held out her hand, allowed Nate to drop what he was holding in her palm.

"What's this?" Monica asked.

"The wedding band you bought me when we were first married."

Monica looked at it closer, surprise on her face. She remembered the day that seemed like a lifetime ago, when they'd stood over the jewelry counter, smiling, and chosen that ring together. She could not help but feel the slightest bit of sadness. "Why are you giving this to me?"

"After the other day, the hateful way you looked at me, I knew we were done, finally, and we'll never get back together again. I'm correct about that, right?"

"That's right," Monica said without hesitation.

"That's what I thought," Nate said, appearing genuinely disappointed. "Then I guess I'll be leaving."

"Wait," Monica said.

Nate turned back.

"Did you leave me only because you thought the baby was yours, or did you stop loving me? It doesn't matter either way, but . . ."

Nate paused before answering. "Like you said, it doesn't matter either way, because we're done for good this time."

"Yes, you're right, Nate. We are done for good."

70

Caleb hoisted three plastic garbage bags off the ground and tossed them in the Dumpster outside the building that housed his brother's law office. He took off his work gloves, stood, and stared at the stars for a moment. It was a beautiful evening, and Caleb was appreciative. Earlier today, he had taken the cash back to Kwan and paid him off without having to beg Austin again for money. He vowed never to borrow another penny from that man.

Caleb started back to the office, when his cell phone rang. It was Blue. "Workin'?"

"Yeah."

"Beers when you get off?"

"Naw, kinda tired," Caleb said. "Think I'm just gonna go home and crash."

"You handled yourself the other night. Thought you woulda lost a step, but after all those years, you was still on."

Caleb smiled, even though he knew that

maintaining his robbery skills was nothing to be proud of. "Thanks."

"The big dude liked it too. He wants to know if you wanna join in on that building I was checking out the other day."

"I'm good. Told you, this was a onetime thing."

Blue was silent. "How much of that money you got left?"

"A grand, after paying off Kwan."

"How long it gonna last?"

Not long, Caleb knew. "Blue, what aren't you getting? I ain't going back to making a living robbing folks, wondering how long it's gonna be before I go back to prison. I got a family, responsibilities."

"That's why you need to be —"

"Blue!"

"Okay, okay. Just trying to help a brotha out," Blue said, backing off. "This is what I'm gonna do. Take a few hours, think about it. But you gotta let me know, like now, 'cause this is going down tomorrow night."

"I told you, Blue, I don't —"

"Call me back if you down." Blue hung up.

Caleb shook his head, knowing Blue thought he was doing him a favor, but Caleb knew there was nothing further from the truth.

His phone rang again. Looking at the screen, Caleb didn't recognize the number. "Hello."

"Hello, this is Lewis Waters. I hope I'm not calling too late."

"Naw, it's cool. I'm just taking a break from work. Did everything go okay today with my son?"

"Yeah, everything went fine. You have a good kid there," Lewis said. "But I think there's a few things going on with Jahlil that I need to talk to you about."

71

Austin and Monica lay in bed together after making love. They lay on their backs, her head resting on his chest. They stared, satisfied, up at the ceiling.

"Have you spoken to Ms. Coleman again? Did she go back?" Austin said, making small talk.

"She said she was going to, but I haven't spoken to her since then."

"I'm sorry how that all turned out. You sounded pretty upset."

"Yeah, but I know it wasn't your fault. You did all you could," Monica said, kissing Austin's forearm.

"It was just about the most unusual thing I've ever seen," Austin said. "I mean, why would that guy — what was his name? Nate Kenny — why would he do that to her?" Austin said, shifting a little in bed. "The attitude that guy had, the arrogance. How could someone —"

"He's a worthless, evil son of a bitch," Monica blurted.

Austin looked at her oddly. "Sounds like you know him."

Monica hesitated. She rolled over onto Austin's chest and looked him in the face. "I . . . I . . . was married to him."

Austin said nothing at first. He looked at Monica strangely, smiled, then said, "Why didn't you tell me? Are you divorced?"

"We are, and I didn't tell you because it had nothing to do with the case. But I'm telling you now. Is that okay?"

"Yeah . . . well, I guess," Austin said. "Sure."

"Can I tell you something else?"

"There's more?" Austin said, not sure he wanted to know.

Monica parted the curls on the side of her head. She grabbed Austin's hand, pressed his fingers to the parted area of her scalp. "Feel that?"

Austin felt a line of slightly raised scar tissue. "What is it?"

"The healed surgical incision from when I was shot. It was my ex-husband's fault."

"He shot you?" Austin said, shocked, as he slowly pulled his hand away.

"No. But he was responsible," Monica

said. "The things I allowed that man to do to me."

Austin sighed, shook his head.

"What?"

"You sure there's nothing going on between you two? Sounds like there might still be some feelings."

"The only feelings I have for him are vengeance and hatred," Monica said, staring coldly into Austin's eyes. "He popped up at my store this evening."

"For . . . ?"

Monica took a moment to answer. "He gave me his wedding band back."

"You seem a little shook by that."

"I'm not," Monica said, looking not at Austin but into the space in front of her, deep in thought. "But I'm sure those were his intentions. All part of his plan."

"What plan?"

Monica didn't answer.

Austin laid a hand on Monica's wrist. "I said, what plan?"

Monica turned to Austin, smiling a little. "Nothing. It's nothing."

"You sure?"

"Yeah," Monica said, smiling wider. "Of course. Now enough about me and my crazy past. You said there was something you needed to talk to me about."

"I don't know. Maybe what I had to say should wait."

"No. It sounded important. I want to hear it," Monica said.

"Okay, well . . . I want to know if you're seeing anyone else."

Monica chuckled. "Uh, no."

"You dating? Going out or anything?"

"Not really," Monica said, eyeing Austin suspiciously. "No. Why?"

"I know it's only been a short time we've been seeing each other, but I'm kind of feeling you."

"Well, I'm kind of feeling you too," Monica said, leaning over and pecking Austin on the lips. "So that's why you're asking these questions."

"Just trying to find out if I have any competition."

"Competition? This is not a race. There's no finish line. We're just kicking it."

"You know, I'm looking for more than just to kick it."

"Austin, didn't we go over this already?" Monica said, flopping back onto her pillow with a heavy sigh. "Things were going so well."

She crossed her arms over her face, sighing more heavily.

Austin wasn't a fool. Monica's body

language was undeniable. She answered his question by not answering. Austin climbed out of bed, walked over to the chair in the corner of Monica's bedroom, and grabbed his slacks.

"Wait," Monica said.

His back to her, Austin halted.

"Do you know how many good guys there are out there?" Monica said.

"A lot."

"No. A couple, and one of them is standing in my room, trying to put his pants on and walk out of here."

Austin turned. "You trying to say something?"

"I'll remain open-minded to the possibility that if things go absolutely perfect between us, then maybe a relationship with you wouldn't be the worst thing in the world." She smiled.

Austin set his pants back down on the chair, climbed back into bed, wrapped his arms around Monica, and gave her a kiss. "That's all I'm asking."

72

Caleb parked the van along the curb in front of the building where he used to live with Sonya and Jahlil.

It couldn't be true, he told himself as he stormed up the filthy, graffiti-riddled stairwell and headed down the darkened, trash-lined hallway, toward the apartment he had been thrown out of a year ago. He heard TVs playing loudly behind some doors, and yelling behind others. This was constant every night.

As Caleb approached his old apartment, he realized there was yelling coming from the other side of his door.

Quickly, Caleb fumbled with his keys, trying to stick the correct one in the lock. They fell to the floor. "Hey! What's going on in there?" he yelled, snatching up the keys, not sure who the yelling voice belonged to, but he thought it sounded like his son. Hurrying, Caleb pushed the right key inside the lock, turned it, and threw open the door, hearing a loud thud as he did. Caleb's eyes landed on Jahlil standing angrily over his mother. Sonya was on the floor, her arm raised over her face, as if afraid she would be struck.

Blind with rage, Caleb rushed across the living room, snatched his son by his shirt, reared back, and punched him across the face. The boy crashed into a bookcase. Caleb heard Sonya screaming as Caleb stormed toward the boy and pulled a fist back to punch him again.

Suddenly, Sonya was behind Caleb, clawing at his arm, screaming, crying, "Don't! Don't hurt my baby!"

"He put his hands on you!" Caleb yelled, staring angrily at his son. Jahlil was bleeding from his mouth. His lids were low, but Caleb could see the hatred with which his son glared at him. "All that I did for you!" Caleb said. Then he yelled to Sonya, as she continued to yank on him, begging, "Do you know what he's been doing? Do you?"

"Please!" Sonya cried. "Just let him go."

Caleb released his son, and the boy stepped around Caleb and his mother and ran out the door.

Furious, Caleb started after him but was grabbed by Sonya.

"Just let him go. Just let him, Caleb," Sonya cried.

His chest heaving, Caleb forced himself to calm down. He turned Sonya by her shoulders. "How long?"

"What are you talking about?"

"How long has he been like this!"

Her eyes bloodshot red, her body feeling almost lifeless in Caleb's hands, she said, "I don't know what you're talking about."

Caleb forcefully let Sonya go, almost pushing her backward, hating her that second, hating himself, hating this life. He grabbed the closest thing within reach, a candle, and flung it across the room, shattering the glass jar it was encased in.

"He's selling drugs!" Caleb yelled, turning to Sonya. "That's why he got the shit kicked out of him. He's robbing people and selling drugs."

"No. Please don't say that," Sonya sobbed.

"You know why? Because he and some girl are having a baby in two weeks."

"No. You're lying!" Sonya said, crying harder, turning her back on Caleb. He rushed over and spun her around.

"No! You can't fucking hide from this. You put me out so I can't keep an eye on my son, this happens, and you try to tell yourself it's not true? It is true. It's true!" Caleb said.

"He's doing everything I didn't want him to do, everything I did when I was his age. But that has to stop, and it has to stop now."

73

Nine a.m. the next morning, Bug sat parked outside the apartment complex Jahlil was trying to move into. "I'm telling you, don't you think you ought to at least call your old man?" Bug said.

Jahlil had crashed on the futon in Bug's bedroom last night.

"I ain't thinking about him or my moms. What I need to do is move up out of there."

"What the people say? They gonna let you get the place?"

After what happened last night, Jahlil told himself he needed to move now. He figured that his father wouldn't sign for him to get the place, so he thought about Lewis. The guy seemed pretty cool. Maybe he would understand. Lewis could say that he was Jahlil's uncle. Jahlil would tell Lewis he didn't need his credit, just sign, because Jahlil wasn't old enough. All Jahlil needed was the apartment people to agree to let him have the place even though he was $3,500 short on the year's rent.

Jahlil sat slump-shouldered in the passenger seat of the car, looking sadly at Bug. "They said I needed the entire year's rent, if they were even gonna consider letting me in."

"You ask them about doing a six-month lease?"

"They weren't hearing it."

"Just wait then, or move somewhere else."

"I can't wait, and I don't wanna move nowhere else," Jahlil said, sitting up, angry. "I gotta go now, and this is where I want me and my family to live. I gotta make it happen."

"How you gonna do that?"

Jahlil's cell phone rang before he had a chance to answer Bug. He picked up. Shaun was on the other end.

"You gotta come and get me. I gotta go to the hospital." There was panic in her voice. In the background, Jahlil could hear loud cursing.

"What's wrong! Is the baby okay?" Jahlil said, motioning for Bug to start the car.

"Just come and get me!" Shaun said.

When Jahlil walked into Shaun's apartment, he saw her leaning against a table as though she thought she would fall. Sweat covered her brow. She looked nauseated, as though she would drop to her knees and vomit any moment. A small weekend bag sat at her feet. She wore a jacket she was unable to close because of the size of her belly.

Her mother stood in the dining room yelling. When the older woman caught sight of Jahlil, she focused her anger on him.

"You! You the little motherfucker that got my daughter pregnant?" She was a bony, miserable-looking woman, with thinning black hair brushed back and held together with a rubber band. "She's seventeen. She ain't raising no baby in this house like she grown."

"Come on, Jahlil," Shaun said, grabbing him by the hand.

"Do you hear me? Don't be bringing that bastard child back in here, 'cause I ain't letting either of you in," Shaun's mother screamed.

Jahlil halted and turned menacing eyes toward the older woman.

"We better go," Bug said, pulling Jahlil toward the open apartment door.

"You right," Jahlil said, taking Shaun's arm, turning her, and heading out.

"Did you hear me?" the mother said, shuffling closer in her slippers, now waving a spatula in her right hand. "The locks gonna be changed, so don't come back here with that baby. Throw it in a Dumpster where it belong, but don't bring that bastard back here."

Shaun and Bug were already in the hallway, but after hearing what was said, Jahlil stepped back inside the apartment and slammed the door behind him. He locked the door and angrily hurried toward Shaun's mother.

Jahlil heard Bug outside trying to get in, his muffled voice begging, "Jahlil, let's just go, man!"

He ignored Bug's pleas and raced toward the woman, stopped just in front of her, snatched her by the front of her robe, jerked her toward him, and reared back his fist.

The woman cowered, raised both her arms, shut her eyes, and cried, "Don't hurt me!"

Jahlil wanted to strike her, wanted to beat her, he was so angry. Not just at her, but at himself, at his life, at the loss of his friend Toomey and everything he had done to land him in the awful place he was in. Jahlil saw himself throwing Shaun's mother to the ground, straddling her, pummeling her with his fists, taking all his hate and frustration out on her. But what good would that do him? Jahlil thought, his shaking hand still raised over his head. It would only make things worse, if that were even possible. Jahlil slowly lowered his arm and fought back the curse words he wanted to say to the woman. He spat at her feet, then walked out of the apartment.

74

Lewis stood in the large room with the old vinyl floor tiles, the chairs, and the four sofas. He had been taken to this visitation room in the psychiatric facility by a nice red-haired woman. She told him Freddy would be brought in momentarily.

Lewis paced the room, regretting his decision to come. But regardless of how often he tried to focus on other things and to spend time with the troubled teen, Jahlil, he could not stop worrying about Freddy's threats. He wondered how the man was doing. He could only imagine how his childhood friend would look after all he had gone through. Was he really crazy, or was Freddy pretending? The last time Lewis had spoken with him was on the phone. Freddy had said that he thought Lewis sold him out. That Nate Kenny and the police were only able to find Freddy in Atlanta because Lewis pointed them in that direction. Freddy said he blamed Lewis then but said nothing about coming after him. After speaking to Kia, Lewis had realized that what she said was true. Freddy never said things he didn't mean and never planned things he didn't accomplish. He only had a GED, but Freddy had said he would study like crazy and earn his real estate license, and he did just that. When Lewis was jumped by a group of boys in high school, Freddy had promised Lewis he would make each one of them pay. One by one, he caught them alone, walking home from school, out after a party, or in the boys' room taking a piss. He caught them off guard, beat the hell out of them with a baseball bat. It was the same baseball bat that he had killed his own father with at eight years old.

Before that awful event, Freddy would sometimes tell Lewis how much he hated his father, how often his father would beat his mother, and then Freddy would mutter something like, "One day I'm gonna kill him."

Lewis had always laughed that off, told Freddy he couldn't hurt a fly. Lewis knew better now. That was the reason he was there.

The door to the visitation room opened. Freddy was led into the room by a big man wearing a white medical coat covering his uniform.

The two men stopped in front of Lewis. Freddy was released. The man next to Freddy said, "I'll be right over by the door. If you need something, just say."

"Yeah," Lewis said, eyeing Freddy. His old friend looked like he was ready to go to bed, wearing slippers and a house robe. His beard was long, his hair short, his eyes vacant.

"You gonna say something, or you just gonna stare at me like you crazy?" Freddy said, opening his arms.

Lewis stepped forward, reluctantly embraced Freddy, and pounded him softly three times on the back like he used to with the flat of his fist.

When he stepped back, there was now a smile on Freddy's face. "Look at you, looking all clean. Life must be good. Have a seat. Tell me what's been up with you."

Although he looked out of sorts, Freddy didn't sound crazy, Lewis thought. He actually sounded saner than he had in a long time.

"I ain't come here to chat, Freddy. Monica been up here to see you?"

Freddy laughed, lowering himself onto a wooden chair. "Yeah, she was all scared, looking like I was out to get her or something."

"Think that might have something to do with the fact you came in her house and almost killed her?"

"I ain't mean that. I told you and her that," Freddy said, the smile gone from his face.

"What else you tell her?"

"What you mean?"

"You tell her you coming after me?" Lewis said, then leaned down closer to Freddy, lowering his voice. "Just what the fuck you mean by that?"

Freddy was smiling again, chuckling. "Just like I thought. We known each other since we was shorties, but it takes me talking some craziness for my best friend to come visit me."

"You saying you only told Monica that just to get me to come up here?"

"You ain't ever come before," Freddy said. "Have you?"

Lewis all of a sudden felt relieved. "No," he admitted. "Shit went crazy between us. I didn't even think you would've wanted me to come up here."

Freddy stood, stepped right up to Lewis, stared him in the eyes. "How many friends you think I got? I had Kia, but she dumped me and killed my baby."

Lewis could still see that Freddy's heart ached thinking his baby was dead. For a split second, he thought about telling Freddy the truth, but that would cause him more pain than good, knowing he would miss at least the first couple of years of that child's life.

"I got back with Joni," Freddy continued. "I loved her. We was gonna be together forever, then . . ." Freddy trailed off. The muscles tightened in his jaw as he looked painfully away from Lewis. When he looked back, it appeared he was trying his best to calm himself. "I had Joni, but now she's dead. You my only friend. I wanna see you from time to time."

"So you ain't mean what you told Monica?"

"Naw, man. I ain't mean that," Freddy said, grinning again.

"You sure about that?"

Smiling wider, Freddy said, "On my mama's grave, I'm sure about that."

75

After work, Monica and Tabatha sipped martinis at a new, swank bar on Rush Street called Spiro. Monica was staring obliviously off into space again.

"Where your head at, girl? You've had that vacant glare on your face all day at work. I was really considering sending you home." Tabatha smiled.

"Oh, *you* send *me* home. That's a new one."

"On the real, you need to tell me what's on your mind."

"Men," Monica said, taking a drink.

"Ah, the new guy. Attorney at law Austin Harris. You make him sound like a good guy, a guy who's looking to settle down. What's the problem?"

"That is the problem," Monica said. "He's known me a week, and the last time we spoke, he was talking about the future, and forever, and the rest of our lives and stuff. I started to itch. I think I was breaking out, 'cause I'm allergic to that kinda talk now."

Tabatha laughed. "Please tell me you didn't kick him to the curb."

"Not yet."

"Why, not yet? Why can't you just let it happen with this guy?"

"Nate."

Tabatha stared at Monica with her mouth open. She stood up from the bar stool, took three paces away, came back, sat back down, and said, "I know you didn't just say that fool's name in here, and say it like you were giving some serious thought to anything concerning his ass."

"He came by to see me at the store last night, said he knows we're done for good now, and gave me this," Monica said, setting Nate's wedding band down in front of Tabatha.

Tabatha picked it up. "His wedding band?"

"Yeah."

"I have two questions. One I know the answer to, so I'll ask you the other. Why the hell you carrying this around with you?"

"Don't know. Guess I never took it out of my purse," Monica said, sipping from her martini. "What's your answer to your other question?"

Tabatha set the ring back in front of Monica, shaking her head. "I was gonna ask why he came by. But the answer is because he's messing with your head, playing the old Jedi mind trick on you, girl."

"I don't know what you're talking about."

"He begs you to come back, you're gonna say no like you always do. He tells you he no longer wants you, any woman's first question is 'Why not?' " Tabatha said. "You haven't been able to stop thinking about this, have you?"

"I don't love him anymore," Monica said. "I promise."

"You sure?" Tabatha said, sounding skeptical.

"Yeah. But I hate myself for what I allowed him to do to me. I keep thinking I should try to do something to get back some of what he took from me. I don't wanna hate myself anymore."

"How would you do that?"

"I don't know. But I'm always thinking about it," Monica said.

"And what, that's stopping you from being able to give the lawyer guy a fair shot?"

"Something like that," Monica said. "He's a sweet man. Supposed to be picking me up tonight to take me somewhere. Said it was a surprise. I just hope he ain't taking me somewhere so he can propose."

76

Jahlil left Shaun at the hospital after spending the whole day there. The nurses admitted her, telling Jahlil there were some minor complications with the pregnancy and the baby might have to be delivered within the next day or two.

"She wasn't supposed to have it for at least another two weeks," Jahlil told the nurse attending Shaun.

"The baby will be fine," the nurse said. "We're going to keep Shaun here, run a few more tests, see what the doctor says, and we'll let you know as soon as he decides."

Jahlil visited Shaun in her hospital room after he was given the news.

"They told you what's going on?" Shaun said.

"Yeah."

"I'm scared."

"Don't be," Jahlil said, rubbing a hand across her hair. "They said everything gonna be all right."

"I ain't scared about that. If my momma kick me out, where am I gonna go? You get the place yet?"

Jahlil hadn't yet found the nerve to tell her he hadn't. "You don't gotta worry about nothing, all right? You just get better." Jahlil leaned in, kissed Shaun on the cheek. "I love you."

He caught the bus home. By the time he got there, it was already late into the evening. He walked into his bedroom and went into his closet. He knew his father would be at work, but he was thankful that his mother wasn't there. Last night, Jahlil imagined that his father must've walked into the apartment right after Jahlil's mother hit the floor. To him, it must've looked like Jahlil had hit her, but he hadn't.

They were arguing, as they always seemed to have been doing lately. She walked up on him, screaming, and he had simply pushed her off him. He didn't mean to push her so hard, didn't know she would fall, but she did. That's when his father came in and punched him.

Jahlil thought his father was wrong to have done that to him, but he never treated Jahlil the way he should've. His father never loved him, and that was just one more reason Jahlil needed to be out from under their rule.

Setting the shoe box on his bed, Jahlil opened it, took his money, stuffed the roll in one pocket, and grabbed his gun, shoving it in the opposite one. He had to do what was necessary.

77

Lewis closed the storybook after he realized that Layla and Tammi had both fallen off to sleep. They lay in their twin beds on either side of him. A Princess and the Frog lamp stood burning dimly on the nightstand, allowing him to admire just how adorable they both were.

Before he'd met Eva, Lewis's life had been in shambles. He had just been released from a short stint in jail, miraculously dodging a possible five-year sentence. But he was homeless, jobless, and broke.

He'd had too many problems and too few solutions. But one day, he walked into the DCFS building, looking for an answer to one of those problems, and he found Eva. She worked there as a case adviser and had found Lewis the job he had now. To him, she had also given herself, and her daughter, which provided everything else Lewis needed — love, companionship, stability, and the desire to be a better man. With Layla, Tammi, and Eva, Lewis felt stronger, more confident, and more loved than he ever had in his entire life. He was happy that the business with Freddy was nothing more than talk. He didn't want to have to tell Eva about his involvement with Freddy for fear of losing her, but more than that, he didn't want her or the children getting caught up in the hell that Freddy often pulled those who surrounded him into.

Lewis set the storybook under the chair he was sitting in, and leaned over to kiss his daughter on the cheek, then kissed Tammi good night as well.

Lewis walked through the hallway of the house he now owned, the house that had been given to him by Monica. It was where she once lived, where they had lived together when they were a couple. But that was some time ago. Now he was with Eva, and she spent as much time here in Lewis's house as he spent at hers.

When he stepped into his bedroom, Eva was on his bed, wearing one of his T-shirts and a pair of his pajama bottoms, sifting through a number of papers.

Lewis sat on the bed beside her and kissed the side of her neck. "You have a closet full of your own clothes here, why you wearing my stuff?"

" 'Cause your stuff feels better," Eva said.

"I think wearing no stuff would feel best," Lewis said, lifting up her T-shirt and sneaking a kiss on the side of her belly. "How's the search coming? Find anything that could help Jahlil?"

"Think so," she said, digging out a page and holding it so Lewis could see. "There's something called the TANF program — Temporary Assistance for Needy Families. I think it might be perfect for him."

"What is it?" Lewis asked, taking the paper from her.

"It says," Eva read, "its purpose is 'to assist needy families so that children can be cared for in their own homes, to prevent out-of-wedlock pregnancies, to encourage the formation and maintenance of two-parent families, and to reduce the dependency of needy parents by promoting job preparation and marriage.' " Eva turned to Lewis. "What do you think?"

"I think you're the best, most thoughtful woman in the world. And I think that program sounds perfect for Jahlil. I can't wait to tell him tomorrow."

78

Austin walked around his car to open the door for Monica.

She took his hand and allowed him to help her out. She looked beautiful, wearing a casual lavender dress with black heels.

She looked up at the house before them; a number of cars were parked along the curb. "Where are we?"

"I told you, it's a surprise," Austin said, closing the door and walking Monica up the path toward the house.

She stopped before they made it to the first stair.

"Okay, the intrigue was nice, but I'd really appreciate it if you told me where we are."

"Monica . . ." Austin smiled.

"I need to know where you're taking me. Please."

"It's a small family gathering," Austin said. "My ex-wife —"

"Your ex-wife!"

"Yes, my ex-wife throws these impromptu dinners, invites the family and friends, and I wanted them to meet you."

Monica looked back over her shoulder at the car as if she were considering breaking away and making a dash for it. "Couldn't you have told me that before now?"

"We'll have a couple of drinks, something to eat, and we'll leave. What's the big deal?"

"Who said I was ready to meet your family? Don't you think you're taking this a little fast?"

"Here we go with that again," Austin said, digging his keys out of his pocket. He grabbed Monica's hand and started back to the car. "You wanna just leave? Fine. I didn't know you'd be so against this."

"Stop it!" Monica said, yanking her hand away and halting in the middle of the sidewalk. "It's not that I don't want to meet them. You keep talking about a future, about a relationship together, but what kind of foundation are you building when you keep me in the dark about things like this?"

Austin thought a moment. "You're right," he said. "I'm sorry. I shouldn't have sprung this on you. What do you want to do?"

Monica took more time than Austin felt she needed. "I want to go in there and meet these people. But don't do this to me again,

Austin."

"Okay," Austin said, taking Monica's hand, and walking her back in the direction of the house.

Fifteen minutes later, Austin stood in the dining room, very close to Monica, both of them holding drinks. He had already introduced her to his ex-wife, Trace, who had been very gracious.

"I just love your dress," Trace said.

"Thank you. You have a beautiful home. I'll have to get the number of your interior designer."

Trace smiled. "I think you already have his number. He did all this," she said, looking at Austin. "You two have a nice time."

"She seems nice enough," Monica said. "Why did you let her get away?"

"I guess I didn't know a good thing when I had it. That's not the case anymore," Austin said.

Monica leaned in and gave him a quick kiss on the lips.

This was what he had been missing, Austin told himself. The house was filled with neighbors and co-workers from both Trace's job and John's. The couples stood talking, drinking, and laughing, and during that time, Austin would sneak peeks at Monica, hoping she was enjoying herself, hoping that this would bring her one step closer to possibly wanting something with him.

After speaking to his old neighbor, Jim, from across the street, Austin walked over to Monica, who was having a conversation with a blonde Austin didn't know. "Excuse me, ladies, but do either of you want anything from the kitchen? I'm going for a bottle of water."

Both women declined, and Austin touched Monica on the arm before making his way through the thin crowd of people into the kitchen.

When he stepped in, Austin was surprised to see his brother Marcus there, holding a half glass of liquor.

"Wow," Austin said. "Thought you said you weren't coming. You know Reecie was invited."

"I know. That's why I changed my mind," Marcus said. His speech was mildly slurred. "She can't avoid me now."

"I guess we'll have to see about that. How long you been here?"

"About two and a half drinks long," Marcus said, his eyelids hanging low.

"Sounds more like three drinks long," Austin said, opening up the fridge and grabbing a bottle of water.

"Caleb coming?"

"Don't think so," Marcus said. "You know he doesn't really go for stuff like this."

Austin cracked his bottle, took a drink from it, and leaned against the kitchen counter. "So, what are you going to say when you see your wife?"

"I —" Marcus began.

Just then, the kitchen door swung open, and Reecie stepped in. "I'm sorry. I didn't —" she said, turning, about to push her way back through the door.

"No, you don't," Austin said, hurrying over to grab her. "I think it's time to stop acting like children and address this problem. I'll be just outside in the dining room. If I hear any screaming or dishes being thrown, I'm coming back."

Marcus watched his brother walk out, leaving him in the kitchen with his cheating wife. Even though he still loved her, he couldn't stand the sight of her that moment.

"How have you been?" Reecie said, seeming almost ashamed to look directly at him.

"Why did you cheat on me?"

"It was dinner, Marcus."

"Were you fucking him?" Marcus said, his speech slurring more.

"No. He was just a guy who had been asking me out for the last year, and I finally said yes."

"That's why you put me out? So you could start dating that guy?"

"No," Reecie said. "I put you out because you had been out of work for two years."

"I told you, I couldn't help that!"

"How do you know? You sure as hell didn't try to help it. Yes, I made enough to support the three of us, but why would you make me? For two years, I came home from working all day, made dinner, played with Sophie, and had to hear you complain about the economy when you weren't doing anything but sitting at home on your ass all day."

"I was painting! And I was keeping an eye out for design jobs. It wasn't my fault that there weren't any out there."

"Really, Marcus? And how did that help us?" Reecie said. "I was in it by myself. I begged and begged you to find work anywhere. It wouldn't have mattered. McDonald's would've been fine. At least I would've known that you were trying. But when you refused, it told me that you had given up on us. You were only thinking about yourself, and I couldn't take it any longer. Your ass had to go, if only to teach you a lesson," Reecie said, waving a hand. "You had to go."

Marcus stood, leaning against the counter, holding his drink, his head slightly fuzzy from the alcohol, but he still felt the full impact of what his wife said. "And the guy?"

"It was a date with no intentions of anything more than dinner and a few laughs. I realized it was wrong after the fact, but when was the last time you took me out for dinner?"

"I didn't have any money."

"If you'd just suggested it, I would've paid."

Marcus lowered his head. He felt his wife approach him. She took the drink out of his hand, set it down, and intertwined her fingers with his.

"I'm sorry about what happened in the restaurant. Like I said, I was wrong."

"And I'm sorry for making you feel you needed to have done it," Marcus said, meeting her eyes. "I'm sorry for being selfish, and for giving up. Can you forgive me?"

Reecie leaned in, kissed Marcus's lips. "I can, if —"

"I got a job interview next week, if that's what you're about to say. It's not as a graphic designer, but —"

"It'll do just fine," Reecie said, hugging Marcus. "Whatever it is."

■ ■ ■ ■

Half an hour later, Austin sat parked outside Monica's house. The two were passionately kissing when Austin suddenly pulled away.

"What?" Monica said, looking flustered, breathing hard.

"What are we doing?"

"We're making out. Why'd you stop?" Monica said, leaning in to continue. Austin pulled further away.

"We're making out in my car, when you have a nice, comfortable bed in your house. And I'm sure you have some eggs and bacon in your fridge you can hook up in the morning."

Monica smiled. "Oh, so you wanna go in my house and get in my bed."

"Yup."

"And in the morning, your audacious ass think I'm gonna be cooking you eggs and bacon."

"I didn't say that." Austin smiled.

"Oh yes, you did."

"Oh yeah, I guess I did. I'm just saying, if you wanna cook breakfast, I'll definitely eat it."

"You know this would be like three nights in a row we've spent together."

"Yeah. I know."

"But this would be the first time you've spent the night. That's a big deal. That sounds like we'd be starting something that could lead to, dare I say, a relationship."

"I can understand why you'd worry about that happening," Austin joked. "You look at how handsome I am, how successful, oh yeah, and how great I am in the sack, and you worry that if you let me spend the night, it's over for you. You won't be able to resist me anymore. You're scared, and it's perfectly understandable." Austin chuckled. "This is what I'll do. You can invite me in, and we can see what happens, or you can jump out of the car right now, and not have to worry about us having the best sex of our lives, you falling deeply in love with me, and us wanting to spend the rest of our lives together. But you have to decide now. What will it be?"

"I have to decide now? Like right now? I can't think about it?"

"Nope. Right now," Austin said.

"Fine." Monica gave Austin a peck on the lips and opened her door. She climbed out and started up the path to her house without looking back.

Austin waited a moment, a slowly fading smile on his face, thinking Monica would look back, but she didn't. He was dumbfounded. What had he done or said wrong? It was a joke. Didn't she know that? Should he get out of the car, chase after her, tell her he was sorry? No, he told himself, watching Monica as she climbed her stairs and unlocked her front door. He would only make a bigger fool of himself.

As Monica pushed open her door, Austin asked himself if this was it for the two of them. He realized it very well could've been and was surprised how saddened he was by that possibility.

Staring up at her, he realized he didn't care about making a fool of himself. Austin grabbed his door handle, was about to pull it open, run after her, when he saw Monica turn, just inside her house, push her dress off her shoulders, then let it drop down to the floor. With a seductive smile and a curl of her finger, she invited Austin in.

79

Caleb sat in the cargo area of a white van, on the way to the electronics store. He had finally called and told Blue to include him on the job. Three men sat with him. One was Blue. The other two were men Caleb didn't know. They looked angry and starved for money, like they had been in prison, were unable to find work, and were doing this job as a last resort to pay for a bad drug habit or debt or to care for family. They looked like Caleb.

After the incident with Jahlil, seeing Sonya on the floor like that, Caleb knew action had to be taken. He knew money wouldn't be the answer to all his troubles, but it was what Sonya demanded in order to even think about letting Caleb back into the house.

Blue had told Caleb that each man could walk away with ten grand. That would get Caleb and his family out of their neighborhood. He could rent a house somewhere, a place big enough for them and Jahlil's girlfriend and the new baby. There would even be enough to make some improvements to Caleb's business, maybe buy a new van, new uniforms, or possibly hire another employee. All those things would make his company appear more "established," and ultimately win him new contracts.

"You all right?" Blue asked, as the van rolled over a pothole.

"Yeah," Caleb said, not sure if he actually meant it. He looked up at one of the men who sat on the opposite side of the van. A sheer stocking cap was pulled over his freshly braided cornrows. The man must've felt Caleb's stare. He looked up with evil eyes. Caleb didn't look away. He thought about the moments years ago, after he was released from the penitentiary, standing outside the prison's gate, looking back at the guards who had controlled his life for the previous five years.

Now, as Caleb was being driven closer to the robbery site, he asked himself whether his time in prison had really affected his son. Had that turned Jahlil into the boy he was now? The boy who cut school, who sold drugs, who robbed people, who hadn't thought enough about his future not to have a child at sixteen?

If that was the reason, wouldn't that have meant that Caleb was responsible? He forced the thought out of his head to find that he was still staring at the man sitting across from him in the van.

"You got a motherfuckin' eye problem?" the man said.

"Sorry," Caleb said, looking away, returning to his thoughts.

Hopefully, with this money, Caleb could build his business into something, so that his son, and maybe even his granddaughter, would never have to worry about their future.

Caleb smiled at the thought of his success, and the pride his family would feel for him. But he had to question the way he was trying to accomplish his goal.

Didn't he have these same intentions so many years ago, when he, Blue, and Ray Ray robbed that convenience store? When Ray Ray lay there dying in his arms? That moment, a vision appeared in Caleb's head. He was on the floor of that same store, holding his dying friend, Caleb's arms, his shirt covered with Ray Ray's blood. But the face he stared down into this time was his son's.

Caleb looked up as if startled from a dream.

"What's up?" Blue said, sensing something wrong.

"Stop the van," Caleb said, softly.

"What?"

Caleb called up to the driver. "Yo, stop the van!"

The driver looked back over his shoulder, a questioning look on his face.

"Caleb," Blue said, "you need this money. Ain't that what you said? Don't be making no hasty decisions you gonna be —"

"I said stop the motherfucking van!" Caleb yelled. "I'm getting off." He turned to Blue. "Get off with me, okay? We've been here before, and we know where it's gonna lead."

Blue smiled, shaking his head. "Naw, man. I'm about to get this money, but I ain't going back to prison. Promise you that."

The van pulled over to the curb. The driver threw an arm over his seat, yelled back at Caleb, "You getting off or what?"

"Blue, please," Caleb said.

"You the one with the family," Blue said. "I understand why you bailing. But it's just me. I can roll the dice. Now get out of here, before dude start driving again."

"Blue —"

"Get the fuck off the van," the driver yelled at Caleb. "Or I'm pulling off."

Blue smiled. "You hear the man. Get the fuck off the van, Caleb."

80

It was dark and late, and as Jahlil walked, he looked into the windows of the storefront businesses that lined Fifty-Fifth Street. He was thinking the wrong thing, planning a way to get him out of his messed-up situation.

Jahlil walked slowly past a gas station, saw a big man behind the register look out at him as though he knew what was going through Jahlil's mind. Jahlil turned his face away, pulled his hood over his head, and kept on walking.

He strolled past a restaurant. The idea of busting through the door, gun drawn, yelling at the terrified diners, popped into his head, but there were just too many people. Police would come, Jahlil would be arrested, driven off to jail, and that would defeat everything.

No, Jahlil thought, if he was going to do this, the situation would have to be perfect.

He looked down at his watch. It read 8:55 p.m. Most of the stores would be just about to close. The employees would be gone. Maybe there'd be just one person closing. This was the ideal time.

He walked in front of a small jewelry store and stopped. He didn't see anyone inside, but the lights were still on, and he saw envelopes on top of one of the glass cases, as if someone was in the middle of doing something with them but had momentarily walked away.

Jahlil looked up and down the street. No one was watching. He approached the store, checked it. The door was unlocked, so he pulled it open. A bell went off that announced his entrance, startling him. From the back room, an overweight, middle-aged woman appeared, saying, "Sorry, we're closing and —"

Jahlil had the gun out of his pocket, pointed at the space between the woman's eyes before she could finish her sentence.

She screamed and threw her hands in front of her face.

"Shut up!" Jahlil yelled, his fists shaking around the gun. He was in it now, and there was nothing he could do but finish. "Is there anyone else here?"

"No. No. It's just me," the woman said,

frightened.

"Don't lie to me!"

"I swear to God."

Jahlil quickly, nervously scanned the store. "Where's the money?"

"Please!" The woman said. "Don't hurt me."

"I said where's the fucking money?"

"In the safe."

"Get it."

"It's time-locked. It won't open till tomorrow morning."

"Then the jewelry," Jahlil said. "Get me some of that, and hurry up," he said, looking over his shoulder.

"Oh, God. That's in the safe too," the woman cried. "Please, just leave, and I won't tell anyone. Just —"

"Shut up!" Jahlil said again, not knowing what to do. Yes, he could leave, but he would have nothing. He would be in the same situation he started in. He needed the money. Something told him the woman was lying. Not knowing what else to do, Jahlil spun to the door, locked it, and shut off the interior lights.

"Oh Jesus, don't!"

Jahlil hurried over to the woman, the gun still pointed at her. "Get in the back."

"Why? Why!" the woman screamed.

"Because I don't believe you!"

The room was small. There was a folding table, three chairs, and a watercooler. A huge safe sat against a wall, a blinking red light on it.

"Open it," Jahlil said.

"I . . . I told you. It's timed —"

"I don't give a fuck!" Jahlil yelled. "I said walk over there and open it." He jabbed the gun at the woman, which made her move toward the safe. She stood in front of it, trembling, as if waiting on directions for what to do next.

"Open it!" Jahlil ordered again.

The woman cried louder, lowered herself to her knees. She grabbed the cross that was hanging from her necklace, kissed it several times, then pressed her palms together and begged. "I can't. Just please, please . . ."

She was telling the truth, Jahlil now told himself. But where did that leave him? He didn't have the money he needed to save his girlfriend and their baby from her mother, the money he needed to save himself from his father and the awful life he'd had so far. He was a failure in school, was responsible for the death of his best friend, and didn't see any other future for himself other than a continuation of the horrible life he was living that moment.

Jahlil looked over at the woman, sobbing, mumbling prayers, thinking that she was on the verge of dying, that Jahlil was actually going to kill her, when there was nothing further from the truth. This was not what he wanted to do. It was too much for him, had always been, but he did it because he had to.

"Sorry," Jahlil said under his breath. He turned to go, took a step, but felt the room spin, his knees buckle, and it felt as though he was going to fall. He stumbled but steadied himself on the edge of the folding table. He was dizzy, and he knew it was from the stress that had been plaguing him for so long.

He grabbed one of the chairs, lowered himself into it.

"Are you —" the woman began, but Jahlil quickly raised the gun at her again. "I was just asking if you were okay," the woman said, smearing the tears from her face.

"I'm not okay," Jahlil mumbled. He looked over at the safe. "You sure you can't get in there?"

"I promise. Before God, I promise."

Jahlil slumped in the chair. He wore no facial expression. He exhaled deeply, wiped his nose with the back of the hand holding the gun, then pointed it back at the woman.

He stood, not believing he was about to utter the words in his brain.

"I need for you to roll over and lie on your stomach," Jahlil said.

The woman's face went completely white. Her eyes bulged and she appeared to gag on her own breath. She coughed up a fright-filled "Why?"

Jahlil took two more steps toward her, his arm outstretched, the gun aimed at the side of the woman's skull. He would have to do this, he urged himself. There was no money, but she had seen his face. She would call the police. They would come, take him away, throw him in prison, and he would never see Shaun again, or his little girl. He would be just like his father, and he would rather die than do that. "Because I fucking said!" Jahlil yelled, his hand shaking around the gun, his finger taut on the trigger.

The woman quickly flipped onto her stomach, sobbing louder now. Her arms were stretched over her head, her palms still pressed together. She was praying again between her crying; Jahlil was not able to make out what she was saying.

He stepped closer, stood over her, lowered the gun to an inch above the dark curls of her head. He could see the white skin of her scalp and he started to feel dizzy again.

Do it! Do it! he pushed himself. He had killed his best friend — taken him to that house, gotten him killed. It might as well have been him that pulled the trigger. And before that, he blew off Craig's head when he thought the man was going to kill his father. He had taken a life before. Why was it so damn hard to kill this woman? Press the tip of the barrel to her head, look away, and pull the trigger, Jahlil told himself. There would be blood, brain, and bone on the floor, but the woman would never tell it was him, and he would not go to jail for this. So that's what he would do.

Jahlil extended the reach of the gun till it stopped against the back of the woman's skull.

She screamed, but Jahlil heard nothing, for his mind was a million miles away. He was a year in the future, where his little girl was crawling around on the living room floor before him and Shaun. Ten years in the future, where the three of them lived in a little house. Times were hard, but they stuck together as a family. And eighteen years in the future, where he and Shaun were dropping his daughter off at the university where she received a full scholarship.

Jahlil felt a slight smile on his face, then it

quickly turned to a frown when he realized all those moments would be tainted by the memory of his pulling that trigger and murdering that woman so many years in the past in the back of that jewelry store.

He snapped out of his daydream, felt tears on his face, and was almost deafened by the still-ongoing screams of the woman.

The gun still to her head, he thought of telling her to shut up, then make her promise that she would never go to the police, but he knew she would say anything to save her life at that moment. The only thing he could hope is that she wouldn't be able to give a good-enough description for the cops to find him. Knowing he did not want this woman's death on his conscience, Jahlil pulled the gun from her head, then ran out of the store.

81

It was morning, and Caleb glanced down at his watch when he heard Blue's voice mail pick up. "Yo, Blue, I know you're not avoiding me 'cause I bailed on you last night. Give a brotha a call, and stop playin', okay," Caleb said, leaving his fourth voice mail in a half hour.

Caleb pulled on a shirt as he walked out of Austin's guest bedroom into the kitchen.

He clicked on the small TV that sat on the kitchen counter, as he took the carton of eggs and a package of bacon out of the fridge for breakfast.

"And in breaking news," a reporter announced, "suspects have been taken into custody in connection with a West Side robbery last night. The computer and electronics store was in the process of being robbed when a security guard stumbled upon the suspicious activity. Three men, Terrance

Picket, Steve Smith, and Bobby "Blue" Oliver —"

The egg Caleb held dropped from his hand and smashed on the kitchen floor. He hurried over to the television to see the mug shots of all three men.

"Dammit, Blue!" Caleb said, slinging the plastic bowl he was holding across the room. "Goddammit!"

82

Jahlil sat on a bench on the high school campus.

He was still shaken from the robbery he had attempted last night but was happy that he was able to get out of there before the police had come. Jahlil assumed they hadn't been informed, and even if the woman had called, she didn't know his name or where he lived. To her, he probably looked like every other sixteen-year-old black kid in Chicago. No cops were banging on his door when he came home last night or when he woke up this morning. And no squad cars were there at school awaiting Jahlil today. He assumed he was in the clear.

When Jahlil had walked into the apartment last night, he wanted to apologize to his mother for the argument they had and for putting his hands on her.

He walked quietly through the rooms, stopped at her partially opened bedroom door. He knocked softly, and when she didn't respond, Jahlil pushed the door open and stepped in. She was asleep.

Jahlil lowered himself to his mother's bedside, listened a moment to the sound of her sleeping, and hoped that none of the horrible things he had done up to this point would come back on him. He would be better now.

He leaned over and softly kissed his mother on the cheek. "Sorry for everything, Ma, but I'm gonna be better. I promise," Jahlil said, now planning to make the future he had envisioned last night with his family a reality.

This morning when he awoke, his mother had gone.

At school, for the first time in over a year, Jahlil was attentive in class. He raised his hand, answered the few questions he could, and had a real desire to learn the answers to the ones he couldn't. He took notes, copied down his homework assignments, and didn't once talk in class when he wasn't supposed to.

After his social science class, as Jahlil was walking toward the door, his teacher, Mr. Bronson, asked him if he could come over to his desk.

Almost immediately, Jahlil felt himself

covered with a nervous sweat. He walked over to the teacher, but the man didn't say anything to him, just watched as the last few students filed out of the classroom.

Jahlil stood there, feeling light-headed. He stared out the classroom door, waiting to see police officers bust in, throw him to the floor, and handcuff him. That's what this was, Jahlil told himself. The woman had told, and now it was all over.

When the last student exited, Mr. Bronson simply said, "You were very active in class today. Let's keep that up, okay?" He smiled.

"That's it?" Jahlil said.

"That's a lot compared to how you've been behaving. Don't you think?" Mr. Bronson said.

"Yeah," Jahlil smiled. "Yeah, it is."

Jahlil chose to eat his lunch outside alone today. The weather was warm, the sun was out, and the compliment his teacher gave him made him feel good, as though he was capable of anything.

Across the campus Jahlil saw Bug walk out of the lunchroom door. When Bug caught sight of Jahlil, he squinted across the hundred or so yards, as if to make sure it was him. When he seemed sure, Bug started quickly in Jahlil's direction. He didn't look like himself. He looked angered, distraught, and saddened all at the same time.

"Yo, what's —" Jahlil said, but Bug hurried right up on him, and with both hands pushed Jahlil in the chest.

Jahlil fell backward onto the grass.

"You promised me!" Bug said, near tears. "You fucking promised!"

Jahlil pushed himself up on his elbows. "What are you talking about?"

"I just lost one best friend, and now I'm gonna lose you."

Jahlil stood, brushing grass from his backside. "Bug, what the hell are you talking about?"

"Don't play stupid. Last night, you robbed a store. You robbed —"

"What? How did you know about that?" Jahlil said, shocked, throwing himself at Bug, grabbing him by his shirt.

Bug shook his head, dug into his pocket, and pulled out his phone. He tapped the tiny buttons, waited a second, then turned the screen so that Jahlil could see. What Jahlil saw was a surveillance video of him pointing his gun at the woman in the store, yelling something at her.

"It's all over YouTube, man," Bug said, angrily.

"YouTube? How the —"

"Police put this stuff on the Internet, askin' for tips."

Why didn't he check for cameras? Jahlil thought. Why in the hell didn't he check?

"It already got like five thousand views. Even some of the kids inside seen it and sending it to their friends. You promised you wouldn't do it again, Jahlil."

"I ain't promise nothing," Jahlil said, angry, pounding himself in the head with the side of his fist. If that was all over the Internet, then it was just a matter of time before someone contacted the police, told them it was him. If that was the case, Jahlil didn't have time to stand here and explain to Bug why he had made the worst mistake of his life. Would he run? Would he try to somehow take Shaun with him? Would he even tell Shaun? His mother? His father?

"Did you hear me?" Bug yelled. "Why?"

"Because I had to!"

"You could've come to me, or your folks. You could've —"

"And what the fuck would you have done, Bug?" Jahlil lashed out. "Or them? Ya'll ain't done nothing before. Why would this time be any different? Tell me, Bug. You yelling all in my face, telling me what I should and shouldn't be doing when you ain't got the fucking problems I got."

Bug was silent, his eyes forced down.

"Good-bye, Bug," Jahlil said, turning and quickly walking away.

83

Monica sat opposite Daphanie at a down-town Starbucks.

She didn't really know why, but she'd had the urge to call the woman, find out how she had been doing since reuniting with the baby, and the infant's father, Trevor. Daphanie said she didn't think it was wise to speak to her on the phone then and asked if they could meet out.

Sitting before Monica, drinking from a cup of black coffee, the woman looked tired and sad.

Daphanie frowned. "Things are horrible."

"But you're with your baby."

"Am I? The baby is home with the nanny, not because I wanted to leave him, but because Trevor won't allow me to take him away from the house. If the nanny is not there, I'm not allowed to be alone with the baby. I can't feed him unsupervised, bathe him, care for him, love him, change his diaper — my own fucking baby!"

"That cannot be," Monica said.

"He doesn't trust me with him. He hasn't said it, but I know he thinks I'll try to take him or hurt him or something, I don't know," Daphanie said. "It's torture being there, watching that woman he pays try to give my baby the care he should be receiving from me."

"If you can't stand it there, maybe you should —"

"Leave? Monica, I have no money, no job. I'm behind on my mortgage. I'm already getting calls from the bank about them foreclosing. I can't go anywhere."

Monica had millions in the bank, but she wasn't going to help the very woman that tried to steal her ex-husband away. Besides, Daphanie said, "Even with all the restrictions, I know I can't leave. At least this way I can be in the same house as my baby." Daphanie dabbed a tear from the corner of her eye with one of her napkins. "If Nate wasn't so damn stubborn . . . I know he could get my baby back."

Something told Monica not to say anything about the offer that Nate had presented her, but she spoke regardless. "He said he would try to get your baby back if I come back to him."

Daphanie looked up from the napkin pressed to her face. "What? What did you say?"

"Nate said if I come back to —"

"You're gonna go, right?" Daphanie said, sitting up, scooting her chair closer to Monica, hope in her eyes.

"Of course not!"

"But my baby . . . Nate said he could —"

"He just said that, trying to play games. You know him almost as well as I do. The attorney already told you there's nothing that can be done, that the contract is binding. Nate only said that trying to get me back with him."

"Then go!" Daphanie said. "This is for my baby. Don't be so fucking selfish!"

Monica leaned back in her chair, feeling as though she had been slapped. "What did you just say to me?"

"My baby was taken away and you have a chance —"

"Get it straight. Your baby wasn't taken. You gave him away. You were made a fool of by Nate, and now you want me to sacrifice for your benefit. I'm smarter than that."

Now it was Daphanie who appeared to feel she had been assaulted. "Heifer, smart is the last thing you are," Daphanie said, leaning in over the table, lowering her voice to a bitter whisper. "Nate told me everything about you. He married you just to have his child. He cheated on and divorced you, and you went back to him. You got shot in the head, and just when you wake from your coma, he tells you he's leaving you for me, 'cause you can't give him a child. And what's most pathetic, I look in your eyes, and I can see you still have feelings for him."

A tear rolled down Daphanie's cheek. She angrily brushed it away as she stood from the table. "Yes, I'm the fool he used once, but I'm trying to get his ass back for that. You're the fool he uses over and over again, but you sit there like a scared little bitch, afraid to do shit about it."

Daphanie shouldered her purse, wiped at her face again and said, "Fuck you, Monica. Don't ever call me again till you're woman enough to give that motherfucker Nate what we both know he deserves."

84

Lewis felt good as he turned the corner onto his block.

At work, earlier this afternoon, Eva had called him into her office. She was sitting behind her desk when he stepped in.

"Close the door," she said.

Lewis did. Eva stood, walked over to him, took one of his hands, and said, "Jahlil was approved for the TANF program."

"Really," Lewis said, happy. "If you only knew what this is going to mean to him. I'll call his father and give him the good news after work."

"I'm so glad."

"I've been where he is," Lewis said. "If there was someone like you who did for me what you're doing for him right now, I could've . . ."

"Shhh," Eva said, pecking Lewis on the lips. "You're the one that's doing it, I'm only helping."

Lewis shook his head. "Do you know how much I love you?"

"Yeah, but tell me again anyway."

"So much that it's gonna take me the rest of my life to prove it to you."

Eva smiled. "I love the sound of that. I'll be here."

A smile still on his face, Lewis pulled up to his house but stopped short when he saw a man at his front door, making an effort to look into his living room window. Lewis drove the Escalade into the driveway, climbed out, and said, "Hey, can I help you?"

The man was Lewis's height but bigger, broader. He was clean shaven, clean-cut, but wore baggy jeans and a plaid button-down shirt, the tails hanging out over his belt line. He turned, startled, a smile immediately coming to his face.

"Pete home?"

"What?" Lewis said, walking over to the man, glancing at the car that was parked in front of his house. It was a late-model black Chrysler 300 with tinted windows.

"Pete here? I was supposed to meet him. This is his address, right?" the man said, digging into his jeans, pulling out a scrap of paper, looking down at it, then handing it to Lewis. Lewis eyed it quickly, then gave it back.

"Right address, but no Pete lives here."

"Damn," the man said grinning wider. "My bad. Must've wrote it down wrong. Sorry to bother you, brah."

"Don't worry about it," Lewis said, continuing to watch as the man climbed into his car, drove off, and turned the corner out of sight.

85

Caleb waited twenty minutes before he finally saw Blue being walked over to sit on the other side of the thick glass window Caleb was sitting in front of.

Caleb read the lips of the guard when he told Blue, "Five minutes."

Blue's wrists were cuffed, but he picked up the phone to his left, placed it in the crook of his shoulder, and pressed it to his ear.

The first words came hard to Caleb. "Sorry, man."

"What you got to be sorry about?" Blue said, trying to smile. "You did the right thing. I was the one who fucked up."

"I wanted you to come with me. If only you woulda —"

"But I didn't, and that's what is, so I don't want you thinking about that. You got more important stuff you gotta take care of, like your family, right?"

"Yeah," Caleb said.

"So do that, all right, man?" Blue said. "Do that, and I'll see you when I get out."

"Yeah, okay," Caleb said, feeling sorry for his friend.

"Love you, man," Blue said.

"You too," Caleb said, watching as Blue hung up the phone, stood, and was taken by the guard back to his cell.

Later Caleb could think of no one else he wanted to go to, no one else he could share the news about Blue with other than Sonya. He stood in the kitchen of her apartment and told her how if he hadn't walked off that van, he would've been sitting in a cell beside Blue.

Sonya walked closer to Caleb. "You what? You were going to break in somewhere and rob them? For what?"

"What have you been saying about me all these years? Why did you leave me? Because I'm a failure, because I don't make any money."

"And this was the way you were going to prove me wrong?"

"We need money! Did you hear what Jahlil is doing?"

"We've gotten it before!"

"And how do you think that happened?"

Caleb said, stepping away from Sonya. "When the rent was way behind here, when you needed all that to catch up on everything else, how do you think I got that to give you?"

Sonya appeared afraid to ask. "Tell me you didn't rob —"

"I borrowed the money from a shark, but I had to rob to pay it back."

"What the fuck, Caleb!" Sonya said, throwing her hands up. "You're going around stealing money but saying you wanna live back here, be back in Jahlil's life. What do you think you'll be teaching —"

"I had to do it, okay?"

"You don't have to do nothing!" Sonya said, emotional. "What if you didn't get them the money —"

"They took me," Caleb said, his voice low. "There was another man who owed them. They killed him, right in front of me. Me getting them back what I owed wasn't a question."

Sonya moved closer to Caleb, stopped just in front of him. He could tell she saw the pain and shame in his eyes. She touched his face, laid her palm to his cheek.

"That's what you were saying you did for us, borrowing the money?" Sonya asked.

"I love you, Sonya."

"Don't ever do that again," Sonya said, softly.

"I love my family."

"Shhh," Sonya said, touching a finger to Caleb's lips.

"I'll do anything for you and Jahlil. I just wanna come —"

Sonya leaned forward, pressed her mouth to his, and quieted him with her kiss.

Caleb lay in Sonya's arms, in their bedroom, after making love. He glanced at the clock on the nightstand. It read 7:06 p.m. He lay his head back against Sonya's breast, regretting the fact he'd have to go clean Austin's offices soon. "Have you talked to Jahlil? Is he still mad at me?"

"I left before he woke up this morning, so I haven't spoken to him yet," Sonya said. "But you know how he is. He won't be mad for long."

"I hope so," Caleb said. He was afraid to mention what was on his mind for fear of rejection, but he needed to know where he stood in all of this. "Is there a chance . . . a chance that I can come home?"

"Caleb . . ."

"Sonya," Caleb said, rolling over so he could look directly into her eyes. "Do you see what's happening? I'm not gonna just sit here and lose our son. I'm his father, and my place should be in this house so we can be a family again. Can we at least try?"

Sonya lay her head back, closed her eyes, and sighed. When she looked back up at Caleb, she said, "We can try."

Caleb kissed Sonya and got out of bed. He grabbed his work pants from the floor, slid them on, and pulled out his cell phone.

"Going to work?" she asked.

"Don't want to, but I gotta," Caleb said, punching numbers into his phone.

Sonya climbed out of bed, covering herself with her bathrobe. "Let me make you something to eat before you go. Who you calling?"

"Jahlil. I think it's time that all of us sit down and talk."

A knock came at the front door.

"That's probably him," Sonya said.

"Why would he knock?" Caleb walked into the front room, Sonya following behind him.

Caleb pressed his face to the door, looked out the peephole, then turned to Sonya. "It's one of Jahlil's friends."

He opened the door. The boy Caleb believed the kids called Bug was standing in the doorway, holding his cell phone. He looked Caleb in the eyes, then around at

Sonya standing just behind him.

"Mr. and Mrs. Harris," Bug said. "I don't wanna be a snitch, but there's something I need to show you."

86

"Do you respect me, or do you think I'm a fool?" Monica asked Tabatha. She had driven over to Tabatha's house after her meeting with Daphanie. She was standing on Daphanie's front porch. "And I need you to be honest with me, Tab."

"Uh, can I at least get a hello?" Tabatha said, holding the door open and stepping aside to let Monica in.

Monica paced two lines across the living room carpet and wound up standing in front of Tabatha again. "Everything I went through with Nate, the years I was married to him, what he's done to me, what I let him get away with — you think I'm a fool, don't you?"

"Monica, no. Why would I think that? Nate was your husband. In marriages things happen that —"

"That I shouldn't have let happen," Monica finished.

"I didn't say that."

"If your husband had slept with his secretary, had set up that whole scheme just to get you to divorce him, would you have taken him back like I did Nate?"

Tabatha frowned, shook her head. "Girl, the moment I found out he was taking pills to make himself impotent on purpose so he couldn't make love to me, I would've divorced his ass and he would've never seen me again."

"You would've?" Monica said.

Tabatha nodded her head.

"See."

"That doesn't make you a fool, and you know I respect you."

Monica walked into the hallway and stood before the full-length mirror, staring at herself.

"Did you hear what I said?" Tabatha asked.

"All that he's done, how does he always come out so clean, when everyone else is left covered in it? You should've heard her, Tab."

"Heard who?" Tabatha said, walking over to Monica, standing behind her in the mirror.

"I met Daphanie," Monica said, stepping very close to the mirror, staring at herself, speaking slowly as though falling into a trance. "She was pathetic and miserable, kind of like I am now. It's all because of Nate." Monica parted her hair where she'd had her surgery. When she turned her head just so, she could see a lot of the scar. It sickened her, but it would be with her the rest of her life, reminding her that she almost died for that man and he cared nothing about that. "But at least Daphanie is angry enough, woman enough to want to go after him."

"What are you talking about?" Tabatha said, worry in her voice. She took Monica by the shoulders, turned her so they were face to face. "Snap out of it, okay? You're starting to freak me out."

"If my life were a book, every woman who read it would think I was fucking pathetic. That I am a pushover, a coward, and not woman enough to stand up and get that motherfucker back for all he's done to me."

"No, they wouldn't."

"Yes, they would! I would think the same thing," Monica said, brushing Tabatha's hands off her. "I'm tired of feeling this way. I'm tired," Monica said, walking over to the sofa, grabbing her purse, and heading for the front door. "It's about time something is done."

"Monica," Tabatha called, but Monica continued toward the door, only stopping when Tabatha yelled her name again at the top of her lungs. "Monica!"

Monica halted, her fist around the doorknob.

"I don't know exactly what you're thinking," Tabatha said, "but it sounds like some revenge shit. Stay away from Nate. I think you're forgetting you almost lost your life dealing with that fool."

"No," Monica said, "I haven't forgotten. I think about it every day."

87

Austin sat at home in the dark living room, in front of the television. It was on, but instead of watching it, he stared at the clock on the cable box.

He wished that Marcus had not moved back home, or that Caleb was around. He would have someone to talk to about this, but then again, he figured he was better off alone. They wouldn't see the fool he was making of himself.

The clock read 10:30 p.m. Austin picked up his cell phone again from the sofa seat cushion next to him.

He punched the number for the recent call list and pressed Dial, since Monica's number was the last one he had called. Actually, the last six calls had been to her number.

They'd started a little more than two hours ago, while Austin sat alone at the table in the restaurant, where he was supposed to have met Monica.

It was the best table in the house, the table Austin secured by pressing a fifty-dollar bill in the hand of the host when he entered. A bottle of the restaurant's finest wine sat chilling in the center of the table, along with a single candle Austin had gotten sick of staring at by twenty-five minutes after the time Monica was supposed to have arrived.

That's when he called her the first time. She didn't pick up.

Austin left a message, hoping nothing had happened to her.

After another half hour and another four unanswered phone calls, Austin requested and paid the check.

Outside, while he waited for the valet to retrieve his car, he stood on the sidewalk, still hopeful, still looking for Monica's Jaguar. It never showed.

He drove home, took off his jacket after stepping in the door, and without bothering to turn on the lights, he sought out a bottle of liquor.

Now sitting in the dark room, he poured himself a third or fourth shot. He had lost count.

He had been stood up. There was no other explanation. As he lifted the shot glass to his lips, he wanted to hate Monica. He wanted to tell himself he wouldn't spend another moment thinking about her.

The doorbell rang. Austin knew who it was.

He got up, answered it, left the door open, and walked back to the sofa.

Monica walked in wearing jeans, sandals, and a knit top, which told Austin she never had planned to meet him for dinner tonight.

"Why are you sitting alone here in the dark? Don't you wanna turn on some —" Monica said, reaching for the switch on the wall.

"Don't," Austin said, sitting down. "Why did you stand me up?"

Monica walked further into the living room and had a seat across from Austin. She appeared uncomfortable with what she was about to say.

"There's something on my mind."

"And what better way to express that than to be a no-show," Austin said, pouring himself another drink. He looked up at Monica. "Want one?"

"No, and I wish you wouldn't have another."

Austin chuckled, then drank half the glass. "Now you're trying to tell me what to do." He set the glass down. "I care for you."

Monica looked as though his admission

pained her.

"I don't want to end things," Austin said.

"That's why you're here, right, to tell me that you wanna end it?"

"Yes, I guess," Monica said, as if ashamed.

"And what if I said you couldn't? What if I said I won't let you?"

"Then I'd say you don't have that kind of power over me, and I'm ending it regardless."

Austin closed his eyes and sighed. Opening them, he said, "So what's wrong with me?"

"It's not you, it's —"

"Don't give me that 'It's not you, it's me' shit," Austin said. "I pushed too hard? I wanted it too much? What?"

"Yes. I guess."

Austin traced the rim of the shot glass with his finger. "I won't apologize for that. I'm a good man. If you were a good woman, not just some . . . bitch who toys with men's emotions, you would realize that."

There was silence, and a somewhat surprised look from Monica.

"I'm sorry," Austin apologized. "I didn't mean that. It's just —"

"No need," Monica said, standing up, walking over and sitting down beside him. "I know you didn't mean it, and I know you're a wonderful man, a man I would be honored to call mine. I'm just not ready to start a new relationship without working some things out first. Do you understand?"

"It's him, isn't it? Your ex-husband, that bastard, Nate Kenny. You're still in love with him."

"I'm not."

"But he's one of the things you have to work out, right?"

"Austin, I wish I could tell you everything, but it's complicated."

Austin sat on the edge of the couch, looking away from Monica.

She slid off the sofa and knelt in front of him, so he'd have no choice but to acknowledge her. She parted his knees, pushed between them, and stared him directly in the eyes. "I promise, if I were fully available, fully able to give myself to you, I would do it. God knows, with the horrible luck I have with men, I would be a fool not to."

Austin stared back into Monica's eyes, as if searching for the truth. "Okay, fine. But once you work those things out, will you promise to give me a call, check to see if I'm still available?"

Monica laughed, and despite the pain he was feeling, Austin could not help but laugh a little too.

"You're so cute," Monica said. "Now I'm wondering if I'm making the right decision."

"You aren't," Austin said, standing, taking her hand and helping her up. "But I understand, and I appreciate you being honest with me."

Austin walked Monica outside to the porch, gave her a hug, and said, "Good-bye, Monica."

Monica smiled sadly and said, "Why don't we just say so long for now."

"Okay. So long for now."

88

The first thing they did was call the hospital to speak to Shaun. Caleb asked if his son was there.

"No," Shaun said.

"Do you know where he is? And don't lie, this is important."

"No, sir," Shaun said. "I promise."

After that, Caleb and Bug drove around the high school, around the mall parking lot, and to the neighborhood basketball courts. They got out of Caleb's van and asked some of the boys shooting hoops if they had seen a boy fitting Jahlil's description. All of them shook their heads. No one knew where he was.

Back inside the van, Caleb turned to Bug. "Is there anywhere else you think he'd be? Anywhere?"

"I'm telling you, Mr. Harris, I took you everywhere I can think of."

Caleb struck the steering wheel angrily

and forced himself to calm down. He thought a moment, pulled out his cell phone, and dialed the man he had met at the DCFS office.

Lewis answered the phone. "Sorry to be bothering you like this, but I'm wondering if my son is with you," Caleb said.

"No," Lewis said, sensing the concern in Caleb's voice. "But I was just about to call you with some good news I had for Jahlil."

"That's gonna have to wait," Caleb said. "He's in trouble. I've been driving around looking for him. I'm wondering if you know of anywhere he might be."

"I'm sorry, he —" Lewis paused suddenly. "Hold it! There was a place. A park by this apartment complex he wanted to move to."

"A park?" Caleb said.

"Yeah," Lewis said. "It's just outside of Beverly, over by —"

"The apartments near the park," Bug said. "I forgot about that place. But I know where it is. I can show you, Mr. Harris."

"Did you hear that?" Caleb said into the phone. "Jahlil's friend is gonna show me where it is. We're going over there right now."

"Can I meet you there?" Lewis said. "Maybe I can help out somehow."

"Fine. We'll see you there."

■ ■ ■ ■

Lewis had already arrived by the time Caleb got there. He was standing beside his SUV. Caleb and Bug got out of the van.

"Is he here?" Caleb asked, looking around.

"I think so. I walked up the hill some and saw someone sitting on a bench with his back to me. It looked like Jahlil, but I didn't know what to say to him. He's probably mad at me for telling you about what he told me, so I decided to just wait. I didn't wanna make things worse."

"Good," Caleb said. "Which way did you say he was?"

Lewis led Caleb and Bug up the hill toward the park. After a minute, the boy sitting with his back to them came into sight. He was sitting on a bench, with his head down. An overhead park lamp cast light down on him.

"I think it's him," Lewis said.

"It is," Caleb said, saddened.

Caleb, Lewis, and Bug continued walking till they were twenty feet behind Jahlil. Jahlil suddenly spun around on the bench, whirling his gun in front of him, pointing it at his father, his friend, and Lewis.

"Whoa," Caleb said, holding both his

hands out in front of him. "Son, son, son, what are you doing?"

"What are you doing here?" Jahlil said.

"I just wanna talk."

"You just beat the shit out of me like I'm not even your son. I don't wanna talk to you."

"Jahlil, maybe —" Lewis started, but Jahlil said, "I don't wanna talk to you either. You told him the stuff I told you to keep a secret. And you," Jahlil said, pointing the gun in Bug's direction. "I know the only reason they here is because you told them. Tell me I ain't right."

Bug didn't say a word.

"I ought to shoot your asses right now. All of you."

"Jahlil! Don't talk like that," Caleb said, taking a step forward, till he was stopped by his son redirecting the gun at him. Caleb froze.

"I'm going to jail, ain't I?" Jahlil said.

"Jahlil —"

"I haven't done nothing right," Jahlil said, more to himself than anyone else. He stared past the three people in front of him, the gun still pointed forward. "I haven't done nothing right, and now I'm gonna go to jail so I won't be able to do nothing right no more." He paused for a long moment, a tear falling from his eye, then Jahlil took the gun and shoved the tip of the barrel under his chin.

"No, Jahlil! No!" Caleb rushed forward.

Jahlil extended his free hand to stop his father. "I need to see Ma."

"Jahlil, please. We love you. Don't do this!" Caleb said.

"I need to see Ma!"

"She's not here. She's at home."

"Then call her!" Jahlil ordered. "Or I'm gonna do this right now."

Caleb pulled his cell phone out, then turned to Lewis. "I need for you to take Bug and go."

"You sure? I could —"

"I'm positive," Caleb said. He turned to Bug. "You go with Lewis, okay? He'll take you back to your car. I'm going to call Jahlil's mother. But I just need for you and Lewis to go. I'm his father. I'll take care of this."

89

Lewis had dropped Bug off at his car twenty minutes ago, but now, as he walked into his house, he was still thinking about Jahlil, still beating himself up for not telling the boy earlier that he had been approved for the aid he needed. If he had known that, maybe he wouldn't have gotten himself into whatever trouble he was in. Maybe he would've been saved from being locked up.

Lewis closed the door, thinking that the only positive in this was that Jahlil was still a minor, wouldn't be locked away for too long, and still had a chance to turn his life around. If Lewis had any say in the matter, he would be around when Jahlil was released, and he would help in every way he could to get the boy back on track.

As Lewis walked deeper into his house, he called out to Eva. "Hello. Anyone home?" he said, not hearing Eva or the kids stirring around. The only light that burned on the first floor was the lamp in the living room window, which Lewis thought was strange, since Eva's car was parked in the driveway.

He walked into the kitchen, not bothering to turn on a light, and pulled the fridge open. He glanced in, but he had no appetite. Jahlil was too much on his mind, and all he really wanted to do was go upstairs, kiss his two little girls good night, then ask Eva to hold him, while he told her what had happened with the boy.

Lewis took the stairs up to the second floor and walked down the hallway to the girls' room. He quietly pushed the kids' room door open to find that they weren't there. What was going on? Lewis thought, stepping out of the room and heading down the hallway toward his bedroom.

When he got there, he noticed the door was closed. He didn't know why, but he hesitated a moment, his hand outstretched toward the knob, afraid to open it.

Forcing himself, Lewis turned the knob, threw the door open, and clicked on the ceiling light. What lay before him was total devastation. The bed blankets were all over the bed, and all the pillows had been thrown to the floor. Both lamps on both nightstands had also crashed to the floor, the bulbs broken, the shades crushed. The bedroom mirror over the dresser was shattered; the drawers had been yanked from their housing, clothes strewn from them.

Had they been robbed? Lewis thought. Had the girls and Eva been taken? He felt himself starting to panic. His breathing came hard and fast, the room starting to spin around him, as he yanked his cell phone from his pocket, trying to think of who to call.

Then, sadly, he abandoned his suspicions of robbery when his eyes fell again upon the bed.

"No," Lewis said, shaking his head, as he stepped cautiously closer to it. What he hadn't seen at first on the burgundy blanket and linen, but plainly saw now, were the dark wet spots in the center of the bed.

"No," Lewis said, again, leaning slowly over the mattress, his hand trembling, as he touched the tip of his fingers to one of the spots. He pulled his hand back and examined it. Blood.

Lewis's knees gave. He stumbled to the floor, begging, praying that what he thought happened was not true. His cell phone rang in his hand.

Startled, he stared at the screen. *Unknown caller.* "Hello!" he shouted.

"Is this Lewis Waters?"

"Yes. Who is this?" Lewis asked, desperately.

"This is Detective Shaw, Chicago PD," a man's voice said. "We need for you to come to the U of C Hospital emergency room."

"Why? What's happened?"

"Please, sir. You need to come. Now."

90

For the last half hour, Caleb had stood ten feet away from his son, who sat on the park bench. He would not let his father approach him or say a word, till his mother arrived.

When Sonya finally did show, she stopped next to Caleb, took one look at her son, and said, "Oh, my God." She started to go to him, but Caleb grabbed her by the arm, held her back.

"You have to give me the gun, before I let her come to you," Caleb said to Jahlil.

Without hesitation, Jahlil held the gun out to his father. Caleb walked over and carefully took it out of his son's hands, clicked the safety on, and pushed it into his pants pocket.

Sonya rushed to Jahlil and wrapped her arms around him.

"I'm sorry, Ma," Jahlil said, hugging her back. "I'm sorry."

"No, baby, you have nothing to be sorry

for," Sonya said, crying.

Caleb stood beside his family, feeling like an outsider, not knowing what to say or do. The feeling was far too familiar, and he knew his lack of involvement had contributed to his son's situation.

"I just wanted to take care of my family," Jahlil said, pressing his face into his mother's shoulder, hiding the tears that started to fall.

"I know, baby. I know," Sonya said.

"But I still need to, so you need to take me somewhere, Ma. Somewhere they can't find me."

Caleb wondered if he had heard his son correctly, and he saw that Sonya had hesitated after hearing what Jahlil said too.

"What do you mean, son?" Sonya said, pulling away just a little. "So who can't find you?"

"The police."

Sonya turned, gave a concerned look to Caleb.

"Jahlil," Caleb said, "you're gonna have to —"

"No. You don't have nothing to say to me. You hit me."

"And I'm sorry about that, son, but —"

"You left me, and when you came back, you said you'd never leave again, but you did. And then you treated me like shit, and then you hit me," Jahlil said, stabbing a trembling finger at his father. "So you can't say nothing to me."

"But I can," Caleb said, knowing this was the point where he had to step in and assert himself as this boy's father, even if he had never done it before. "I have the right to say something to you, because I love you, and I know what you're going through."

"You don't know what I'm going through!" Jahlil yelled, climbing off the bench and stepping away from his mother. "How could you? You were never there. You hardly know me."

"But I do," Caleb said. "I've known you since the day we brought you home, and I knew you could've turned out just like me if we weren't careful. I prayed that would never happen, but it did. I been through exactly what you're going through now, and a lot of it had to do with my father not being there for me. But when I needed him most, he came back and did something for me that I will always be thankful for. And I'm going to do the same for you."

"What . . . what are you talking about?" Jahlil said, looking to his father, then to his mother.

"Jahlil," Sonya said, tears coming harder

down her face with what she was about to say. "You can't run. You just can't. You'll be looking over your shoulder every day, and that's no way to —"

"What are you saying?" Jahlil said, looking around, as if for a direction to run.

Sonya took Jahlil's hand, pulled him close to her. "You have to turn yourself in, baby."

"No. No! What about Shaun? What about my baby? I don't even know if she'll be okay."

"You don't have to worry about that, son. I spoke to Shaun tonight. The baby is fine," Caleb said, stepping over and standing on Jahlil's opposite side. "And like I said, I'm gonna do for you what my father did for me. When I went to prison, he took you and Sonya in, cared for you, protected you. Now I want to do that for your family. Let them stay with me and your mother, and know that while you go through this, you don't have to worry about them, and when you're done, they will be here, waiting for you."

Jahlil looked into his father's eyes, and for the first time in years, Caleb saw what he believed to be trust coming from his son.

"Will you let us do that?" Caleb said.

Jahlil threw his arms around his father, hugged him tight, and cried.

"I'm sorry, son," Caleb said, but unable

to hold the tears back. He cried with his son. "I'm sorry I hit you. I'm so sorry."

Sonya stood beside them, sobbing, till Caleb reached out for her and pulled her in, where the three wept together.

An hour later, Caleb stood up from the bench where he was sitting beside his son. He looked out toward the street. He thought he saw a flashing light. He was right.

After the family had cried together and held each other, they had all decided that it was time to call the police.

Sonya didn't want to be there when they came to take her son away, so she said her good-byes then, and still crying, she left.

Caleb would stay, talk to his son about the gift of fatherhood. He told him he would bring his family to visit and make sure Shaun sent pictures and emails as often as possible. They talked about a few of the good memories they had together and even laughed once or twice. But for the last ten minutes they sat in silence.

Now, as Caleb dreaded, he saw the lights from the two police cars that pulled up over the curb and across the sidewalk and drove up the grassy hill. They stopped some forty feet away.

Caleb placed a hand on his son's shoulder.

He felt the boy trembling badly under his touch. "It'll be all right, son," Caleb said, softly, as the doors opened on the first police car. The officer who drove pulled his gun and pointed it at Caleb and Jahlil; the other officer stepped forward and said, "Is this the boy we're taking into custody?"

Caleb turned to Jahlil, who looked back at his father, fear in his eyes. "Be strong," Caleb told him. Then he turned to the officers and said, "Yes, this is my son, the boy you're taking into custody."

91

Lewis stood outside of the small emergency patient room where Eva was being treated.

Upon arriving, Lewis had been told by a haggard-looking, dirty-blond nurse that Eva had been raped and brutally beaten by two men.

"What? No!" Lewis had said, feeling tears threatening to come to his eyes. "Who did —"

"I don't have those answers, Mr. Waters," the nurse had said. "But you can see her if you want."

Now Lewis entered the treatment room. When he saw Eva, he raced to her, tried to hug her, but Eva recoiled in fear, as if he had been one of the attackers.

A different nurse, this one short and dark-haired, standing in the corner of the room, pulled on Lewis's arm. "She's still in shock. Take it easy with her."

Eva's eye was blackened and swollen.

Dried blood and bruises were all over her face, and her jaw was twice its normal size.

"Who did this to you?" Lewis said, begging for an answer, but Eva did more crying than speaking. Whatever words she did mumble, Lewis could not understand.

Moments later, the dirty-blond nurse reappeared, wearing latex gloves. "I'm gonna need for you to step out for a moment. We need to do a rape kit."

"What's that?"

"The doctor is outside. He wants to talk to you."

Lewis stepped into the hallway, where a balding man explained to Lewis they would be testing Eva for STDs and gathering DNA that hopefully would help them find who did this to her.

"Will she be okay?"

"Her jaw is broken," the doctor said. "We're going to have to wire it surgically, but other than that, and whatever she'll have to get past psychologically, she should be fine. I'll tell you more when we find out."

The doctor left Lewis in the hallway, where he just wanted to slide down the wall to the floor, drop his face in his hands, and cry.

"Are you Lewis Waters?" a hulking man in a trench coat asked.

"Yeah."

"Detective Shaw. I called —"

"Who in the hell did this to her?" Lewis said.

"That's what I want to ask you. Does your girlfriend have any enemies? Anyone out there that would want to —"

"No," Lewis said, thinking the question ridiculous. "You need to find who did this. You need to find them!"

"That's my intention."

"And my two little girls. They weren't at my house when —"

"Your neighbors have them. Are you sure there is no one that —"

"I'm positive," Lewis said.

Detective Shaw gave Lewis a glare that suggested he was lying. "If something comes to mind, call me," Shaw said, handing Lewis his card before walking away.

92

Standing outside the back of the hospital on what looked like a loading dock, Lewis needed time to get his head around all this. It was dark and quiet back there. He walked to the edge of the platform, looked around the very dark corner of the building, faintly saw a row of what looked like parked delivery trucks and other hospital vehicles.

He stopped there, thankful for the silence, and stared up at the moon. Why Eva? he thought. Of all people, why would anyone want to harm her? Then a disturbing thought: Maybe it wasn't Eva they were after. The detective had asked Lewis if Eva had any enemies. She didn't. But he did.

Lewis turned to race back into the hospital when he felt the barrel of a gun pressed into the space between his shoulder blades.

" 'Sup, motherfucker?"

The voice was immediately familiar, even though Lewis couldn't place it. Lewis's breath stopped in his chest. He raised his hands slowly to shoulder height.

"Did you tell him anything?"

"Who are —"

"Shhh," the voice said. "The cop — I'm sure he asked you who raped your girl. Did you give him names?"

"I don't have no fucking names," Lewis said, finally realizing where he'd heard that voice. It came from the guy he'd found outside his house the other day. "Who did —"

"Shut the fuck up! I'll kill you right now," the man said. "This stops here if you don't go to the police. You do, we gonna pay another visit to your house, and this time we do those two little girls that was down the hall. Know what I'm sayin'?"

Enraged, Lewis made a move to turn, get the gun, kill the man behind him before he was killed. But the gun was quickly taken from Lewis's back and pressed harshly to the back of his skull.

"Don't, motherfucker! He told us not to kill you, but I swear . . ."

Breathing heavily, his hands still raised, Lewis asked again, "Who did this?"

It took a moment, then, "This is payback from Freddy, for my sister, Joni."

93

Last night Caleb had called and told Austin what happened with Jahlil. Immediately his brother had met him at the police station and assumed the position of his nephew's legal counsel until a criminal attorney arrived.

At the station, Austin was made aware of the charges — breaking and entering and intent to commit armed robbery. They were pretty serious, but Jahlil was only sixteen years old, and he had no previous criminal record.

Because of the severity of the charges, Austin wasn't sure Jahlil would get off with just parole, but he was sure the criminal attorney would fight as hard as he could for that or, at least, for as short a stay as possible in lockup.

Today Austin stood on his front porch, surrounded by his brothers — by his family. It was a glum, gray day, the day after he had broken up with the woman he could've been having a very good relationship with, and the day that his brother Caleb was moving out.

Boxes of Caleb's belongings sat stacked on Austin's porch, ready to be hoisted into Caleb's van.

Marcus stood staring at Austin, then back at Caleb. "We been through it all, huh?" he said, sadly but attempting to smile.

"Yeah," Caleb said, slapping a hand on Marcus's shoulder. "But we're still here. I guess that counts for something."

Austin saw the concern and worry in Caleb's eyes. He always knew when his little brother was troubled, could spot it when they were just kids. "Jahlil is going to be fine. I found him the best attorney."

"I know," Caleb said. "And I can't ever repay you for this. Never."

"Considering all the crappy treatment I gave you in the past, why don't we just call it even," Austin said, opening his arms.

Caleb smiled a little and walked into his older brother's embrace.

"C'mon, Marcus," Austin said, waving him over.

Marcus smiled and joined his brothers in the small circle, their arms wrapped around each other's shoulders, staring into each other's faces like they did as kids when they'd huddle while playing street football.

"I don't have to tell you guys how much you mean to me, do I?" Austin said.

"Naw, you don't," Caleb said.

"But we wanna hear it anyway," Marcus said.

Caleb gave Marcus a shove. Marcus grinned and shoved Caleb back a little.

"Marcus," said Austin, "after Dad left and Mom died, you were the one that kept the three of us together. I think I can speak for Caleb in saying that we probably wouldn't be here right now if it wasn't for you. You've been the best brother that either of us could've asked for, and if there is ever anything you need, don't hesitate to ask. You hear me?"

Marcus grinned. "I already know that, Austin. But it is nice to hear from time to time."

Austin turned to Caleb. "And you, I know times have been hard, but let me tell you this, I will never, ever let you or your family go without. I will never let anything happen to them. Do you understand me?" Austin said, emotion starting to overwhelm him and make his voice quiver. "I got you! Do you hear me?" Austin said, tightening his grip on his brothers. "I love you, and I got you guys."

94

Monica had found what she thought could've been a wonderful man. A man she could've fallen in love with and yes, even though she fought the idea, could've possibly spent the rest of her life with. Maybe. But she tossed that away, for what? she asked herself, as she parked her car and climbed out of it.

For the opportunity of a lifetime, she told herself, as she walked up the path toward the house in front of her. She had given years of her life, of her love, only to have been mistreated, to have been criticized and treated miserably, because she was unable to have a baby. She had been lied to, cheated on, disrespected, and almost killed because of her association with one man, Nate Kenny, and unfortunately, for the life of her, she could not leave him alone until she could somehow repay him for all the hell he had brought upon her.

Monica hadn't told Daphanie about this move, but Monica knew the woman was willing to aid her in whatever capacity was needed.

Monica had already started her search for Tori Thomas, Nate's ex-secretary, and mistress, and one of the many women he had wronged, and last night, while online, she had found her on Facebook, sent her a message. *Hi. It's Monica Kenny. Want to know how you've been. Have a proposition for you. It's regarding my ex-husband, Nate, so you know it's not good. Respond if you're interested.*

The plan — Monica was not certain of it. Her mind was not as calculating as her ex-husband's. It was why she might need to call on Daphanie and was reaching out to Tori, to help her devise a scheme that would bring at least as much pain and suffering to Nate as he had brought to each of them.

Monica approached the stairs to Nate's house confidently, climbed them, placed herself in front of his door, and rang his doorbell. Only then did the enormity of what she was about to do, what she might risk, club her over the head.

As Monica waited for the door to be answered, she realized she could turn, run away now, try to forget all that tormented her about her past with Nate. Her life as it was was not that bad. Or she could follow through with her intentions and risk his once again coming out on top, as always, leaving her with far less than she had right now.

Think quickly, Monica told herself, feeling a bead of sweat form at her brow and roll over her forehead.

She heard the lock turn on the other side of the door, and Monica quickly wiped at her brow. It was too late. Her decision had been made for her.

The door opened. Nate stood behind it, wearing slacks and a polo shirt. Upon seeing Monica, he smiled but looked surprised that she was there.

"You, uh . . . what are you doing here?" Nate asked.

Monica stared into his eyes. It was like staring down the devil himself. "What you said to me the other evening in my store — were you serious?"

"About coming back to me? About us being a family once more?" Nate said, genuinely looking as though there was nothing more he wanted in life. "Yes, Monica. You know I was."

Monica swallowed hard. "Then I want to come back. I still love you," Monica forced herself to say. "I want to come back and for us to be a family again."

95

Lewis took the day off from work to spend at the hospital with Eva. He sat there by her bed, tormented by the fact that he was the reason she was raped. He so badly wanted to admit that to her but could not bring himself to do it. What good would it have done?

She lay in bed quiet for Lewis's entire visit, half sedated from the pain medication for her wired jaw, half still in shock from the ordeal.

Lewis kissed Eva's cheek, told her he would be back to see her later, then left the hospital. He drove toward home but found himself unable to deal with the overwhelming feeling of powerlessness.

Eva was the woman he loved, the woman he would one day marry. For Freddy to have sent someone to break into his home, rape and beat Eva, and then think that Lewis would stand for it — the man obviously didn't know Lewis like he thought he did.

He grabbed the wheel of his Escalade, whipped a U-turn across three lanes of oncoming traffic, and headed downtown toward the one person he thought could help.

Nate Kenny sat poised behind his desk, his eyes focused intensely on Lewis.

"And you said they didn't touch Layla," Nate said, with concern a father would show for his own daughter, for Nate had had the child in his care for a couple of months and had grown to love her as his own.

"No."

"And you're sure this was Freddy Ford?" Nate said.

"Yes."

Nate closed his eyes and lowered his chin onto his intertwined fingers. "I'm sorry," he said. "Freddy Ford is my problem. I created him, and for him to do this to you, to the woman you love . . ." Nate said very softly, then suddenly slammed the side of his fist against his desk with enough force, it seemed, to reduce it to splinters. He stood and paced, troubled, over to the windows.

Lewis watched him, thinking about the man's statement, that he had created Freddy Ford, and Lewis was thankful that Nate finally took responsibility for that. It had truly been all his doing.

Nate turned to Lewis. "Was there anything else said by these men?"

"Nothing more than I told you."

"Do you want me to go after them?"

"I . . . I don't know," Lewis said, then wondered how anyone could find them. There was no information given. All there was was the warning Joni's brother gave, and the fact that Freddy knew where Lewis lived, and how to hurt him.

"Lewis," Nate said, walking over to him. "Do you want me to go after them? I'll call my investigator."

Lewis stood. "No. This is done. I don't wanna risk something happening to Layla or Tammi or something worse to Eva. We're gonna work hard, and I know we have what it takes to get past this. But what about you?" Lewis said. Despite the feelings he had for Nate — which at times closely resembled hate, considering all they had been through — they still shared a bond. Freddy had come after Nate once, shot him four times with the intention of killing him. Lewis didn't want to see Nate hurt again. "If he'd do this to me, and we used to be best friends, what do you think he'd do to you? You have a child too. What's to stop him from . . ."

A frown came to Nate's face. "Understand this, Lewis. If that man again tries to come after your family, or even considers trying to hurt me or mine, he will know the full, unrelenting scope of my rage, and I promise you, he will wish every day, for the rest of his miserable, tormented life, that he had never been born."

96

Freddy Ford walked beside the man in the white uniform, into the visitation room.

Inside, there was another man standing, waiting. He was broad shouldered and muscular. He was of medium height, appeared to be in his early thirties, and wore sagging jeans, a T-shirt, and a denim jacket.

Freddy walked with the attendant over to the man. Freddy wore jeans, slippers, a bathrobe, his chest bare underneath. He heard the attendant tell the man, "I'm not leaving the room. I'll be right there by the door. If you need me, just say."

The other man nodded, crossed his arms over his chest, and focused on Freddy as he approached.

Freddy scratched his beard, looked over his shoulder then sat. The man lowered himself into a chair across from him, staring Freddy in the face.

"It's done," the man said. His name was

Scott. He was Joni's younger brother by two years. He had run in gangs since thirteen, had been arrested several times, and spent more time in prison than out.

"You ain't hurt her too bad, did you?" Freddy asked.

"Too bad?" Scott said. "That was my sister and I loved her, and she's dead now!"

"That was my girl, and I love her too!" Freddy raised his voice. He looked up and saw the attendant's eyes on them. He lowered his voice. "Scott, I feel you, but she ain't the one who had your sister killed, okay? We just sending a warning right now. The other comes in time."

"How much time?"

"You got what I asked for?"

Scott sunk his hand into the inside pocket of his jean jacket, brought out a small, thick envelope, and passed it to Freddy. Freddy quickly pushed the package into the pocket of his robe.

"How much?" Freddy asked.

"Two thousand. It's all I could get right now."

"It's gonna take more."

"I'm working on it," Scott said, standing.

Freddy stood, gave the man some dap, and a half hug. "I'm missing her too, but we gonna take care of that, okay?"

Scott stepped back, and stared at Freddy with conviction. "We better."

Freddy nodded and sat back down.

Scott walked toward the attendant. The man opened the door, walked Scott out, and left Freddy sitting in the room alone. That was against protocol, but then again, letting Scott in the facility with that wad of money was against the rules, and agreeing to what Freddy approached the attendant with was as well.

A moment later, the visitation room door opened again, and the tall dark-haired attendant stepped back in. He quickly walked toward Freddy.

"You got it?"

Freddy handed him the package. "It's only two grand."

"You said —"

"I know what I said, but ain't nobody no millionaire. We'll get you the rest eventually."

The attendant — the name plate on his chest read Kelly — hid the money in one of his pockets, grabbed Freddy by the arm, then said, "Don't play games with me. I'm putting my ass on the line trying to break you out of here. *I* don't get all the money! You can rot behind these walls for the rest of your life."

430

ABOUT THE AUTHOR

RM Johnson is the author of eleven novels, including bestsellers *The Harris Family* and *The Million Dollar Divorce.* He holds an MFA in creative writing from Chicago State University. He currently lives in Atlanta, Georgia.